LIAM DAVIS & THE RAVEN

Love Inscribed #1

ANYTA SUNDAY

First published in 2014 by Anyta Sunday
Buerogemeinschaft ATP24, Am Treptower Park 24, 12435 Berlin

An Anyta Sunday publication
www.anytasunday.com

ISBN 978-3-947909-23-0

Content Edited by Teresa Crawford
Line Edited by Lynda Lamb
Copy Edited by HJS Editing

This book contains explicit sexual content.

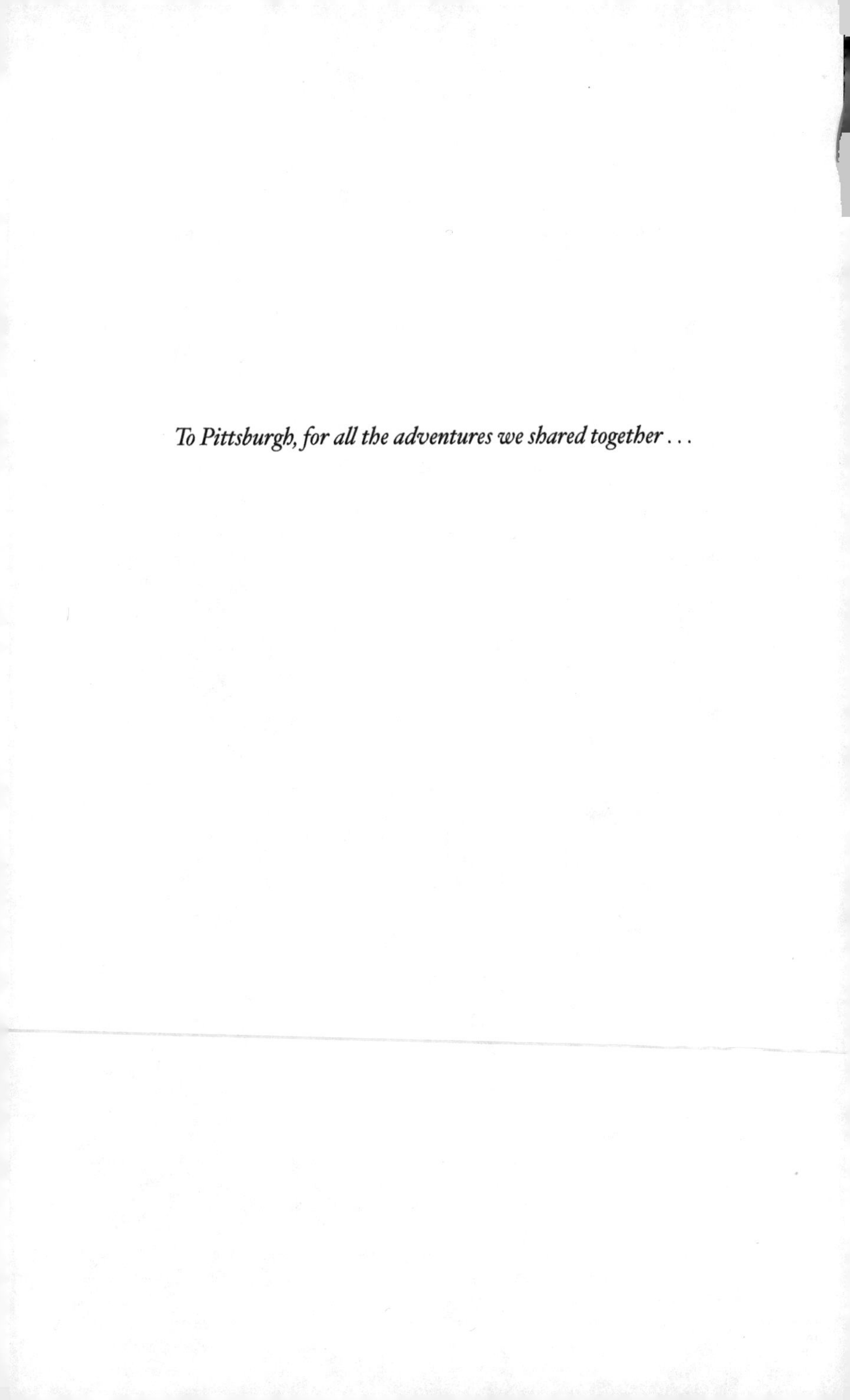

To Pittsburgh, for all the adventures we shared together . . .

CHAPTER ONE

Freddy Krueger was the reason I was sitting in the back of some guy's car, speeding to the University of Pittsburgh Medical Center.

I replayed the evening's events over and over, but if I had really thought about it—difficult with the burgeoning concussion—the point of no return had passed that morning . . .

Man Dead a Week in Central Pittsburgh Apartment

I lingered at the newspaper stand with the *Pittsburgh Post-Gazette*—paid for and tucked tightly under my arm—nudging the strap of my messenger bag. The headline begged me to come closer and check out the lurid report.

A breeze folded the corner of the paper, hiding half the columns and making it impossible to read at my current intellectual-who-shouldn't-care-for-sensationalist-reporting-but-no-one-has-to-know-I'm-actually-riveted distance.

Pushing up my glasses, I glanced to either side of the empty pavement. Empty, save the vendor, but he was tucked behind his stand scratching at his Sudoku. Quickly, I sidled closer to the rickety red rack. I lifted the flap of paper and scanned the first paragraph:

A man has been found dead in his apartment. Police say he appears to have been dead for close to a week. The body was discovered after neighbors complained about insistent whining from the deceased's near-starved cat....

"Ya gotta be kiddin'!" the vendor chimed in a heavy Pittsburgh accent, pushing in his racks under the safety of overhead balconies. I lurched away from the rack, from the cat that, despite being "near-starved," hadn't yet started chewing on his owner...

"Ya know it's goin' to rain," he said, stretching a finger toward the thick gray clouds in the distance. As if to emphasize his point, a gust rolled down the street, rustling the papers and whistling through the gutter grates.

"Better be on my way, then." If I hurried, I'd miss the downpour. The clouds appeared lighter around the city's prominent Cathedral of Learning, close to where I was heading.

Maybe I'd be lucky.

Readjusting the strap of the messenger bag carrying my essentials—laptop, pens, notebook—I hurried toward campus while scouring the articles on the first pages of the *Post-Gazette*.

Some of the headlines lacked zest and catchiness, something that I wouldn't let happen with *Scribe* this semester if I got promoted to features editor.

When I got promoted to features editor. If I wanted the apprenticeship at my father's firm, I had to prove I could hold an editorial position—for two consecutive years.

I swallowed the lump of excited nerves that'd been bundling in my throat all week and hurried toward the large, concrete block of hideousness that housed the magical world of the student magazine.

Just a few pathways stretched between me and my reporting assignments for the semester. Maybe I'd be reassigned the student politics column I wrote last year. Or, since the final year of my undergraduate studies had finally accepted me into its embrace, maybe the chief would give me my promotion—

Clash! Thunk!

I hit metal and tumbled, landing with a smack against the pavement. The newspaper ripped. A tingle of pain burst through my wrists and everything blurred. An amused voice sounded from my left, and I shifted into a crouch, brushing the grit off my grazed palms.

A guy in a black-and-silver wheelchair sat with his arms folded. "If you wanted to catch my attention, you could've started with 'hello'."

"I didn't see you," I said, plucking up my glasses and getting to my feet. The frames were a little scratched, but not too bad. I slid the glasses back on.

The spiky-haired guy smiled. Tattoos of hummingbirds trailed up his arms, and his pierced brow was spectacularly arched.

"Sorry," I said, collecting the paper and folding it. "Are you all right?"

"Better than you are." He rolled his wheelchair back a few feet and then forward again. "Chair's good too. Word of advice, watch where you're going next time."

Well . . . he had a point. I should be more observant, especially considering I prided myself on noticing details others tended to overlook.

Someone behind me caught his attention, and he waved. Sparing one more amused glance my way, he rolled around me and up the path.

A splash of rainwater hit my nose. The clocktower in the distance chimed the hour.

I jogged the remainder of the path just as the splashes snapped into a downpour.

Sopping, I scurried into the concrete block of hideousness.

Surely, the day could only get better.

WITH ITS FLAKY wallpaper and threadbare carpet, the *Scribe* boardroom provided a wonderful view of the proudly-towering neo-gothic Cathedral of Learning. Twelve clever minds seated at an oval table readied to make the room my favorite place in the world.

I slipped into the room, and a whiff of tension hit the back of my nose with a tickle. Editor-in-Chief, Harry Benedict, settled his steel gaze on me, flustering me at once. *Yes, sir, I know exactly what you're going to say—*

"Nice of you to finally join us, Liam. Make it a goal this semester to pay as much attention to punctuality as to your impeccable reports."

Jack Briggs and Marc Jillson—kings in here because they ran the most successful opinions and party page columns of the last decade—sniggered across the notebook-studded table.

Jack calmed down and Jill came snorting after. Hannah, next to him, shifted her notes, though she should have lifted her notebook to protect her face from the discharge rushing her way.

I swung off my messenger bag, shrugged out of my wet sweater, and palmed the cool metal back of the last free seat as the chief gave Jack and Jill a bland stare that shut them up quite nicely.

"Let's continue, shall we? Right." Chief Benedict opened the frayed leather binder before him, thumbing the worn spine with tender strokes. "This year we are going to have a few structural changes."

My pulse picked up, ringing in my ears. The chief came sharply into focus. He stroked the beard he'd spent the last year cultivating—to stop pulling the hair on his head—and scanned the paper before him. *Changes.* Yes. This was it. His gaze lifted straight to mine. Any second now, he'd promote me to the position I'd worked toward my entire undergraduate education.

He pursed his lips and leaned back in his chair. One by one, he looked at us: content editors, copy editors, and columnists. But he lingered on me, and surely that was a spark in his eye?

"Tell me, what are an editor's best attributes?"

Was he drawing this out on purpose? Perhaps he was demonstrating how to hook an audience. Heat thickened in the room, the frictional anticipation of twelve ambitious student journalists. Come on, chief. *Look at me. Let me answer, and then we can get on with the promotion.*

The chief laid his gaze on Jack. The lucky son-of-a-gun. "Vision," Jack said, shrugging his broad shoulders like it was obvious. "The ability to see beyond what the magazine *is* to what it *could be*."

"Good. What else?"

Chief was really going to milk this today, wasn't he?

Jill's turn. He whipped his sandy bangs out of his brown eyes with a jerk of his head. His slightly upturned nose made him look as arrogant as he was. "He must be able to draw in readers with eye-catching headlines and choose the most evocative photographs and captions."

"He *or* she. Good." Chief Benedict swiveled his gaze to me with a subtle raise of his brow.

I returned it. "They must also understand the technical aspects of publishing."

The *Scribe* quarters were my second home. Maybe even my first, since I knew it better than my own apartment. Some nights I stayed here until the wee hours of the morning and didn't leave campus at all. I knew this place. All the ins and outs. Everything.

Chief knew that too.

He narrowed his eyes, and glanced at his binder. Again, he stroked the spine with his thumb. "*And*," he continued, "editors must not only be exceptional writers. They must be creative. They must be able to see the team's creative vision, then help *materialize* that vision."

He picked up a sheet of paper, and the light from the windows behind him made the paper transparent. What did it say? Were those names? If the chief would just tilt—

"With that in mind, I'm doing something a little . . . unexpected this semester." He rested the paper back in the folder. "I'm reassigning most of you to new positions. Something that I feel will challenge you, broaden your horizons, and make you better columnists and editors."

Getting the features editor position would definitely be a good challenge. I straightened my glasses and pulled out the pen I always, *always* carried in my pocket. Grabbing my notebook, I was ready to take notes of the new structure.

Jack rolled his eyes and pulled at the black Desperado T-shirt that hung loosely on his frame. If he were an ounce less of a prick, he'd be an interesting guy to have a conversation with; as it was, he needed taking down a peg or two. If I ever got to be executive editor, I could do it, too. *Oh yes, my pen is mightier than any sword* . . .

"Jack," Chief Benedict said suddenly, "say goodbye to the opinions column and hello to politics."

I stilled, my pen scratching to a halt against the fresh page of my notebook. "Jack, politics?"

"Me, politics? But you need me for the opinions—"

The chief drew a sharp line in the air that silenced Jack. "Hannah will take over opinions for the semester." Jack gripped the table, his lips parting as if to start protesting again, but the cold, staunch stare of Chief Benedict made him hold his tongue. Instead he jerked back violently in his chair and raked a hand through his short black hair.

I blinked down at my page. *Just a minor blow*. I didn't need to run the politics column if I got the features editor position. That would take up most of my time anyway. I probably wouldn't have time to contribute regularly.

The chief kept delegating the new positions, earning some wide smiles alongside the disappointed scowls.

"Marc, you're news editor." Jill turned a dark shade of crimson. News editor was a tough but rewarding job, and the chief made a good decision giving the job to Jill. Pain in the ass though he was, he definitely had potential that needed nurturing.

And what nurturing do I need?

"Liam Davis," Chief Benedict read from the sheet.

My pen cut into my palms. This was it. After countless nights working to deadlines, writing, re-writing, editing, I'd finally be *Scribe*'s features editor.

"You won't be working in an editorial capacity this semester."

The pen fell from my grip, clattering on my notebook. "Wh—what? But I—I'm the best."

"And you don't lack modesty."

I blinked, struggling to focus on his next words through the ringing of his last words.

" . . . an exceptional editor, I'd like to see you expand your skill set. And this goes for all of you. I'm trying to challenge you to approach topics that are out of your comfort zone. . . ."

Won't be working in an editorial capacity.

". . . commit yourselves to this, and you'll be better prepared for the real world of publishing once you're through here at the *Scribe*."

Won't be working . . .

" . . . Liam, I'm challenging you with the party page."

The *what*?

Was this a joke?

Jill shot to his feet, knocking over his chair. His nose flared again, and sweet, shy Hannah flinched as spittle flew out of Jill's mouth.

"You're giving the most popular page of the magazine to him? *Liam effing Davis*? How can you give someone who doesn't have a single friend outside *Scribe* the *party page*? That's a recipe for a stuck-up, frigid disaster. Someone who has no life will not be able to give this column life!"

"That's quite enough, Mr. Jillson. Contrary to popular thought, your opinions are not always welcome."

I placed my pen in the center of my notebook and stared at the chief. He'd known what I'd really wanted. He'd even talked me through what the position meant and how to be the best. Why did he give me *this*? Had I offended him somehow? The chief wasn't the passive-aggressive type; he'd have told me if I rubbed him the wrong way.

Jill threw his hands up. His mouth opened but his raging voice was the last sound I wanted in my ear. Calm and easy did it. We could discuss the issue and politely make it clear the chief had made a mistake. "Jill—"

"Marc, to you."

I shifted in my seat. "*Jill*, you don't like me, that's clear, and believe me when I say the feeling is quite reciprocated. But you're also protective of the party page, and I can appreciate that." The chief raised both brows close to his hairline. "Unfortunately, sir, he has a point. I don't have enough jackass in me to run the party page as well as Jill can."

"I seem to sense the potential." Chief Benedict laced his fingers together and leaned forward, his elbows resting on either side of his binder. "But it's quite simple, Liam. Do you want to be on the *Scribe* staff this semester?"

What kind of question was that? "Of course—"

"Then we're settled here." He brushed his beard again. "Now, before we discuss the particulars of this year's first issue, I want to remind you all that this year's *Best College Article* deadline is at the end of next week.

"Pick only what you believe are your top three pieces from last year. Two external judges from prominent newspaper agencies will be reading and ranking your articles. One from our own *Post-Gazette* and another from out of state. So please, consider wisely which pieces you'll submit . . ."

DRENCHED AGAIN, this time in afternoon rain, I let myself into apartment twenty-three, and lowered my bag next to my forgotten umbrella at the door. If I'd taken it this morning like I'd meant to, would the day have turned out differently?

Maybe I wouldn't have fallen over, gotten soaked, and arrived late to my meeting. Maybe that would've put the chief in a better mood. Maybe he would've changed his mind about me doing the party page?

I stripped out of my wet clothes and padded to the laundry room to start a load.

But it was what it was. I *had* fallen over, arrived late and wet—and tonight I'd have to do research for my first column.

They're only parties. I can handle it.

I just have to be professional and choose an angle that will work for me. The politics of student parties, perhaps?

Back at my bag, I pulled out my notebook and, bypassing the dining table by the large arched windows, moved to the couch. I took out the flyers I'd grabbed from bulletin boards on campus.

The folded bunch rested heavy in my hand. One by one, I leafed through them. Bling Bash. Derelict Dance. Nightmare on Shady Avenue. Booze Banger.

I shook my head at a crude drawing of a shot glass nestled

between breasts. "Doesn't that sound awful?" The only answer was an echo of my voice. Even the rain pattering against the window lessened.

Thick clouds layered the apartment in dark shadows so I turned on a light before sliding out my laptop.

I read through an email my mom sent me, and looked over her application to work as a nurse in a retirement home. After sending it back to her with a few minor suggestions, I began choosing my top three articles from last year for the BCA competition.

The article I knew had to be submitted centered on the importance of student activism on campus. "By far my best work," I said, shifting my feet over the cool hardwood floors.

I really needed to get a rug, warm the place up some more.

I hesitated before composing an email to my father. I wasn't sure what his reaction would be when I wrote to him that I didn't land the features editor position. We didn't talk often, and the last time we saw each other face-to-face, while I was visiting New York, he calmly sat me at his desk, shaking his head.

"Everyone has different abilities. I'm sure you'll find something you're good at, but you don't have the right . . . personality to work as a journalist here."

I leaned forward, steepled my fingers together and rested my elbows on his desk. "I want a apprenticeship at this company. I'll do whatever it takes."

My father leaned back in his chair, frowning. "When I was at university, I held the student newspaper's features editor position for two years. A tough feat, the competition was stiff. Do the same, and you have a apprenticeship." He scribbled something in his diary. "But, Liam, there will be other things for you out there if you fail."

"I won't fail."

I shut down my laptop. I wouldn't tell him anything just yet. There had to be a way for me to land the features editor position.

I picked up the flyers once more. Carrying them around the

narrow kitchen island, I popped a slice of bread into the toaster. It sparked.

Zing! A small shock shot up my arm.

I jerked my hand back and dropped the flyers on the bench. Shaking my hand, I glared at the toaster. *I ought to write a report on the dangers of second-hand electrical appliances!*

Jill's snigger came to mind, and it stopped my chuckle short. Why did his words niggle at me so much? True, I *didn't* have any friends outside my professional circle. My life consisted of writing, reading, editing, and studying. I was lucky if I remembered to eat. But sacrifices had to be made if I was going to land my dream job. I didn't have time to waste on getting drunk and making friends at Booze Bangers.

My toast popped, and I carefully plucked it out of the death trap.

A shiver rolled over me. Who would know if I suddenly died? No one would be there to miss me. My mom maybe, but her calls were irregular at best—who knew when she'd figure it out? Most likely it'd be Chief Benedict who noticed something was wrong.

Except . . . if I died *today*, he might think I didn't want the party page, that I quit.

No one would know!

I didn't even own a cat that would meow until the neighbors were annoyed enough to investigate. How long before they found me? Longer than a week? Would only the smell of my decaying flesh tip them off?

I shook my head and, drawing in a steadying breath, unplugged the toaster.

It hardly solved the issue, but it'd do for now.

My gaze dropped to the bright orange flyer on the bench, now covered in crumbs from the toast I gripped too hard. *Nightmare on Shady Avenue* party. Maybe I should go. Maybe it'd calm me and make me see how good I have it.

Make me see that worse nightmares exist.

ALONG WITH DEAFENING MUSIC, multiple kegs overflowed.

One didn't need to see them to know it, either. The run-down Victorian house reeked of beer and something more acidic. I prayed it was vodka and not the regurgitated remains of someone's dinner, but I wasn't about to investigate. No, I planned to find my angle for the column, write my notes, and get out of here.

I steered around a large crowd chugging beer from jugs, vases —even a watering can—and perched myself on a carpeted step at the bottom of the staircase in the foyer. Here would have to do; there wasn't anywhere else to sit. That, and I wanted to avoid banging into Jack and Jill, who I'd briefly encountered fist-bumping each other in the kitchen.

A couple making out against the wall shared the lower steps with me, and their suppressed moans harmonized with the vocalized pleasure of other couples. Seemed the foyer was the place for hooking up.

Taking out my notebook, I scribbled some notes. *Rooms large with dim lighting. Half the guys wear black-and-red striped pullovers. Some have fake hands with long, sharp fingers. . . . Nightmare on Elm Street is projected in the living room, and the slashing terror lights up the wall.*

I twisted away from the grim images. There was a reason I'd always been sensible enough not to watch it.

A girl in a white dress at the bottom of the stairs twirled. She lit up the dim foyer and her smile lifted with a laugh as she followed her Freddy boyfriend around the corner. Her laugh continued, making me think of Linda. How long was it? A year since she'd broken up with me? Time really flew by.

Doesn't have a life. How can he give the column life . . .

The pop rock thumped louder. Freddies swam around me and I blinked. Refocusing on the notebook, I slowly let go of a breath. Why couldn't I get Jill, or the *Man Dead a Week in Central Pitts-*

burgh Apartment, out of my head? I struggled to gulp down a fresh lungful of air and push back the vision of myself dead and rotting.

Maybe I should get a cat.

Yes, I'd go to the shelter tomorrow. Then all will be good. Great, even. Perhaps the cat's fur will help soak up the nasty echo. . . .

I clicked my pen, a habit Hannah found irritating when I did it at the office. But pen-clicking soothed me and brought out the creativity in me. The frustration built until there was nothing left for me to do but make my pen gush everything and anything out.

Click. Click. Click!

Angle. My angle. What could it be?

Click. Click. Click!

A girl in dark pants, shit-kickers, and blue streaks in her chocolate hair walked in the front door.

My stomach clenched and my finger paused at the top of the pen. There it was, over the girl's shoulder.

My angle.

My pen hit the paper, and the ink flowed.

Jock. Big-boned. Broad shoulders. Tall. Runs fingers through hair as though he's attractive and knows it. Walks into party like he has all the time in the world, slow but oddly graceful. Ears look like they've had a serious clubbing. Lashes like a girl's, long and dark—suggesting his blond hair is unnatural. Laugh lines around the mouth, a deep crack in his skin where a dimple might be. Casual jeans, dark green T-shirt, beat-up leather jacket. Bag slung over shoulder. Black, non-descript. Wears so much Axe body spray, it's detectable across the room.

His gaze clasps on a male making out in the foyer. Hurt flashes in his eyes. A raw, pained look. But he swallows it back as if he doesn't care. Or isn't entirely surprised by what he's seeing. He stops in front of the slighter male who has his tongue locked in—

I pushed my glasses further up my nose. Huh.

—another guy's mouth.

I paused my pen on the page as I stared for a moment. Then

My Angle spoke, and I was back to pushing the pen. I shouldn't have left my recorder at home. *And I really should take a shorthand-writing course.*

"Wow. I really do always go for the wrong person." His voice was heavy and creamy, edged with the same hurt his eyes reflected.

The slighter man, long bangs swept over his forehead, pulled out of his kiss, looking to My Angle and then glancing to the side, toward my brown canvas shoes. Reproachfully, as if My Angle were the one in the wrong, he said, "What are you doing here?"

"What are *you*?"

"I was going to tell you," Long Bangs said.

The music grew louder, and I slipped down a step to hear them better. My Angle glanced at me briefly, his jaw twitching. *Green eyes.*

"Well, Chris, seems now you don't have to."

I transcribed the rest of the argument, the idea for the column piece articulating in my mind. Yes. It would be about breaking the illusion that college parties are superficial. Raw, real, uncensored emotion lived here. I'd call it *University of Party, Lectures in Life*.

A thrill rushed through me as I envisioned the column, complete with insignia in the form of a keg.

I clapped my notebook shut and zipped it in the inside pocket of my jacket. My pen went back to my pocket, and I strode out of there, leaving the party, the booze, and the breakup behind me.

I had my angle. I was done.

I sucked in the fresh night air and made my way down Shady Ave. A few drunken students roamed the street, some dressed in black and yellow, cheering for the Pirates; others—like myself—quietly slipped through the shadows.

At the lights on the corner of Shady and Fifth, someone stumbled to my side. He was a guy about my age, with dark coppery spiked-up hair and much higher cheekbones than mine. He smoothed his tight, net T-shirt to his flat stomach. "Could I borrow your glasssses?"

I subtly pulled back from him. "Excuse me?"

"My contact came out. Can't see the numbers. Looking for"—he lifted his hand and splayed his fingers—"five-twelve Shady Ave. Should be 'ere somewhere."

The pedestrian signal turned green. I could hurry off and get myself home, but that wouldn't be particularly *Caring Citizen* of me, would it? This was just a guy that needed a hand. If *I'd* lost my glasses, even sober, I'd be half blind.

"I'm keeping my glasses right where they are," I told him, gesturing him to walk across the street. "But I can walk you home."

"Shovel-wrist," he mumbled.

Was that chivalrous? Hard to tell with the slurring. I let myself believe it was a compliment and nodded. "You're welcome."

With an uninhibited sigh, he hung on my arm and we crossed the street.

"I'm Mitch, by the way," he murmured, tightening his grip and sagging his weight against my side. "I donna usually drink. Donna think I should again, either."

"I suspect you'll be thinking that all day tomorrow as well," I said.

He stumbled so I slowed my pace. Along with alcohol, he smelled like something sweet—like he shampooed with cotton candy. When the brass numbers 512 shone under the lantern light, I steered Mitch up the stairs and to his door.

He dug a hand into his pocket and pulled out his keys, dangling them in my face. "Got 'em."

"So you do."

He chuckled as he fumbled for the right key and opened the door.

"You good from here?" I asked. Surely he'd at least find his apartment inside?

He nodded, and in an awkward—rather flexible—move, he kept the door open with his foot and threw his arms around my neck.

Vodka-laced lips met my cheek, followed by a low chuckle, whispering over my skin as he pulled back. "Night!"

The door shut, and I blinked under the lantern light. Well. Interesting night.

I turned and jogged down the steps.

For a second, I thought I heard my name whispered in the breeze, but the scuttling of leaves over the pavement reassured me I was imagining things.

Liiiiam. I walked faster. My imagination was getting the better of me—

A fractured shadow of Freddy's sharp-fingered hand stretched long and menacing under the streetlight.

I picked up my pace to a trot. I didn't like to think of myself as a scaredy-cat, but that didn't stop it from being the case.

The clanking of steps got closer, and the shadow grew, splitting more under the light. Breath hit the back of my neck. I jumped, looking over my shoulder.

Freddy's scarred face loomed toward me, and I skedaddled to one side. "Am I a magnet to the intoxicated tonight?"

I steered away from him and his awful mask. Time to get home—

Glittering steel shot out and sliced down the side of my arm, tearing my sleeve.

Pow!

Pain bloomed in my gut. "What the—?" A punch hit my jaw, and I stumbled back. My heel hit something and I fell, slamming the back of my head against the concrete.

Two or three blurry Freddies spiraled above me. A sharp metallic taste filled my mouth and slipped down the back of my throat. *Who the hell was this guy? Was he trying to rob me?*

"Leave me alone." My wispy, weak voice didn't match the

intensity of my request. "Take my wallet." I twisted and spat out blood.

Another jolt of pain ripped up my side, and I curled into it.

Stand up. Get away—

I struggled to push myself up, but no sooner had I heaved myself onto all fours than Freddy kicked my side, and my arms buckled.

The streetlight darkened, shadowed by his figure crouching next to me. Freddy twisted his steel, gloved fingers, taunting me with the light dancing on their sharp tips. "Let's see how you like this up—"

Wham!

Freddy choked on his words and fell. I scrambled away, wincing at the throbbing, dizzying pain in my head. There were only shades of blue and soft ground under me as I crawled. I made it a few feet before I collapsed.

Blurry, the silhouette of a hooded figure loomed. He hauled Freddy up by his shoulders and kneed him until he crumpled to his boots—

My head throbbed again. Who was that? I strained to make out more, but all the blues around me bled into one, and I lost consciousness.

CHAPTER TWO

Two voices swam around me. Male and female. There was a gentle rumbling. I groaned, clutching my head as I peeled my eyes open. I was in the back of a car.

I jerked upright.

Bad move. My head pounded.

Dark hair streaked with blue blurred in front of me, and the female spoke, "We're taking you to UPMC, just hang in there."

I rubbed my eyes under my—still intact glasses, thank God!—and let my vision clear.

The voice belonged to the girl from the party, the one who'd come in with My Angle behind her. "I'm . . . fine. Just a bit disoriented." And confused. What happened? That Freddy guy attacked out of nowhere; if it hadn't been for that hooded guy showing up . . .

I shivered and shifted my focus. Sitting in the driver's seat was My Angle—I couldn't see him well, but I recognized his scent. Axe.

"You're My Angle!" I said, the words distorted and easy to mistake.

Blue Streaks laughed. "Wow, Quinn, he must have had quite a fall to think you're an angel." She turned to me with a cheerful grin. "That'd be Quinn, and I suspect he's more spawn of the devil than anything."

That earned her a whack across the arm. "I just found out my boyfriend's cheating on me," he said in a deep voice that vibrated in the air and stirred the hairs on my arms. "Just like that I'm apartment-less, and instead of holing myself up in your room with Super Mario and Pringles, I'm dropping this guy off at the emergency room. You can be nice to me, Shannon."

She laughed as she shook her head, hair falling in waves over her shoulder. "No. Not happening again. Even after cleaning my sheets, I still had crumbs in my bed for weeks!"

"What's a few crumbs to my grief?" Quinn asked, turning the car onto College St. and passing my apartment; it was the only floor with all the lights out. "Why not think of it as an opportunity?"

"Opportunity?"

"Think of it as a chance to exfoliate or something."

"Eww, boys are so gross."

"One person's gross is another's creative." Quinn angled the rearview mirror. He winked at me. Or was it a trick of the light? Maybe I'd hit my head harder than I thought. "Help me out here, man," he said. "Together we can prove just how damn awesome us guys are."

Shannon snorted, and Quinn growled, low and playful.

"I think it depends on the guy," I said, tenderly touching the back of my bruised head. Luckily I didn't feel any blood.

Shannon agreed and settled a hand on Quinn's shoulder. "This one straddles the line between grossest and most awesome guy in the world." She gave him a fond smile and swung her gaze my way. "You hanging in there all right?"

I nodded and rested my head back on the seat.

"We'll be there in a minute."

I shut my eyes as she continued bantering with Quinn. The sound of their voices comforted me, and I suddenly began to laugh. Quietly at first, but then the bouts got louder and my breathing became more labored. Tears tickled the edges of my eyes.

"What's so funny?" Shannon asked, and Quinn frowned in the rearview mirror.

Funny? No idea. Nothing. Everything.

I shrugged and burst into another uncontrolled bout that squeezed my stomach so hard it hurt.

"Jesus," Quinn said with a half-laugh, sending me into another episode. "I think I better drive faster."

ANTISEPTIC AND LINOLEUM, the smell markers of a hospital. The walls were covered with pictures of superhero-doctors that must have been donated by a local school. I took off my glasses and cleaned the lenses with my shirt.

"I'm *fine*," I said again to the rather tired-looking Doctor Carter who was scanning her clipboard of notes. "I don't need to stay here."

It wouldn't be the end of the world to be admitted overnight. Hospitals didn't bother me like they did some. But my laptop was at home and my report needed writing. Ideas gnawed at me, sentences rolled through my mind—and it didn't help that My

Angle, Quinn, was right there. My column seemed to be hanging in front of my nose, but I couldn't write it with doctors prodding and poking and policemen asking questions.

I slid the glasses back on.

Other than a bit of tenderness and slight headache, I really *was* fine. Perhaps still a *little* jumpy from the attack, but on the whole, I was okay. Certainly good enough to go home.

I smiled at the doctor as she narrowed her eyes and gave me an assessing once-over.

Shannon and Quinn stirred somewhere near the door, talking in hushed whispers. Except, they really weren't so hushed.

"Lee should stay here," Quinn said, "to be on the safe side, right?"

"Pretty sure it's *Liam*. Let's see what the doctor says, but we're not leaving until we know he has a ride home if he needs it."

"Fine with me. Not like I have a home to go back to anyway."

Shannon sighed, but it sounded fake. "If you promise there'll be no Pringles, I *suppose* you can crash with me and Travis."

Doctor Carter glanced over my shoulder at the two of them. "If one of your friends here will take you home and keep an eye on you overnight, then I'll sign the release forms."

"Oh. No, I—" The urge to laugh overcame me again. "They're not my friends."

"Do you have someone to call? To take care of you?"

"Well, I . . ." I pushed my glasses higher up my nose. My shoulders slumped forward. Of course the answer was no. I leaned forward and asked quietly, "For future reference—though I'm hoping this will not occur again—would it be enough to say I owned a cat?"

The doctor let loose a small smile as she shook her head. "Sorry, no."

There was more shuffling behind me, and then Quinn yelped. I turned to see him rubbing his side and glaring at Shannon.

"Fine," he said, and then looked up at Doctor Carter. "I'll stay with him, if he wants."

"You would?" I asked, sliding off the bed and reaching for the notebook inside my jacket.

"Sure—as my darlin' here just pointed out," Quinn looped an arm around Shannon, tugging the back of her hair until she jumped. "I'm homeless anyway. Why not crash at your place?"

OF COURSE I said yes to Quinn's offer. Why not? I had the space in my apartment, and I could finally write my piece.

It didn't hurt his case that he was built like one of the superheroes in the pictures that lined the hospital halls. I mean, for tonight, while I was still a touch jumpy, having him between me and any possible Freddy visitation wouldn't be a bad thing . . .

"Nice place," Quinn said, following me into my apartment, his shoes squeaking over the threshold. There came a *ziiip*, and he slung his leather jacket over the wooden coatrack in the corner.

"Yeah. It's all right." I took off my jacket, removed my notebook, and kicked off my shoes. My socked feet skated over the floorboards but I caught myself before toppling over, and I continued the short house tour. "Living room and kitchen here. Bathroom just down the hall next to my room."

Quinn walked to the closed door in the living room and knocked. "And in here?"

He didn't wait for an answer; he twisted the handle and let himself in.

I waited for him to finish taking a peek, but he didn't turn around. I tucked my notebook under my arm and crossed over to him. "What is it?"

"Okay, Liam," Quinn said, glancing at me out of the corner of his eye. "I'm officially jealous. I'd be happy with a *room*—you have a *study*?" He shook his head.

"I don't use it as much as I should. If you really need a room, you can use it."

Quinn snorted.

"I mean, it's a little draughty," I said.

"You're serious?"

"Why wouldn't I be?"

Quinn turned and leaned his back against the doorframe, staring. What was with that intense look? I folded my arms, dropped them, refolded them, and glanced at my darkened study, which was mostly an empty room with a wall of bookshelves and a dusty desk in the corner.

"You don't even know me," he said. "What's more, I don't know you."

"You knew all your previous roommates?"

"No."

I pushed up my glasses. "Then I don't understand your issue."

He blinked and glanced back into the room. "How'd you score this place, anyway?"

"It's one of my father's apartments. I can use it while I'm studying."

"Why do you talk like that?" Quinn asked. "Father instead of plain old dad? And 'hoping this will not occur again'? That type of thing?"

I unfolded my arms, catching my notebook as it dropped. "I haven't really noticed I speak in any particular way. But I chose 'father' instead of 'dad' because this"—I gestured to the apartment—"we're not close. I was the product of an affair he had, and we don't really consider each other family." If he considered me family, he'd have offered me the apprenticeship without any stipulations.

"And yet," Quinn said carefully, "he lets you use his place."

"He can afford it. That way he figures he's square with my mom."

A frown etched its way between Quinn's brows, and I sensed unnecessary sympathy.

"We're all fine about the situation. There are no hurt feelings hidden anywhere. It is what it is."

"Huh," he said, his gaze dipping to the notebook in my hand. "Okay. What's that?"

I turned the notebook over in my hand and slipped it under my arm again. "My work. Which I'd really like to get started on." I walked back into the living room, turning another slip into a large stride. If I weren't careful, I'd end up with another concussion. "There are some blankets in the cupboard next to the bathroom. You can sleep on the couch. I'm going to work from my bed tonight."

Quinn's steps came heavy behind me. "Right. Well, I guess I'll come in on an annoyingly frequent basis to make sure you're all good. But first"—he pinched the notebook from under my arm—

I twisted sharply, lunging for my notebook. The half-head he had on me gave him an advantage. He whipped the book out of my reach. A dull ache throbbed in my ribs, stopping me from jumping for it.

"Let's see what your work is, shall we?" He leafed through the pages, scouring their contents. "You can sit down if your side is hurting."

"I'm fine. Or I will be when you give me back my notebook."

His long lashes lifted as he glanced at me over the notebook. "I saw you tonight at the party. You were watching my fight with Chris. You were writing something . . . what was it? Ah, here we go." Clearing his throat, he read aloud, "Jock. Big-boned. Broad shoulders. Tall." He chuckled. "Jesus, this reads like a catalogue. I'll have one through four, please."

His chuckling stopped abruptly. "Wait a sec, you're describing *me*, aren't you? *Runs fingers through hair as though he's attractive and knows it?*" Quinn's voice faltered. "I'm not all *that* attractive. I've got weird ears . . ." He raised both brows and shook his head.

"Which you haven't failed to note here either. *Ears look like they've had a serious clubbing.* Ouch, Liam."

I shifted my weight onto my other foot. "Those are mere physical notations. To create a picture. I certainly wasn't deriving any conclusion about you as a person from your looks."

Quinn looked up sharply from the notebook. "No, not based on my looks, but my actions. The details you use to describe my break-up scene says as much. *And then his eyes clasp on a male making out in the foyer. Hurt flashes in his eyes, but he swallows it back as if he doesn't care. Or isn't entirely surprised this is happening at all.* Wow. I don't even know what to say to that."

I opened my mouth to assure him he would remain anonymous—that the notes were more for me than for the column. They were just to recreate the atmosphere in my mind, so I could analyze it and explore my theme. Sometimes I'd transpose the emotional elements onto a fictitious character to play out an example—but enough details were changed . . .

No sooner had half a syllable passed my lips than Quinn spoke, "Actually, I do have something to say."

He tossed the notebook onto the couch and used his fingers to count. "First impressions of Liam. Moves with the grace of a giraffe in stilettos. Brown eyes behind thick, black oblong glasses —like you're going for the Clark Kent look, which you might pull off if your dark hair weren't such a tousled mess and your front tooth wasn't chipped."

He took a step toward me, stirring air over my skin and sending an unfamiliar shiver down my spine. "Has glossy skin—almost elf-like, but with an uneven tan that, judging by the pastiness of your upper arms, you got by accident. Perhaps reading a book in the sun too long?" Another finger uncurled. "Has a sharp nose that's reddened by the constant pushing up of glasses. Wears slacks and a short-sleeved shirt that was hurriedly put on. Fresh, but not ironed."

Quinn inched even closer, his eyelashes lowering as he raked a slow gaze up and down my body. "Fidgets with the pen in his pocket when he's uncomfortable or nervous."

I immediately let go of my pen and dropped my arm to my side. "Keen observation skills." I picked up my notebook from the couch. "And it was a newspaper, not a book."

"And I was born with ears like this."

I looked at him and nodded. "But I was right about the hair. Bleached."

Quinn closed his eyes and shrugged. "And everything else."

I slid backward toward the hall and my room. "Look, you provided a theme for my column. You're my angle, that's all."

"Yeah," he murmured quietly, but my skilled ears heard. "Being someone's angel would've been too good to be true."

"LIAM? WAKE UP."

I jerked upright. "Huh?" I blinked, grabbing at the open laptop that had slipped off my lap.

Quinn murmured something along the lines of "figures" and then passed me a glass of water.

I took the water and drank it all. I swiped my arm over my mouth. "Must have drifted off." Quinn plucked the empty glass from my grip, and I unlocked my computer screen. I'd only written three paragraphs? "Gah! Thanks for waking me! I didn't get half my thoughts down."

And why is that surprising, considering you can only concentrate on the attack? Who jumped me, and why? And even more importantly—

My gaze flickered from the bright computer screen to Quinn's tired face, lined with shadows. It made me glance at my radio clock on the bedside table. 2:00 a.m.

"Who was the hooded figure?" I asked.

"Hooded who?" Quinn ran a hand through his hair but this

time it didn't seem so self-assured. He swallowed, his large Adam's apple jutting out. "I don't know what you're talking about."

I cocked my head and studied him. He held my gaze squarely but there was a slight twitch to his jaw. "There was a guy who came and tossed Freddy off me. He was wearing a hooded coat, I think. I didn't see his face."

"I didn't see any guy in a hood," Quinn said, and spun on his heel, moving toward the door. "It was just you, lying unconscious on the grass. Thought you were passed out from too much alcohol. But you didn't smell like it." He paused, one large hand clutching at the doorframe, and looked over his shoulder. "Why didn't you tell the police someone else was there?"

I rested my head against the cool wooden headboard. It stung a bit where I'd bruised it, so I lifted it off again. "I'm not sure, exactly. It didn't feel right. I guess I wouldn't want him to get in trouble. He might have given Freddy as much as I got."

He stilled, and then turned his head away. He disappeared around the corner, his steps thumping through the apartment.

My opened document begged me to re-read it and get back in the zone—but by the beginning of the third paragraph, the hooded figure hijacked my concentration. Something about him nagged at me.

The journalist in me just had to know who he was.

CHAPTER THREE

I gripped the brown folder containing my three best articles from last year, and carried it into Chief Benedict's cozy corner-office overlooking the street that lined the Cathedral of Learning.

"I'd like to hand in my submission for the BCA competition," I said, handing my folder to him over his desk.

He lowered what he was reading, scrubbed his hand over his beard and snagged the folder from my grip, eyeing me carefully. "You're calling it close to the deadline, I told you about this a week ago." He glanced at his silver clock that matched the desk and chairs. His gaze fell to the folder and he thumbed it open. "I remember these."

I let out the breath I was holding. The chief remembered them. That was a good sign. A very good sign—

"But don't get your hopes up. I don't think they'll do."

"Sorry?"

The chief pulled the plastic spine off the folder and took out one of my articles. "These are perfectly solid reports, Liam."

"Then what's wrong with them?"

"Nothing wrong. But they fail to hit 'just right'." He waved the article. "Do you trust me to replace this with what *I* think is your best work?"

"I respect you, Chief Benedict, but I can't lie. I'm not sure. What do you think is my best?" Which one had he removed? I leaned forward—

Dump!

Chief Benedict threw it into the large wastepaper basket beside the desk. He clapped his hands together once. "*The Ghosts of College Past, Present, and Yet to Come.* That's your best. Such a creative defense of universities from capitalism."

I balked. Yes, the story had been fun to write and I enjoyed giving my politics page a Christmas flair—but it was so . . . so . . . *light*. "*That*'s my best work?" I shook my head.

Chief Benedict pulled the hair at the tip of his beard. "It was wide-reaching, engaging, it hooked readers who rarely read the politics page. You were showing us the issue, not telling us—it's one of the best I've read from any student in a long time. And if you'll let me, I'd like to place that one in here."

"Fine," I said slowly. "But I disagree. I think the other two will rank higher."

"Let's see, shall we?"

My hand found its way to the pen in my pocket, and it was clicking the top with erratic rhythm. I gave the chief a nod and stepped back toward the door.

"Just a sec," he said.

I paused.

"Do me a favor, would you?" He stood and lifted a stack of old *Scribe* magazines, then sauntered around the desk and handed them to me. "Take these back to the archives."

I took the stack and looked him in the eye. "I wanted the features editor position. I thought I'd worked hard enough for it."

"You work plenty hard, and it's going to happen."

"When?"

"Next year, perhaps."

I breathed in deeply. A whole year away? That would be too late. I'd never get the chance to hold the position for two consecutive years! "What about next semester?"

"I'm not quite convinced you'll be ready."

"I will be. Let me prove it to you."

Chief Benedict crossed his arms over his checkered shirt as he stared at me, calculating something. He lifted a hand to rub his beard again and then let out something between a sigh and a chuckle.

"Okay, Liam, how about this: at the end of the semester you'll write a feature piece for the magazine. You can write it on any topic. If it stuns me, if it shows me you've grown as a writer, I will promote you to features editor next semester. You have my word."

Resting the stack of old *Scribe* editions on his desk, I withdrew my notebook and pen. "When exactly?"

The chief glanced at his calendar. "In my inbox by Friday at midnight, December fifth. Sound fair?"

"Midnight?"

"For any last-minute changes I know you'll want to make." He reached out a hand, and I didn't hesitate to lock him into a warm shake. With a nod, the chief let go.

I hugged the stack all the way down to the basement, to a room lined with filing cabinets sorted by year. A long table stretched down the middle, and I dropped the magazines onto it.

A sneer behind me jerked me around, knocking half the pile to the floor.

Jack and Jill stood in the doorway. Jill sauntered in and tossed a magazine at my face. I caught it and straightened my glasses. The most recent *Scribe*.

"Are you serious? What am I saying—of course you are. You can't be anything *but*. *University of Party, Lectures in Life?* I knew chief made a mistake. Knew it. Students are sniggering at that piece of shit all over campus. Just go to the cafeterias and listen."

I gripped this week's *Scribe*, my fingers trembling. Why was I so jumpy? I'd never let the guy get to me before.

Freddy, holding out his steel-gloved hand under the streetlight, flashed in my mind. I shivered. Jill was a prick, but he wasn't Freddy.

I straightened, and opened the magazine to my article. People were laughing at this? But this was *quality*.

"Come on, Jill," Jack said, shrugging my presence off like I didn't matter, like there were better things to do with the day. "Maybe his next one will be better. Even I found switching to politics articles tough."

"Yours was actually pretty good," I said. Jack and Jill might get off on making me feel like a failure, but I considered myself above that. A true journalist would look at Jack's article objectively. And objectively, it was good. I liked how his article explored the corruption of the prison system. "The details you gave about life in prison were horrifying and gripping."

Jack grew quiet, and Jill glared at me.

"Gripping?" Jill said. "Insensitive prick. His brother is in there!"

I raised my hands. "I didn't know. My comment was not meant to disregard—"

"Just shut it, and make the next party page better," Jill said evenly, as if it cost him a lot to control himself. "Don't want to have lost all my readers when I take the page back." He stalked out of the room, with Jack following him.

I slumped against the table, pushing more old *Scribe* magazines to the floor.

Jack's voice tunneled down the hall. "*Scribe*'s not the place to get aggressive, man."

"Well . . . but . . . he shouldn't have been so dismissive about—and anyway, the party page. It's my thing. I worked my ass off for it. It's hard for me to see anyone else with it. And it's *true*. The guy doesn't know what it means to cut loose . . ."

Turning to my column in this week's *Scribe*, I re-read it. It was a good column. It offered insight. Had depth.

I shook my head. Jill was wrong.

Dropping the magazine onto the desk, I bent over to clear up the floor. Tonight I'd attend another party and write my next piece. Something that would inspire more than cheap laughs, but conversation and—

My hand stilled on a *Scribe* from two years back, which lay open to the middle. A picture of a hooded figure's blurry silhouette stared back at me. I frowned, and my pulse pumped faster as I snatched the magazine closer.

"The Raven Saves Again," I read.

I scanned the familiar article. *I've read this before.*

Last weekend after partying with friends at Rigg House's Swalloween party, Nick O'Connor did what he did after every party, and walked back across campus to his dorm. Only the short walk didn't turn out like it usually did. A few blocks from Rigg House, he was hit from behind. "I was caught off guard . . . didn't see him coming. I lost my balance and fell." *As the attacker went to strike again, a hooded figure leaped out from the shadows and dragged the attacker off, allowing O'Connor to run back to his dorm. . . .* "This guy just came out of nowhere. It was like he appeared from the sky, dark like a raven . . . [He was] wearing this navy hood, like a jacket or something. Couldn't see his face."

Same rescuer as mine. Large hood, vague outline, no face.

Police arrested the suspect and have charged him with assault.

I scanned further down.

This was not the first report of a hooded man coming to a

student's aid. There are rumors the man is a campus vigilante, and he has been the reason for two prior arrests of students . . . He is mentioned on Scribe's opinions page on more than a handful of occasions.

I photocopied the article and searched through all the magazines of the past two years for more reports on The Raven. I found three more mentions of him, including one cartoon strip asking the same questions I was: Who was The Raven? And why did he care?

I skimmed over one of the letters from last year's opinions page. One student wrote a short note to the vigilante, demanding that he "hang up his hood . . . [as] committing one crime to solve another, does not a hero make."

Not everyone was a fan of The Raven.

I filed the photocopies—along with the meager bits of information I'd found Googling him—into the flap of my notebook, and put the stack of magazines the chief had given me—and the new stack I'd collected—into their proper place.

Click. Click. Click.

My finger worked the pen in my pocket.

Yes, that was an idea.

I could use my time at these parties not only to write my reports, but also to ask questions. Maybe others had stories about The Raven? Maybe I could discover his identity and get answers to my questions.

Then I could write a report about him, unveiling the man behind the hood at long last. What would Jill say to that? Likely it'd render him speechless, and I was all for it. I glanced toward my *University of Party, Lectures in Life* column.

Students would eat up news of a campus vigilante. There'd sure be no laughing.

I DODGED a whack from a piñata baton and darted behind the trunk of a neighboring pine.

I should have been looking forward, not over my shoulder and jumping at any little shadow that moved. Freddy wasn't there anymore. He wasn't.

Straightening my shoulders, I jog-walked across the front lawn toward the crisp sounds of live salsa music.

Inside, I asked for the host, Alyson, and was steered into the kitchen to a Hispanic girl. The girl was applying ruby-red lipstick that matched her slippers and the tiny flowers threaded on one side of her dress.

I extended my hand. "Liam Davis, from the *Scribe*. I write the party page—"

She cracked a large smile, and capped her lipstick. "Stephy! Our party's been chosen for the *party page*!"

An animated shriek sounded in response, and from around the corner walked Alyson's sister, who looked exactly like her, from her eyes and mouth to the dress she wore. "Party page. So freaking awesome."

Before I knew it, I was showered with questions, and Stephy handed me a cocktail, which I gripped like a lifeline. "Have fun, and if you need anything, we'd be totally happy to help out!"

I shifted the cocktail to my other hand. "Actually, I do have a question. Have either of you heard any rumors about The Raven? The campus vigilante?"

The girls exchanged a look, and their faces sobered as they faced me again. "We've never seen the guy, but,"—Stephy inched closer, her voice softening—"we were at a party a few weeks back, and Dylan, this guy we know, said he saw The Raven throwing some guy up against the wall."

I pushed up my glasses. "Where was this? Is Dylan here tonight?"

She shook her head. "It happened down Walnut Street. He's away on some field trip."

Alyson looped an arm around her sister. "He got a photo with his phone. He printed it and stuck it in his dorm room. He's all proud of it, but it's really blurry."

"What's his last name and what dorm is he in?"

"MacDonald. Beckman Hall."

"Thank you, ladies. You've been a big help." It looked like I'd soon be visiting Beckman Hall. Who knew, I might even have the mystery wrapped up in under a week.

And now to find an angle for next week's party page.

I slipped out of the kitchen and roamed the large downstairs dining room that opened into a sitting room via a large archway. This party was all about style. No beer here, only cocktails with—I lifted the little umbrella sitting on top of the drink—speared pineapple.

I ate the pineapple.

But what to do with the drink? It probably wasn't professional to drink on the job, after all.

He doesn't know what it means to cut loose, to party. . . .

I stared at the liquid for a moment, and hesitated. Then, shrugging internally, I raised the drink and took a small sip.

Fruity. Not bad.

I took another sip, and scoped out the room. Dancers filled most of it, jumping up and down and spinning about. Wow, actually . . . some of them were good. Such an interesting mix of people too. Very . . . multicultural. Maybe that could be my angle—

Distant voices drifted over the dancing crowd—familiar voices, snarky edged with sweet. Two steps forward and a splash of cocktail on my white shirt, and there they were. Shannon and Quinn.

They danced in the center of the group, looking close and comfortable as they laughed and grooved.

Shannon's blue-streaked hair was pinned up. With dark pants

and T-shirt, she dressed simply, but her confidence made her stand out amongst the sea of cocktail dresses.

"Ouch, Shan, you did it again."

Shannon stepped off Quinn's foot. "Well if you'd let me lead," she said, "it wouldn't happen."

Quinn looked down his thick lashes at her, shaking his head. "That's where I draw the line, darlin'. I need to lead. It's built into my core. Can't change it."

She slapped his shoulder. "Liar. Admit it, you just can't figure out how to do the steps in reverse."

Quinn scowled at her. "I'm not admitting anything. Now turn." He spun her under his arm, his muscles rippling all the way up and under the sleeve of his brown T-shirt. Shannon's hearty laugh whirled with her.

When she came to a stop, she leaned into him. "Now it's your turn." She startled the guy by whipping him around.

"Jesus, Shan," he said as he came full circle, grinning. "You're strong."

I sucked a piece of ice down my throat and coughed. The empty glass was light in my hand. I finished it already? *Let's hope it's not very alcoholic.*

I put the glass on the doily-covered table at the side of the room, and found a spot at the wall to rest against as I shook off any bad effects.

Pushing up my glasses, I sought Shannon and Quinn, locking my eyes onto them as they started another dance. They moved together with little grace, but plenty of humor, and the force of their laughter travelled to me from halfway across the room.

A strange longing to walk up to them and say hello tickled at me. But a "hello" out of the blue? That was hardly appropriate, was it? They were *barely* acquaintances. Sure they'd helped me to the hospital, and Quinn had stayed over one night, but they were just being good Samaritans, that was all. I was a tiny blip on their past radar readings, which they'd likely already forgotten.

Quinn hadn't even bothered to say no to the offer of a room, nor had he said goodbye. I'd woken up to a scrawled note that said I was snoring like a healthy bastard, and that he had a self-defense class to get to. See ya later, and have a good life.

And I hadn't minded, had I? It'd saved me from having to usher him out, since I'd left early for the library to study. And his loss about the apartment, not mine.

So why did I want to go over there now?

I pulled out the notebook I'd wedged into my pocket and tried to ignore the urge. I wrote down Dylan MacDonald and Beckman Hall, then detailed the multicultural aspects of the party. Pages of notes later, I sought them out again. Shannon finished dancing with a spiky strawberry-blond that let her lead, and fell back into Quinn's arms.

"Just can't get enough of this, can ya?" Quinn said, and flinched as if expecting her to—

She whacked his arm.

—yes, just that.

Suddenly, and likely a side effect of the cocktail, I was moving toward them. Maybe it wasn't *so* inappropriate to go over. Fact was, Shannon and Quinn had gone out of their way for me, and I'd never *thanked* them for it. Yes, I should tell them I appreciated what they'd done for me.

I forced my hand off the pen in my pocket and breathed in a lungful of Axe and sweaty air.

I sidled around a dancing pair and, miscalculating my step, bumped into Shannon's back. I gave her a small smile when she turned. "Sorry—"

"Liam!" She threw her arms around me like we were long-lost friends. She squeezed me warmly, a loose strand of her hair tickling my neck. Over her shoulder, Quinn looked puzzled. Like he was trying to figure out who I was—or maybe just what I was doing there.

"Just wanted to say thanks," I said to him, still locked in Shannon's mighty grip.

"No thanks needed," Shannon murmured and pulled back. A new song started and she swayed with the beat. "You must be quite the party goer. Didn't think I'd see you again."

I shook my head and pushed up my glasses. "Not exactly. This is more of an occupation."

"Occupation?" she asked.

Quinn rested his arm on Shannon's shoulder, leaning on her, his head cocked in my direction. "He writes for *Scribe*."

"Yes," I confirmed. "The party page."

Something behind me caught Shannon's attention and a shadow passed over her face as she stopped dancing and frowned.

"Righty," Quinn said, pushing off Shannon, his hand dragging down her arm to tug her hand. "I have it in me for one more dance before I call it quits." He raised his chin at me in a *See ya, mate* way. Or maybe just a *See ya*. "Later, Liam." The green in his eyes flattened. "All the best for finding an angle."

I should've just walked away and left it at that. Except . . . I didn't want things to end there. There was such energy around Shannon, and I was attracted to it. *Curious.* I shifted my gaze from her to Quinn to her again, my fingers clicking the pen in my pocket. "May I cut in for a dance?"

Shannon snapped her attention back to us, and her lips quirked at the edges. "Sorry, thought I saw my brother but I must have imagined it . . . cut in? Yeah, sure, I don't mind."

She untangled herself from Quinn and clapped a hand on my shoulder. "Just a word of warning though, the guy likes to lead."

And with that, she stepped to the side and pushed her way out of the dancing crowd. Quinn's eyes darkened, and he rested his hands on his hips.

"Uh, what?" I jerked my gaze to follow Shannon's exit route. Had . . . had Shannon misunderstood me? I wanted to cut in for a dance, yes. But with *her*.

I blinked and met Quinn's gaze. "Well this is awkward."

His shrug was almost imperceptible, as if it were for him, not me. "I'm guessing that's a no to dancing?"

"It's not a yes. I've never danced with a guy before." Never much danced with a girl, either. Though there was that one time at my cousin's wedding. . . .

"It could be something else to write about." Quinn searched my face for a reply that I didn't have, and then he focused on the crowd around me. "Or maybe there's another more interesting *lecture in life* here. I'll leave you to find it."

He stepped to maneuver around me, and I sidestepped, cutting him off. His surprised breath brushed over my cheek. Minty, fresh, not reeking with alcohol like I expected. "I just meant to come over here to say thanks. That's all. Why didn't you take up the offer of a room?"

He looked toward his shoes and then up again. "It didn't seem like you'd care either way."

"I don't. It just doesn't make sense. You need a room, I have one."

"It might not make logical sense, but . . . you and me, I don't know if we'd get along so well."

I frowned. "It's a room."

"Yeah, but no. Thanks." He pushed past me, his arm knocking lightly against mine. "Hey, Shan, wait up!"

And that's the last you'll see of them.

I moved back to a quiet spot against the wall and sank against it for a moment. Slowly, I took out my notebook. Maybe Jill had a bigger point than I thought. I shrugged the creeping *something* off me, and jotted more notes, including one in the very back of the book. For me, for tomorrow.

Get a cat.

"Oy, Dreamy."

Something pinched my thigh, startling me. My notebook fell from my hand, tumbling into the lap of the guy sitting in a wheelchair. "Gah!"

"Well, that's not the usual response I get from people. But I like it better." He lifted my notebook to me. The hummingbirds on his arms seemed to move as his muscles bunched. He waved the notebook.

I shook my head and took it. I prided myself on being observant, yet this was the second time this guy surprised me. "You're a stealthy one, aren't you?"

He grinned. "Have to be. Look, do me a favor and stand on my other side, would you?"

I frowned, and maneuvered to where he pointed. He wheeled in closer to the wall and glanced over his shoulder.

"What are you doing?" I asked, wrangling my notebook into my pocket.

"Hiding from my sister."

His blue eyes met mine for the briefest moment, and something clicked. "Wait a second. Look at me again."

His grin lifted and that blue was looking at me again. "Why sure," he drawled. "Don't mind if I do."

I sucked in a sharp lungful of air.

"Take your breath away, do I?"

I shook my head and pushed my glasses up. "Nope, but I believe I've met your sister. Your eyes seem to exhibit the same mischievous twinkle. It's Shannon, isn't it?"

"We've got mischievous down to an art form. Now inch a little to the left and don't look down at me. I don't want her or Sullivan to spot me."

"Sullivan?"

"Sullivan. Quinn. You know him too?"

"Well *know* is going a bit far," I said. "But we've met. Why're you hiding from them?"

"They weren't supposed to be at this party. Damn. I knew I should have gone to Penn State. This is worse than living at home." He shook his head and laughed. "Hey, keep your head up."

I jerked my chin up and stared at a couple pressed up against the wall in front of us.

"They're going for it," he said. "*Get a room!*"

The couple acknowledged him with their middle fingers. A deep, hearty laugh left him, rumbling through his chair and through the material of my pants.

"You sound so much like Shannon, it's uncanny," I said, glancing at the crowd around us. So far as I could see, Shannon and Quinn were long gone. "What's your name, anyway?"

He rolled forward and pivoted the chair until he faced me. "Hunter's the name. Travis Hunter. But I prefer to go by the last name now." For a lingering moment he gazed toward his lap. Then he reached out a hand. His shake was firm—a little too firm, as if he were well-practiced at proving his strength to strangers.

"Quite the grip, Hunter. I'm Liam."

"I know."

He did? "How?"

He pointed his index finger toward my pocket; poking out of it was my notebook, my name inscribed into the cover. I pushed the notebook further in. "I write for the *Scribe*."

"So that's where I've seen Liam Davis before. You wrote the politics column last year."

I straightened, my lips stretching into a wide smile. I pushed up my glasses and nodded. "That was me."

"Serious shit. I loved your Christmas piece."

My smile faltered. "Thanks. What do you study?"

"Economics, but I don't want to bore you with any details. I'm also an amateur photographer." He reached around and unhooked a camera bag from his chair. He took out the camera, opened the lens cap and looked through the lens. "Say cheesy balls."

Ugh.

Hunter lowered the camera and checked the picture. His lips quirked. "That usually works for a grin. Try again. How about cheesecake this time?"

Snap! Snap!

"Much better. I have to say, Liam, when you aren't trying to run over the disabled, you're quite a charming guy. Not my type, but cute for sure. Now, if the way is clear, how about we brave moving to the kitchen and getting us some cocktails?"

Two hours and three cocktails later, we were outside bashing the remnants of the hanging piñata, me with a baton, and Hunter with a long branch. Candy and condoms flew out of the donkey's face and rained on us. Hunter stuffed half the condoms into a case at the side of his chair.

"Here ya go, Liam." He rolled over to me and tugged my pen-pocket until I almost toppled onto him. "Whoa, there."

I braced myself on his chair as a bunch of condoms were slipped inside my pocket.

"For whoever the lucky one is."

I patted my notebook. Dizziness coursed through me, making me stumble backward. If Jill could see me now! "No lucky one. Too busy for that."

"That's too bad—shit!" Hunter was looking toward the road. Slamming the driver's door to a beat-up Honda was Shannon, and the scowl on her face said everything. "She found me."

"Game's up, then," I said.

"For today." He rolled over to me. "Liam, meet me at Crazy Mocha Coffee on Ellsworth tomorrow."

I frowned. "Why?"

"Why? Why not? You're here alone. I'm here alone. I'd say it wouldn't hurt either of us to hang out tomorrow."

"Well . . ."

"What? You have better plans?"

"I was going to buy a cat."

He raised both eyebrows.

Shannon called out to him, her hair flying around her face. "Travis. Get your ass here now."

He rolled backward, keeping his eyes on me. "Look, show up if you want to, or not. I'll be there. One o'clock."

JUST A LOAD OF NONSENSE. I didn't like it a jot. With gritted teeth, I highlighted the column I'd spent all morning writing, and deleted it.

I sank onto my couch, closed my laptop and rested it next to me. Without the purr of the fan, it was too quiet in the house. Despite the slight hangover, I didn't appreciate the silence.

I moved into the study where I kept my stereo and tuned in to the local NPR channel. Dust drifted off the speakers as the room came alive with voices.

I sneezed. I should use the room more often. Sitting at a desk was better for my posture than the couch or the bed. *Not half as cozy, though.*

I sighed, then slumped out to the living room and snagged my keys and wallet. The clock in the kitchen read quarter to one.

The column could wait a few hours. Maybe escaping would help refresh my mind.

Fifteen minutes later, I was at Crazy Mocha Coffee. Hunter sat in the corner near the window, leaning back in his chair, leafing through a magazine.

Winding around the tables, I halted a few feet from him when he laughed. "And I thought *I* had a hangover!" He gestured to the seat across from him. "Like the look, man."

I looked down at myself. What was he talking about—

Oh. The seams did look awfully large this side of the T-shirt. My hand flew to the back of my neck, where the tag scratched the palm of my hand.

"Wonderful." I scanned for a restroom, but stopped at the counter. There, with their backs to me, were Shannon and Quinn. *So much for thinking I'd never see them again.*

Hunter cleared his throat. "Yep, guess who decided to tag along. There's no damn getting rid of them." He tossed the magazine onto the neighboring table, and it slid off the edge. After a few breaths, he shrugged. "Grab a seat, and I'll get you coffee if you like."

"Oh, uh, sure. Thanks."

He winked and rolled off. "You betcha."

"Guess I'll just wait here with my T-shirt inside out until you get back, then."

I'd meant the comment for myself, but halfway across the room Hunter chuckled. "Rock the look, man."

"Shan," Quinn's voice sailed across the room, getting closer and closer. "I know it's a pain in the ass, but I'm real thankful."

"Keep buying me hot drinks, and I won't throw you out on the street. Yet, anyway." There came an *oof*, followed by a short laugh. "Hey, I'm carrying coffees here! Wait, isn't that Liam?"

I straightened, wiping my palms against my thighs.

"Liam." Quinn rested his hands on the table as he squeezed into a seat next to me. "Tell me you're not here using Hunter as your angle."

"I'm not here using Hunter as my angle."

Shannon sat on my other side and handed over Quinn's coffee. "Quit it, Quinn. He's Travis's date."

"Wait." Quinn frowned. "*Date*?"

"In a manner of speaking," I answered quickly, "but probably not the way you're thinking. We arranged to meet up here." I pried my hand out of my pocket and rested it on the table. There was no need to be nervous. "To chat."

He relaxed into the seat. "Yeah, you don't look his usual type." His gaze dipped from my face to my T-shirt, where a small grin played at the corner of his lips. He hid it behind his coffee mug, and took a sip.

"Move it, Sullivan," Hunter called, expertly moving his chair while balancing one coffee. Quinn scooted his chair to the side. "Here you go." Hunter carefully slid the coffee to me.

"Thank you," I said, taking the warm cup and sliding it carefully toward me. Before I could enjoy it though, I needed to fix my T-shirt.

"Sure thing."

"I'm just going to visit the restroom," I said, pushing back my chair and hurrying away. When I returned, Shannon was talking to Hunter about why the self-defense course she and Quinn ran was so important.

"Gives these men and women the chance to feel more confident going out," Shannon said. "They learn the skills to defend themselves and get a chance to run away."

Hunter asked, "And you've been running these since . . ." He didn't finish his sentence, but Shannon lowered her gaze and nodded.

"Yeah. It's not enough, but I just need to do something."

"This is the right thing to do, Shan," Quinn said, focusing on his half-full coffee.

I sipped my still-steaming drink. The way Quinn sat there with his prowling grace and deep voice had more than a few males and females glancing his way. The guy could say what he wanted, but he knew how good-looking he was, clubbed ears and all.

He scratched at the top of his shirt, giving me the faintest peek of his chest. I looked at his face, startling myself into splashing coffee over my front—Quinn was staring back at me, one eyebrow raised.

"Gah!"

Hunter glanced over at us, cocking his head at Quinn. "He likes to do that—" With a casual gesture toward me, his hand hit his coffee and tipped it over. He lifted the cup, swearing. "Sorry!"

I moved too slowly, and coffee spilled over the side of the table and onto my thighs. Jumping up, I brushed off as much of it as I could. "Guess it matches my shirt now."

Quinn grabbed a bunch of napkins from the counter and came back to wipe up the rest. He handed me a few extra. "For the pants."

I nodded and took them. But I'd need more than a few paper napkins.

I twisted sharply at the tap on my shoulder. There, with his dark copper hair and shy dimpled smile was the guy I'd helped home the other week. Mitch, was it?

He darted a tongue over his bottom lip, glancing to everyone at the table and back. "Hey. I'm sorry. I didn't mean to interrupt. I just saw you, and . . . I have a feeling we know each other from somewhere."

I peeled the coffee-stained napkins off my thigh and balled them in my hand. "Yes, we met. A week ago. Friday night . . ."

He bit his lip and folded his arms across his skintight V-neck. "Ohhh."

"Are you going to introduce us then?" Hunter asked. He hooked his hands behind his head and smirked up at Mitch.

"Sure, this is Mitch. He lost his contacts while inebriated, so I walked him home."

Quinn made a sound like he was swallowing a snort. Mitch unfolded his arms and shook Quinn's hand, then Shannon's. His shy smile wavered as he took Hunter's hand, and when Hunter let him go, Mitch casually wiped his palms on his jeans.

"Are you kidding?" Shannon asked, narrowing her eyes at Mitch. "You think a spinal fracture is contagious?"

Mitch glanced at his hands, frowning. "It wasn't—"

Shannon shook her head. "It's just rude, is what it is."

"Yeah, okay." Mitch backed up a few steps and glanced at me. "Uh, bye." He hurried away.

Hunter's eyes closed, his hands balled tightly, and his nostrils flared. Shannon reached out and patted his hand, but he whipped it away from her, jerking his chair back.

"What the hell was that, Shan?" he cursed under his breath.

"You always think you need to come to my rescue. I don't need you to. I don't *want* you to. Why is it you can't see that I'm just fine on my own?"

"But—"

Hunter was already rolling around the table and toward the front door. "Mitch, man, wait up a sec."

"Quinn," Shannon said, blinking rapidly as if to hold back tears.

Quinn sidled over and wrapped an arm around her. "You meant well, darlin'. I know."

I should move. Do something. Anything. I was just making things more awkward by watching, even if it was my instinct to observe.

My wet pants still clung to my legs, so I skirted toward the restroom. I passed Hunter at the door just as he caught Mitch's attention.

"Look man, I spilled my coffee before. I know I have sticky hands—I'm assuming that was the reason for wiping them."

"God, yes, it was." Mitch rubbed the bridge of his nose with the back of his hand. "I'm sorry it came across differently . . . "

"No worries."

I made my way to the bathroom and dried my pants as well as I could under the air dryer. After a couple of minutes and a rather quizzical look from an elderly man, I gave up. The pants would have to go into the wash as soon as I got home anyway, and home was only a quarter-hour walk. I'd say my goodbyes and leave. Maybe this was a sign that I should be home working.

I left the restroom and paused this time as I passed Hunter and Mitch. Mitch's gaze slowly travelled down Hunter's tattooed arms. He gave him a cute, crooked smile. "Well, have a good day!"

Hunter flexed his arm muscles as if he were aware of their appeal. "Yeah, you too." He rolled back in a swift move, and I jumped to avoid colliding. "Liam. Nice friend of yours. Sorry about the drama."

"I was tempted to pull out my notebook and start recording it all."

He laughed.

I actually wasn't joking.

We approached our table. Quinn's voice rumbled through the air, his words hitting me with a slam.

"There's just something . . . off about that Liam guy. He's too stiff and awkward. For all his brains, he doesn't have an ounce of smarts around people. I mean, you saw him just now. He couldn't even stick up for that guy. It's no wonder he seems not to have any friends—" Quinn jerked in his seat. "Ouch, what'd you kick me for, Shannon? That's going to leave a bruise."

I stopped at the table, but didn't bother to sit. Why stay where I wasn't wanted? And besides, I had more important things to worry about. Like getting out of these pants and writing my column.

"Ah, crap." Quinn saw his mistake. I stopped him before he gave me an insincere apology. If he was sorry at all, he was just sorry he got caught.

"No, it's okay, Quinn," I said. "For all your social ease, you don't have the brains to know when to shut up. I get it."

His mouth dropped open, and Hunter slapped the back of my leg. "Oh, we're going to get along really well."

I tilted my head at him. "I've got to get going. The party page won't write itself."

With that, I left. Back to my big, cold apartment to hang out with Old Faithful, my laptop.

CHAPTER FOUR

At nine o'clock on Tuesday evening, only Hannah, the chief, and I occupied the *Scribe*'s offices. The bright fluorescent lights flickered tiredly above us, as if complaining about the long day. My fingers ached from typing, but I still had tasks to accomplish. I could work from home, but I cringed at the idea of hearing my clacking fingertips echo in the emptiness; at least there was a coziness here that absorbed the silence.

After rewriting my third party page piece a fourth time, I submitted the print-ready version to the chief.

One thing down, now on to the next: telephoning Beckman Hall. I was going to find out everything I could about The Raven and make one heck of a column out of it.

Hannah startled, drawing my attention to her. "Liam!" She tucked a strand of mahogany hair behind her ear and bit her bottom lip as she glanced at a piece of paper in her hand. "Come take a look at this."

I stretched out of my chair and moved around to her desk. Peering over her shoulder, I read the typed letter addressed to the editor of the opinions page.

The Raven's gonna lose his wings
We'll smile while he sings and sings
Then we'd love to watch him fly
Through a deep, dark, angry sky

"Who sent this?" I asked, grabbing the torn envelope. No return address or postage. Whoever wrote it had to carry it into *Scribe*'s offices.

"I cannot and will not publish this," Hannah said as I lifted up her phone and dialed the chief's extension.

He answered gruffly, and I briefly summarized the threatening letter.

"Bring it in," he snapped, "and I'll take a look."

I hung up the phone. "Chief wants to take a look. Can I take it to him?"

"Yes, of course." With trembling hands, she handed it over and I scanned it for clues. Surely the police would have some tricks to figure out who wrote this? They'd dust for prints and record the threat, should anything ever happen to . . .

I shook off the thought and strode into the chief's office.

He took one look at the letter and sighed. "It's not the first threat that has made its way to the opinions page." He stroked his beard as he read it over once more. "I'll file a report with the police, and we'll do whatever we can." Looking up at me with regarding eyes, he said, "It isn't just these guys"—he hit the letter with the back of his hand—"that want to find the vigilante. The police do as well. Whoever The Raven is, if he doesn't stop what he's doing, he will eventually be caught and brought to justice."

"Justice!" The cry came sharply, and my stomach clenched. "He's saved people's lives. Protected them. He has a cause and he's standing up for it. The Raven's a hero."

Chief Benedict sighed. "He's a hero that has sent quite a few students to the emergency room."

"Only because they asked for it."

"No one asks for it, Mr. Davis."

"So you think it's better that innocent guys get beaten to within an inch of their life? That bats get taken to them and they end up crippled for the rest of their lives?" A hiccup rose up my throat, and my eyes stung with unfamiliar heat.

The chief rounded his desk. I flinched when he drew an arm around my shoulder and gently moved me to a seat.

My whole body shook, and my teeth clenched so tightly that my head ached.

Chief Benedict crouched at my side, one hand still firmly on my shoulder. "No, it's not better," he said. "It really, really isn't. But we must work on other ways of stopping senseless violence. Because violence against violence . . . it will go wrong. What happens to the criminals when The Raven swings just a little too hard? Or lands a kick at just the wrong angle? What happens when blood stains his fingers for good? He won't be the guy with the good cause anymore, and he won't be admired; he'll become a killer and his life will never be the same again." The chief shuffled on his feet as he pushed himself back up. "And what if one day he's outnumbered, and he ends up in the hospital—or worse?"

At some point I'd started clicking my pen, comforted by the rhythm. But there was nothing I could say to the chief. Nothing at all. He was right, and I hated that.

I picked myself up off the chair and gave the chief a sharp nod. "I have a column to draft," I said. I shut the door on him and his sigh, and slid back behind my desk.

But I didn't work on my column. Instead, I stared blankly at my screen and my office "friends."

The Raven saved me, saved many people, and now—now we had to thank him by warning him about the threat to his life. And we had to save him by getting him to stop.

"You okay, Liam?" Hannah asked, shutting her laptop.

I glanced over. "I need to find The Raven and warn him."

She gave me a sharp nod and looked toward the piles of paper on her desk. "If I come across anything that will help, I'll tell you."

"Thank you, Hannah."

Her smile was coupled with rosy cheeks, matching the hair tie she wore to pull her mahogany hair off her face and into a bun.

"Off now, are you?" I asked, picking up the phone, fingers itching to press the buttons and dial. I needed to call Beckman Hall right away.

Hannah pushed back her swivel chair and grabbed her messenger bag as she stood. "I'd better get back to my apartment else Lotte will complain I have no life at all. Not even a slumming-it-on-the-couch-in-front-of-the-TV life."

"But if you're happy, right? It shouldn't matter." I glanced from my laptop screen, glowing with the number for Beckman Hall, to Hannah, who was nervously rounding her desk toward mine. I gave her a small, curious frown and she blinked her gaze away from me. Shyly. Coyly.

I tensed.

What was happening here?

"You're right, it doesn't matter. *If you're happy.*" She blushed and focused on me. "But I do want more than just working. Like . . . like maybe going out on a date sometime."

I clutched the phone tighter as she tapped her fingertips on the edge of my desk. "Liam? Do you maybe want that too? To go out sometime"—her voice shook at the edges—"with me?"

I swapped the phone to my other hand as if it would help me

think of a reply. I wasn't sure how I felt about dating. Hannah was sweet; she always brought and shared oranges and grapes. I enjoyed talking to her during the day, and she often gave insightful thoughts on my work. But going out on a date?

I pushed my glasses up the bridge of my nose, even though they were sitting high enough already. Before I knew it, I'd laid the phone down and was clicking my pen.

Click, click, click.

"I'm not sure, Hannah. How about I think about it and get back to you?"

"Oh, um—"

I brought up my calendar on the desktop and scanned all the meetings, classes and deadlines I had coming up. "How does the end of next week sound?"

She frowned lightly. "So you'll get back to me about us going out not this Friday, but next Friday?"

"No, Friday I'll have to research for the party page, but Sunday would work."

That way I'd have time to weigh up the pros and cons of dating. I'd made the mistake before of dating someone who worked in the office. Bad idea. But I couldn't ignore the warm ache at the thought of someone wanting to spend time with me. Someone who actually seemed to like me.

Someone who would discover my dead body before it started to rot in my apartment.

"Okay, Liam." She gave a small chuckle, then turned and left. "Next Sunday it is."

The door shut behind her with a soft *click*, and I stared at it for a good ten seconds before the chief brought me back to the present, snapping his fingers in front of my face.

The chief left soon after, leaving me and the dodgy light alone in the building. Finally, I picked up the phone and dialed Beckman Hall.

The girl who answered sounded almost identical to Hannah,

and I did a double take before introducing myself. She recognized my name right away. "I just loved the piece you did on ghosts of university past and present and that. Really great."

What was it with that Christmas piece? Had no one any real taste? I cleared the strange mix of delight and disappointment from my throat, and my voice came out deeper than its usual baritone. "Thank you. I'd like to speak with a Dylan MacDonald?"

"Just a sec." She must have covered the phone because, though I couldn't make out what she was saying, I could make out voices. A long moment later, she said, "I'm sorry, Dylan came back sick from his field trip. He might have glandular fever. He's gone back home and I don't know when he'll be back. Do you want me to leave a message on his door? Or, he has a friend crashing in his room for a couple days . . . maybe he can help answer your questions?"

I declined the offer. Dylan would have no idea who I was or what I was after, and I didn't want to leave details in a note on his door. I certainly didn't want to involve his friend.

Just before I hung up, the girl spoke again, "So, like, how do you choose what party you write about?"

"Random, mostly." This wasn't entirely true; I chose parties that were close to my apartment.

She continued, "Beckman Hall is having a ball this Friday, would that count as a party?"

I almost declined, but I reconsidered. If I attended this ball, I'd be at Beckman Hall, where a photo of The Raven hung in Dylan's room. Maybe, if I was clever enough, I wouldn't have to wait until Dylan returned to get a glimpse of the vigilante.

I leaned back. "Actually, I think Beckman Hall ball would work splendidly. How do I go about getting a ticket?"

BECKMAN HALL CAFETERIA-TURNED-BALLROOM looked like it

had been sucking on gangster hats, feather eyelashes, fringed skirts and cigarette holders for so long that it started spitting feathered scarves and velveteen gloves to the floor in protest.

Wearing plain black slacks and a black shirt, I slipped easily into the shadows, and no one gave me much more than a passing glance. Now that I was here, all I had to do was write some notes for my column, find out where exactly Dylan roomed, and sneak inside for a quick look around.

A voice cut through the plucking of bass strings, and the familiarity stilled me. Trying to fit myself against a life-size silhouette showcased on the wall, I skimmed the heads of the crowd toward the voice. No. It just wasn't possible. How could he be here?

I blinked at the guy dancing to the lively jazz—black pants, white shirt and suspenders.

Quinn.

It's no wonder he doesn't have friends.

My throat pinched as I swallowed, and despite the . . . rawness that overcame me seeing him, I couldn't look away. Thank God he wasn't gazing in my direction. I slunk closer to the wall, trying to be more inconspicuous.

How was it that Quinn was at almost all the parties I went to?

I'd read up on Beckman Hall, and this ball was famous, but really? It was unfathomable that we would run into each other at a party—three times in a row.

I searched for Shannon, but didn't see her anywhere in the thickening crowds of top hats and suave come-ons. Nor did I spot Hunter hidden in a corner. Was it just Quinn?

I narrowed my gaze on him again. Judging by the chipper smile on his face, he was quite simply having a ball.

The girl he danced with laughed loudly when he mirrored her moves. Something about them had me itching to pull out my notebook and start writing. I couldn't get enough of trying to make sense of this bleached-blond, green-eyed, broad-shouldered, club-eared man who seemed so at ease at these parties. Maybe, if I studied him long enough, I'd uncover the key ingredient to fitting in well in social situations.

Rested against the silhouette, I pulled out my notebook. I had to write a column on the ball anyway, so I *could* start with a description of the dancing. I wouldn't actually use him as my angle or anything; he was just one example of the numerous people swinging their hips. . . .

Quinn kept scanning the crowds as if waiting for someone to turn up, and each time his head swung around my way, I ducked into a crouch and pretended to pick up the pen I'd "dropped."

Inching back up the wall until I was standing again, I skimmed the room trying to spot who he was looking for. Shannon, perhaps? Or maybe he was trying to get back with that guy he broke up with?

When the jazz band started improvising mid-song and the saxophonist burst out into a complex melody, I twisted toward the stage, my gaze sweeping over Quinn—

I froze. He'd stopped dancing, and was focused directly on me.

I couldn't figure out why a jolt of *guilt* zapped me from head to foot. Just because he had friends and fit in better didn't mean I couldn't be here too.

I clapped my notebook shut, slipped it into my deep pocket, and without any acknowledgement, turned toward the exit. I didn't care to exchange words with him. In fact, I shouldn't have even cared how energetically he danced.

I was at Beckman Hall for another reason.

It was time to execute my plan of sneaking into Dylan's room.

I waited until people started to get inebriated. Then I waved a piece of paper and asked students where his room was so I could tack the note to his door.

In fact, what I intended to do was hide out in the hall until the guy crashing in there returned. I'd hook him into conversation and push my way into his room to check out the walls, where the picture of The Raven hung.

A drunk guy with flushed cheeks and a goatee led me all the way to Dylan's room, on the second floor above the cafeteria-ballroom. Jazz vibrated faintly underfoot as Drunk Guy used his keycard to let us both in.

"His room is just down there—" He unleashed a beer-flavored belch, and I gulped for fresher air at my side, which wasn't that much fresher—there was a distinct smell of sweaty guy and stale beer in this dorm.

"Thank you," I said, giving him a quick nod and moving over the thinning navy carpet toward the door he'd pointed at. From here, it seemed to be partially open; light spilled in a wedge into the dim hall.

Brilliant. The plan worked.

"Sure," Drunk Guy said, and shuffled off in the opposite direction with another large belch.

Slowing my step, I calculated my next move. Seemed the guy crashing in there was already here. Now all I had to do was make some conversation while slyly scanning the walls.

Simple enough.

I hoped.

Voices trilled down the hall, followed by laughter and doors opening and shutting. Footsteps followed me to Dylan's door. I moved to the side to let the guy pass, but he didn't. I blinked at the scuffed black shoes as they moved to my side, and—

"Gah!" I startled, lurching into Dylan's door and swinging it open.

"Liam," Quinn said, grabbing my arm tightly to stop me from toppling into the room. He pulled me back to a standing position as the door thumped against the wall, revealing an unoccupied room. Maybe the guy had just gone to the bathroom?

"What are you doing here?" I asked, torn between the need to grab my pen and the need to investigate The Raven so I could leave before the guy returned from his toilet trip.

Quinn frowned at my hurried words and guilt-ridden tone. "Maybe I should ask what *you* are doing here?"

I scanned the hall and made a decision. In the name of truth, in the name of *journalism*, in the name of helping The Raven who'd saved me, I stepped into the decent-sized room and yanked Quinn in with me by his suspenders. I'd have preferred him to turn around and go the other way, but he might have lingered in the doorway and demanded answers, drawing all the wrong attention to us.

Once we were safely inside—the suspenders having come to a hearty snap against Quinn's chest—I carefully placed the door in its original spot.

"Again, what are you doing?" Quinn said, this time with more curiosity.

"Just a bit of research. This shouldn't take more than half a minute."

"Are you . . ." Quinn said, following me around the king-size bed. He stopped at the two desks in the middle of the room. "Are you snooping?"

"I prefer to call it investigating," I said, scanning the corkboard of pictures overhanging the desks. One of these shots might be *the one*. Quinn stood with his arms folded, shaking his head. I glanced and added, "But I suppose I could live with sleuthing, too."

A hint of a smile touched his lips. Lifting pictures to see the ones hidden underneath, I asked, "And what are you doing here?" I couldn't deny I was marginally curious as well.

Quinn shrugged. "Confession: I wanted to find you. I rang up the *Scribe* and some girl, Hannah, I think, said you mentioned you would be here tonight."

"Hannah?" I asked, ripping my gaze from the corkboard for an astonished second.

"Yeah, I know someone who lives here and it was pretty easy to get a ticket. I've been waiting for you to arrive."

"I'd have thought I was the last person you'd want to see. Or if not the last, close to it."

He ran a hand through his hair and bit his lip. "It's just . . . you haven't been at home. Every time I go there you never answer."

Quinn had visited? "I've been working late."

"Fine, but I needed to finally tell you that I'm sorry. What I said last weekend, well, I was a complete prick, and I never should have been so cruel."

I re-focused on the pictures. "Stating a fact isn't cruel."

He winced. "Look, Hunter seems to think you're the best so, you know, I had no right to say what I did." He tried for a small smile and then reached out his hand. "Do you think we can start again?"

My fingers brushed over a blurry picture of a figure in the darkness, wearing a hood. Was this the picture Dylan had taken?

I ignored Quinn's hand as I searched for more. Nothing. The fuzzy photo didn't capture any facial features or give any clue about where to find The Raven.

"So, can we?" Quinn asked again, perching himself on the bed's patchwork quilt.

"Well—"

A scuffling sound outside the room startled me.

I guess I had expected I'd get out of the room without having to confront anyone, because suddenly I jumped a step in Quinn's direction. What was my excuse again? Where was the fake note?

Flustered, I couldn't quite figure out my next move.

Just stand there and take it as it comes, ad lib.

Quinn stood quickly, and we both would have faced the music of getting caught investigating if it weren't for what happened next.

Among the sounds of pants, groans and kisses, came the

sound of a zipper being undone and a girl's plea. "Turn off the light in there."

There was only time for an awkward glance to Quinn, who looked as uncertain what to do as I felt, before a male's arm stretched through the gap in the door, fishing for the light switch—

Click!

Darkness. Slurping smooches assaulted my ears.

I flew to the ground, crawling for a space to hide myself. I glanced toward the door at the live silhouettes of legs imprisoning us in this room. I yanked on Quinn's pant leg, making him drop to all fours too. He came down lightly without a sound, like he'd done this before.

The bed. It was our only option for hiding. The desks were too small, and there wasn't any other furniture.

So, the bed it was.

I slithered under and thought I heard a soft curse as Quinn pressed himself in behind me. "Snooping, snooping, snoopster!" he said.

Thankfully, I could only make out the wooden slats and the corner feet of the bed because, tangled around my legs, was something that felt like clothing and I prayed wasn't dirty underwear.

Quinn sidled in closer until his breath tickled my side and his deodorant filled my nose with every breath. Jazz music beat through the thin carpet and against my stomach, legs and arms, and I hoped it would disguise our breathing.

More groans sounded, and then footsteps moved into the room, followed quickly by discarded clothes hitting the floor, slick kissing sounds, and light slaps. The horrific sounds got closer and closer until, looking over Quinn, I glimpsed two pairs of feet.

Was it too late to start praying they'd do it somewhere other than the bed?

Kaplank! Boing!

"Christ!" Quinn whispered as their bodies hit the mattress.

I pressed my finger to my lips, instantly realizing it was too dark under the bed for him to see my cue, so I fished for his mouth and pinched it shut. His lips grazed the length of my finger as he turned his head in my direction. I yanked my arm back. We flinched as the slats groaned above us, followed by a moan that sounded as if it were trying to harmonize.

"Yeah, oh yeah. That's right. Suck it. Suck it."

My eyes adjusted to the darkness under the bed. The way Quinn was looking at me, as if unsure whether to laugh or scowl, had me wishing for the cloaking darkness to return. He shook his head and rubbed his forehead like he just couldn't believe this was happening.

"All the way in, yeah, you can take it. God, your mouth is fucking beautiful."

Quinn shut his eyes and looked at me when he reopened them. He was mouthing something that I couldn't make out, but I knew he was cussing.

I agreed that the situation wasn't ideal, but we had to live through it. I shoved my glasses up and twisted just enough to reach into my pocket—

The slats thumped and I froze, pressing myself closer to the floor, my hand jammed in my pocket.

The girl spoke. *"Give it here."*

I predicted the coming event, so I quickly wriggled into a better position, pulling out my pen and notebook from my pocket. I might just be able to read some of my notes from earlier. I'd concentrate on the column I had to write, and not on the thumping that—*thump, groan, thump, groan*—had just started.

"God, you're so tight."

Silent laughter shook Quinn's body and grated against my side. Well, while he laughed, I'd focus on the historical elements that were portrayed at this ball and—

Quinn shuffled closer to me and brought his mouth to my ear. His warm hand rested on my pen-clenching hand. "Are you serious?" The words slid down my neck and his breath turned my skin into goosebump soup.

Thump-thump, thump-thump, thump-thump.

"Fuck. Fuck yeah. Ride me, baby."

"You're unbelievable," he whispered again in my ear. He plucked the notebook and pen from my suddenly limp hands, stuffing my much-needed distractions into his back pocket.

"Turn over. Up on your knees."

Thump!

This one was so loud, Quinn flung his arm over me, half curling onto me as if to protect me from falling bed slats.

"I could fuck you like this all fucking night."

"Christ, please don't," Quinn whispered against the back of my neck, where his face was pressed.

"Do you like this? Do. You. Like. This?"

Not particularly. Though I found it somewhat fascinating just how much fun the two of them seemed to be having. Sure I'd had sex before, but it was usually a quieter affair. Perhaps I'd just been with the wrong girl?

What would Hannah be like if we decided to pursue something?

Oh-oh-oh-oh!

The slats jumped and slammed and groaned, and Quinn pressed against me tighter until the groans and cries peaked, and the bed banged one last time against the wall. A shuddering cry ripped out of the male, dissipating into softer pants as they both caught their breath.

It was a stiff few minutes until—thank the heavens!—the two lovers slipped back into their clothes and returned to the ball.

Quinn and I waited no more than thirty seconds—just to be sure they wouldn't come back—before we scrambled out from under the bed.

Quinn peeled off a stiff sock from his side, and we ushered ourselves out of the room.

As soon as we were in the hall, I snatched my notebook and pen from Quinn's back pocket, making him jump. "Just wanted these back," I said, shoving them back into place.

With a stiff nod and a stiffer walk, Quinn led the way out of the dorm.

Outside, I gulped down the cool air as we made our way from Beckman Hall to the street. Transitioning from the most unwelcome noise pollution to the still and quiet night wasn't as refreshing as I'd hoped. "One thing we are good at," I said, walking faster to beat off the chill, "is finding ourselves in awkward situations."

"Yeah, well," Quinn said, tugging my sleeve to stop. I hugged myself for warmth as he caught my gaze. "Here's another awkward moment coming up."

I rubbed my upper arms. "What's that?"

Quinn pulled out a set of keys from his pocket and gestured toward the car in front of us. "You're cold. Jump in. I'll give you a lift home."

I was cold (and still nervous walking home on my own since the Freddy incident), so I accepted the offer. Slipping into the passenger seat of the car, I buckled up. "Was that supposed to be the awkward moment?"

Quinn settled into his seat and gripped the steering wheel. "No," he said. "The awkward part is when I ask you *again* if you forgive me for being such a prick last weekend."

"Oh," I said, looking out onto the dark street, peppered with streetlights. How many Freddies lurked in the shadows? I shivered. *Focus on the forgiving-Quinn-the-prick conversation!* "You want us to start over?"

He shifted. "Uh, yeah."

"I don't see what there is to start, but okay. I'm sure we can forget last week." I studied his flushed face, clubbed ears, and thick lashes. A thought struck me as I took in his strong, Thor-like build. "Are you still apartment-less?"

"I'm staying at Shannon's."

"Right." We stared at each other a moment longer. Even with him a good couple feet away, I still felt tingling where he'd been pressed up against me. "Are we going to get moving anytime soon?" I asked. "I have some notes to convert into a column."

He started the car, murmuring something under his breath with a roll of his eyes, and drove me to my place.

I spent the ten-minute drive noting Quinn's silence and the way his breath kept hitching as if he wanted to say something. When I stepped out of the car, I braced one hand on the roof, the other clenched around the top of the door. I looked over at Quinn. "You want to ask if the room is still free, don't you?"

He raised both his brows, as if caught off guard, and his cheeks reddened. "Again, I'm really sorry what I said the last few days. I was a dick."

"Yes, you were." I let go of the car and slowly backed away. "But we started over. If you want to move in, come over tomorrow afternoon and we can sort it out."

CHAPTER FIVE

Saturday morning, my daily newspaper reading was interrupted by a blaring horn outside my apartment. I peeked out my window. The top of a white van reflecting the morning sun assaulted my eyes. The horn hooted again, definitely coming from this offending vehicle. I shoved my feet into a pair of unlaced gray shoes, grabbed my keys, shut the door and jogged downstairs.

"Some people are trying to read here," I muttered as I stormed over the small patch of grass to the van.

Three feet from the ruckus-maker, I recognized him. *Hunter*. One of his hands reached out the open window and clutched the top of the car. He tapped his horn again, lighter this time and with an acknowledging jerk of his head.

"Liam!" he yelled through the open passenger window. "Finally. Get your butt in here. We're on a mission."

"What are you doing here?" I said, tripping over my laces as I stepped to the car and opened the door.

"I told you already. We're going on a mission." He palmed the passenger seat with a healthy leather slap. "Jump in."

"Isn't it considered polite to call first?"

Hunter snorted. "I didn't have your number. Told Sullivan I lost the directions to your place and he happily gave 'em to me."

"You spoke to Quinn?" My interest in hearing his name was more piqued than it should have been. It might be something to analyze later. I'd see.

I shook Quinn from my thoughts and concentrated on Hunter. "You can't expect me to just go with you. I could be busy."

"Are you?"

"I was reading the *Post-Gazette*, as a matter of fact."

"That'll be there later. Now, ass in seat. Don't make me reach over there and drag your sorry weight in here."

I glanced to his legs. "Could you actually do that?"

Hunter lifted his T-shirt, tucking the end under his chin, and beefed up his arms. A small blue bird seemed to be flying over the guy's well-toned abdomen. I studied his impressive display of muscle, then chuckled at his cocky smirk and glinting eyes. "Trust me, I can pull a lot with this."

He leaned over the chair and grabbed a fistful of my navy T-shirt. I didn't need any more convincing. I hopped into the van and strapped up.

With a laugh, he righted himself in his seat, and started the van. "Now give me directions."

"Me? I've no idea where we're going."

"To Mitch's, of course."

"The guy you were flirting with at the coffee shop?" *The guy whose street was the venue for my attack?*

"I haven't been able to get him out of my mind all week." Hunter waggled his eyes, pulled down on his hand controls, and accelerated out of the parking spot. "I decided it's time for a little serendipity."

I frowned, bracing myself against the leather seat as Hunter careened around a corner. *Freddy Krueger won't be there now. Maybe the place will jog your memory of The Raven.* "You do know serendipity means something pleasant happening *by accident*, don't you?"

"Nah, you're wrong, man," Hunter said, looking over at a four-way and gesturing toward all options until I pointed left. "Serendipity means good luck, and I don't believe you just wait around for it, I think it comes to those who seek it." He shrugged and amended with a twitch of his lips, "in this case, stalk it."

He glanced over at me still clutching the seat; it was my nerves more than his driving—though only just in that order. "Where to now?"

"Just up here to the right. 512."

Hunter made a U-turn and squeezed into a tight parking spot opposite the house. He rubbed his hands together. "Right, let the luck begin."

The way he'd parked, I was in full view of Mitch's house and the lamppost under which . . . my ribs hurt just thinking about it. I sat on my shaking hands. Hunter didn't know all the details of that night; he was only here for the cute guy I'd delivered home. I focused on Hunter instead of the scenery outside my open window. "What's the plan now? Are you going to knock on his front door?"

"Hell no! That'd be a bit creepy. I don't want to give him the wrong idea about me."

I pointedly looked around the van and inclined my head

toward Mitch's apartment across the road. "So what's the *right* idea about you?"

He laughed and whacked me over the back of the head. "Hey, there's snacks and warm Coke in the glove box. Help yourself."

"Seriously, what is your brilliant, serendipitous plan?"

"Say *that* five times in a row." Hunter twisted toward me and the view of 512. "The plan is whenever Mitch shows up, I get out of the car and go over to him. All going well, he'll land right in my lap and we'll wheel off into the friggin' sunset."

It didn't sound like the slyest plan, and there was the whole matter of how quickly he'd be able to move once Mitch did show up—but whatever gave Hunter his luck.

"What's the part of the plan that involves me?" I asked, pulling off my glasses and cleaning them with my shirt. It kept the surroundings comfortably blurry for a few moments.

"You're the entertainment. Who knows how long we're going to be here?"

"I barely got three lines of work in last night," I said, thinking about how I'd fallen asleep with the laptop on and woken up to a string of aaaaaaaa's where a Roaring Twenties party-description should have been.

I slipped my glasses back on and rested my head back against the headrest. Staring at the ceiling, I planned out my column. I really should be spending the day working on that and my English Lit readings instead of lollygagging here, where I'd been attacked—

And saved!

It was the saving part that had me glancing out of the window again. The grass, the air, the silhouette of a hooded figure had all bled into shades of blue.

This week I'd go back to the *Scribe* archives to see if I could find more on the mysterious hood. Maybe I'd overlooked something important.

I peeked at Hunter, who sat gripping the wheel, hunched

forward to get the best view of the old Victorian apartment and anyone coming or going out of it.

I grabbed a Coke from the glove box and cracked it open. It sprayed over my face and the sticky liquid trickled down my neck.

Hunter snorted. "Good one. You're a funny guy, Liam."

I put the Coke between my legs to wipe my glasses a second time. "Funny? I like it."

He laughed harder and gestured for the Coke. I passed it to him, and he took a large gulp.

"Give me my camera," Hunter said, and rested the Coke can in the drink holder. "It's behind my seat."

I reached over and brought out the professional-looking monster. Hunter unzipped the bag and drew out the camera.

"Okay, now this feels like a stalk out," I said, shrinking lower in my seat.

"Stake out?" he said, clicking through pictures on the digital screen.

"No, definitely *stalk* out. This is feeling more and more illegal by the minute."

He passed me the camera. "Take a look. I think it's a good shot."

I stared at my face on the screen, taken at the party where we'd first met. Hunter truly was gifted, this was . . . a great shot. "I look good."

"Yeah, you do. Quinn thought so too."

He did? Awkward. What to say to that?

My mother's somewhat questionable advice came to mind: *When in doubt, deflect.* So I did. "And, um, what did your sister think?"

Hunter's gaze sharpened on me for a while, as if he was trying to understand something.

I lifted my brow quizzically.

"I don't get you."

"What don't you get?"

"A lot of things."

"Then ask me. Sometimes it's the best way to get the answers you're looking for."

"That so?"

I nodded. "For example," I said, "what happened to your legs?"

Hunter looked at his lap and back to me again. "Some guy beat me up on the school quad after basketball practice one night because I like dick. Bad stroke of the bat left me paralyzed from the waist down. Are you gay?"

"Since I've only ever been with women, I'd say not. Did you catch the guy who did it?"

"No. That was the hardest on my family. There was no one to place the blame on, no name to be angry at, to take to court, to send to prison." He shrugged and went back to staring through the window.

I glanced at the stretch of path I'd been kicked on. How lucky I'd been for The Raven. What might have happened if he hadn't turned up? I shuddered as Hunter cleared his throat.

"Are you involved with anyone?"

It was strange to share such personal details, but it was somewhat refreshing too. "There's a girl at work who'd like to go out on a date. I'm still undecided."

"Does she hit all the right buttons?" He swerved a gaze toward my crotch and winked.

"I really don't know yet. She's smart enough, and kind . . ."

"But?"

"But we work together. It could get uncomfortable if things don't work out." I shrugged. "In the girl department, things don't usually work out. It's not their fault. I'm . . . I guess you could say . . . more work-focused." Just thinking of work gave me a little thrill. I really couldn't wait to get back to it.

"How are you so confident?" I asked, glancing at Hunter's legs. "So positive?"

Hunter gripped the steering wheel. A rush of warm wind

funneled through the car. "It's true. I could be a miserable prick and I'd have some right to be. People would forgive me for it too, for a while. But why would I want that? You've only got one life, and I want to make the most of mine. I'm not saying sometimes life doesn't fucking suck, but I choose to focus on good stuff. That's the guy I want to be."

I glanced up in time to catch his wink.

"Any other questions you got there, Liam?"

Actually, I had quite a few. In fact, I'd even written some down a few nights ago in my notebook. I lifted myself just enough off the chair to reach my pocket. "Yes."

"Holy shit. Quinn wasn't joking. I've heard of this infamous notebook. This should be interesting. Fire away."

I leafed to the back where I'd jotted down a few curiosities. "Okay," I said. "I have some personal questions that I'm curious about. I'll list them, but you don't have to answer if you don't want to."

"You want to know how I go to the bathroom, right?" he said, lifting his brows. "And whether my junk still works."

In fact, those were two of my questions, though I'd have phrased them differently. "Yes."

"Well, I have a catheter." He pointed toward his leg. "A leg bag. I presume you know how that works?"

I nodded. "Do you always wear it?"

"I can go a few hours without, but yeah, I wear it most of the time." He watched carefully for my reaction which, other than a brief wince, wasn't much of one. I certainly didn't envy his position, but I understood it.

"As for the other stuff, I have a pretty good routine, but sometimes—once or twice a year—I have an accident." He shrugged like it wasn't a big deal, and I didn't think it was either, but Hunter stiffened and a light blush touched his cheeks. "But that's just life. I know how to deal with it."

"Sure. And what about intercourse?"

Hunter chuckled. "Paraplegics can still have sex. I do, and I really enjoy it." He curled his muscles again. "I'm strong, and other than doing it standing, I can pretty much fuck how I want. Using the chair can make things rather adventurous, too. And—because I know you're wondering—I have my orgasm in the mind. Smelling, kissing, touching, watching a guy come undone . . . you have no idea how much that attracts me."

I wrote down his answer, tracing over it with my pen.

These topics needed to be talked about more openly. It would have made a fascinating article for *Scribe*. Could have been my end-of-semester feature, except that Quinn made it clear he didn't like me using him or his friends as angles for my stories.

"Thank you for sharing. I didn't know much about any of this."

Hunter nodded and glanced toward the street, running a hand through his hair to spike it up. "Sure."

I stared at one of my other questions and licked my dry lips before I asked it. "You've known Quinn a long time, right? Were you and he ever together?"

Hunter cocked his head and studied me, a whisper of a smile nudging the corner of his lips. "When did you come up with *that* question? Never mind—no. Quinn and I were friends, he was the first guy I came out to, but we were never attracted to each other like that."

I ticked off the question with a larger-than-usual stroke of my pen—

Tap-tap-tap.

I jerked at the tapping on my car door at the same time Hunter cracked into a smile.

"So much for our suave stalking," he said under his breath. "He found us first."

Mitch rested his arms on the car window sill and sent us a puzzled look. A dark yellow T-shirt clung tightly to his chest, and coppery hair glinted golden red in the sun.

"I saw you guys," he said, a touch nervously, keeping his eyes on Hunter. "What are you doing around here?"

I deferred the question to Hunter, and pressed myself further back into the seat so they could see each other better. Probably now was a good time to think of an excuse and slip out of the car, leaving Hunter and Mitch to their serendipity.

"I was hoping to run into you," Hunter said, "but I guess this will have to do."

Mitch's cheeks flushed. "Sorry?"

"Look," Hunter said with less confidence in his voice, but with a smile on his face. "I'm just going to put this out there, and you can tell me what you think. You're hella cute, Mitch, and I'd love to go for coffee with you sometime."

I chose then to interrupt, because I really shouldn't have been in the middle of this moment. "Excuse me, Mitch," I said, opening the door and slipping out. "I have the *Post-Gazette* to read. So I'm going to leave."

"That wasn't subtle at all!" Hunter cried out with a laugh to my back, and Mitch chuckled too.

I waved it off and trudged over the road as Mitch clambered into the front seat and shyly asked if they could do coffee right now. Hunter's van rumbled to life, and a few moments later, they were off. I was left staring at the stretch of grass where the campus vigilante had saved me.

CHAPTER SIX

Quinn showed up shortly past five, his hair still wet from showering. He toed off his shoes and dumped his sports bag at the front door, eyeing me with a look that made me think perhaps I wasn't standing straight enough, that made me wonder if something was hanging out of my nose. Casually, I swiped my face and rolled my shoulders back into better posture.

Having a roommate makes all kinds of sense. I rarely used my study anyway, preferring to work on the couch or my bed, and, well . . . in case I did die in my apartment, someone would know about it. Someone who could scream a little louder than a cat, anyway.

I dug my hands into the pockets of my dark gray slacks and

fiddled with my pen as Quinn strolled into the room toward me. The lump that rose in my throat took a few swallows to get down.

"This is the place." I pointed toward the study Quinn had eyed the last time he was here.

For a moment it could have been that night all over again, with the way he charged over to the door and stuck his head inside.

"You'd really still want to live with me?" he asked, sneaking a look at me from the corner of his eye. "You're not kidding?"

"Why would I joke?"

Snorting, he moved over an inch so we could both fit in the doorway. "Yes, why indeed." Without warning, Quinn slung his arm over my shoulders and crushed me closer to his side. "So, roomies then? You going to be good with that?"

"If you cut down on the deodorant," I said, prying myself free, "we'll be great."

Quinn laughed. "Can I get a glass of water? I'm still parched from class."

"Class?" I asked as I headed for the kitchen. "On Saturday?"

"Shannon and I run self-defense classes at the rec center."

I perked up at that. Since my unanticipated meeting with Freddy, I'd been thinking that maybe I should learn some self-defense. "Might be a good idea to take one of them," I said, pulling out a fresh glass from the cupboard.

Quinn leaned against the opposite side of the kitchen island and flicked through the pile of party flyers I had collected over the weeks. "You should come along to one, then."

"I'll check my schedule, but yes, that would be good."

As I turned on the tap and filled Quinn's glass, he blurted, "You don't mind I'm gay?"

I glanced at him over my shoulder and turned off the tap. Facing him, I leaned back against the sink. "Why should I?"

He looked at me, the frown on his brow slow to disappear. "All right. Just don't want you freaking out when you see a guy leave from my room, that's all."

I swapped the hand holding his glass and wiped my wet palm over the leg of my pants. "If I were to 'freak out' as you call it, I'd probably be doing that while he's *in* the room. The walls are thin. But, rest assured, Quinn Sullivan, I'm too busy to care about your shenanigans. As long as the wall stays up, you're all good."

"All good, huh?" For the confident guy he was, he sounded quite relieved. "How much do you want for the room?"

I lifted the glass and drank. By the time I remembered it was meant to be his, I'd already finished it, a few drops of water beading at the corners of my mouth.

Giving him a sheepish smile over the edge of the rim, I put the glass in the sink and filled up a fresh one. "Sorry. You'll probably have to get used to that. I get sidetracked with a thought and, yes, well . . . I'm also a little on the clumsy side."

"Yeah, you don't say."

A bizarre and irrational urge to poke my tongue out at him came over me, but I managed to keep my decorum. "I don't pay rent on the place, so I don't expect you to either."

"No rent?" he asked.

The surprised look on his face startled me into a jerky movement, and I splashed water down Quinn's front, soaking him. I must have handed him the glass a little faster than I should have. He yelped and plucked his T-shirt away from his stomach as the cold liquid soaked to his skin.

"Sorry," I said. "Misjudged that one completely."

"Just a little." Quinn reached over his shoulder and pulled off the shirt. He balled it up and rested it on the counter, then walked slowly toward the bag he'd dumped at the entrance. "Good thing I have my sports stuff here."

"Sports stuff?" I hummed.

Without the loose T-shirt, Quinn looked like a superhero. His toned stomach tapered gently to his hips, and he had a lot more hair on his chest than I had.

I pushed my glasses up.

Fascinating how the slight chill in the air pebbled goosebumps all down his stomach, disappearing at the waistband of his jeans.

Similar to my irrational tingling whenever the word *examination* was mentioned, I got goosebumps just looking at Quinn.

He shifted into a crouch, laughing softly as he unzipped his bag. "Like what you see?"

I lifted my gaze to his. "Yes, I do."

He stopped mid-chuckle. "Um, Liam? You do?"

I nodded. "I'm an observer. It's in my nature."

"In your nature," he repeated, glancing at his stomach. He bit down what looked like a retort, and he ruffled through his sports bag.

His bleached hair glinted under the light.

"What is your natural color?" I asked. I'd been curious about that. Was it the same light brown as his chest hair?

Quinn pulled on a large white shirt. When his head popped through, he stared at me for a moment, his lips wobbling into a grin as he ran a hand through his hair. "It's an unremarkable mousy brown."

I cocked my head, trying to imagine the color on him. Somehow, in my imagination at least, it made him look paler and less . . . Quinn. "Hmm. Probably should keep dying it then."

He murmured something under his breath, and chased it with a shake of the head. Coming back to the kitchen, he said in a rustier version of his voice, "Back to no rent. I can't freeload, I just . . . that doesn't work for me."

Didn't work for him?

What type of person didn't take up the offer of free accommodations? He could save his money for important things like university fees, traveling, savings . . . but instead he insisted on paying for something he didn't have to?

"I have to pitch in somehow," he said, picking a rotting apple from the fruit bowl and walking it to the bin. He pressed his foot on the pedal and dropped the apple in. Then, grabbing two fresher ones, he moved around me and washed them.

How easily he made this place home. How foreign it was to have someone in my kitchen cutting apples into wedges.

Quinn rummaged for a plate while I distractedly thought of a way he could pitch in.

"Apple?" he said, putting the plate between us and taking a wedge to his lips.

I took one. "It doesn't seem practical insisting to pay for something you could have for free."

He was standing so close to me I almost felt his shrug brush against my side. "Sometimes, Liam, it's not about being practical or even logical." He crunched on his apple. "It's about doing what you *feel* is right."

I used my apple to push up my glasses before taking a bite. "Well, I don't get it, but okay. How about you pay for my daily newspapers? That's about three or four dollars a day."

"That's it? No, no, I've got to do more."

It took me another two slices of apple before I had an idea that might work. "Actually, I do have a thought."

"What's that?" He twisted toward me, his hip leaning against the counter. He wiped his sticky fingers against his jeans.

I lingered on that stomach of his. "I could use a man with the body of a superhero."

Quinn hooked a finger under my chin and lifted my face. He raised a slow, questioning brow. "Liam, if I didn't already have some idea how your brain works, you'd be flat on your back right now. Please tell me what you mean."

I shook my head. "I mean, since the night I was attacked, I've been more than skittish going to parties. I'd feel a lot more comfortable if I went with someone who knew how to fight. At least until I learn how to defend myself."

"Are you saying you want me to go with you to parties for rent?"

"Would that be a problem?"

He laughed, and his fresh breath burst in little bouts against my temple. "Not if you refer to me as your superhero from time to time. My ego could get used to that."

I stepped away from the goosebump-inducing Quinn. For whatever reason, whenever he spoke or laughed or moved around, the room didn't seem to echo him. It was like he soaked everything up and added warmth to the room that had been missing since I'd moved in.

"Do we have a deal, then?" I asked.

He folded his arms, but his head was practically nodding in answer. "I'm getting the best end of the bargain here."

"As long as I can quote you on that if anyone tries to throw a fist at you."

"Deal."

QUINN MOVED in the next morning. I insisted he come early so I could let him in before disappearing to the office. Monday, I'd cut him a key so he wouldn't have to wait around for me.

He came ten minutes later than our eight o'clock arrangement.

I yanked the door open to a wet and tired-looking Quinn and company. Quinn stood holding a large box, his hair matted with rain that dripped onto the box. He looked like he might still be asleep.

Behind him, carrying a box in each hand, Shannon gave me a dimpled grin and swept a blue strand of hair off her face with a flick of her head.

Hunter was the first to speak, rolling past Quinn and into my apartment balancing a suitcase on his chair. "Let's dump this before your bed and other shit starts elevator surfing."

He dropped the suitcase at the side of the door, and slapped my ass on his way back into the hall. I jumped at the contact, letting out a noise that seemed to snap the rest of the guys into motion. They all piled in. Shannon rested her boxes to the side and pecked my cheek before following Hunter. Quinn zombied the distance between us and pushed his box into my arms.

"Thanks for the help," he murmured, and then followed it up with a yawn.

The damp cardboard against my chest had me simultaneously grabbing the box to hold it away from me and shaking my head. I'd already removed an entire shelf of books for him and dusted the desk. "Actually, I really have to get to university. I've got a column to look over and some studying for—"

Quinn blinked, resembling a live human for a moment. Sort of. "Dude," he said, "it's the crack of dawn."

"Not really. Technically, dawn would be—"

He reached out and pinched my lips shut with his thumb and forefinger. The pads of his fingers weren't very soft or smooth but rather calloused. His fingertip tickled my lip in a way that gave me the shivers. "It's eight on a freaking Sunday. *Ten o'clock* would still be dawn to me."

My grip tightened on the weighty box. What was in here? Bricks?

"Be that as it may," I tried to say around his fingers, but it came out more a vibration than anything. My voice must have tunneled over Quinn's hand because he jerked his hand back. Suddenly he looked like someone had poured ice water over him.

"Is this work urgent?" he asked.

"The deadline is Tuesday, but—"

"Tuesday. Right. Then this is how it's going to work, Liam. You're going to suffer through a quick move for maybe an hour or so, and then I will take us all out for brunch to say thanks, man.

After that, you can go to uni and type to your heart's content, okay?"

I shifted, changing my grip to the underside of the box. "I'm not a fan of moving. It really bores me."

Quinn veered around me and held open the study door for me. "You're not the only one."

I trudged into the room and lowered the box to the floor. Quinn had a point—if I'd been the one moving in, I guess I'd have appreciated the help. "What do you want me to do? Keep in mind, I'm allergic to power tools."

Well, not allergic *per se*, but I couldn't use one without hurting myself or getting shocked, so allergic seemed an appropriate description.

"Not keen on them myself. But don't worry"—he pointed to the box—"I thought you could help me with my books."

I snapped to attention, already nodding and moving toward some empty shelves in the bookcase. "Now *that* I can handle."

The chuckle Quinn left me with bubbled around the room, and a sudden burst of sunlight escaped a gap in the clouds and flowed into the study.

I soaked in it a moment before busying myself with Quinn's . . . *comic* books. They held a familiar weight. I leafed through a couple as I did with the *Scribe*. They were in pristine condition, no dog-eared corners, no coffee stains, no sticky pages.

Fanning a few dozen, I organized the issues before carefully stacking them onto the shelf.

Each new comic conjured more images of The Raven. Inky blue, graceful, face shadowed by his hood . . . part of my desire to go to the university today was to find more names of people who had seen or heard about The Raven.

Hearing Quinn in the background, I stilled, my fingers splayed over a series of Superman issues. What did Quinn know about the vigilante? I hadn't forgotten the night after the hospital, how he'd stiffened at the mention of someone saving me . . .

Hunter rolled into the back of my legs and yanked me down onto his lap. A comic book flew out of my grasp and clattered against the shelf before slumping to the floor.

"What was that for?" I asked, trying to pull myself off him and reach the comic before it bent for good. His grip tightened around my waist.

"Don't mess with the hummingbirds, man," he said with a grin and a flex of his arms. "They'll win. Look, you have to help me."

Over my shoulder, I asked, "With what?"

"Mitch, of course. He's . . . he's a dream, and I want it to come true."

"How am I supposed to help?"

"I told him you work for *Scribe* and that you wanted him to come say hi sometime."

"Why?"

"Look, Mitch is . . . a bit unsure about this." Hunter tapped the arms of the chair and then prodded my back. "I want you to figure out what part bothers him."

"Why don't you just ask yourself?"

"Because I don't want to scare him off or make him uncomfortable. And I think it's the same for him. He might be worried he'll say the wrong thing or . . . " He sighed. "Sometimes it's easier to talk to someone else about it, you know?"

"I'm sure he has friends he's doing that with—"

"Yeah." The distinct sound of a smile lingered in his voice and a quick glance proved it to be true. "But I'm all about making my luck, aren't I? For that, I need to get inside his head, and you"—he gently pushed me off him—"are my mole."

"And what if the answer's not something you want to hear?"

When I faced him, he shrugged. "And what if it *is*?"

Quinn and Shannon stumbled in, struggling with the base of Quinn's bed. They dropped it with a heavy *thunk* in the middle of the room.

Hunter, holding my gaze, rolled out of the room. "I've got to get to basketball. Shan, are you good to get home on your own?"

Shannon smiled. "No problem, Travis. Do you want me to come with you? I could—"

Hunter raised his hand. "Sis, just don't. I can handle it."

Hunter left and for a few moments the aftertaste of awkwardness lingered in the air. Swiveling from box to bookcase, I concentrated on stacking the DC comic books below the Marvel ones.

Shannon and Quinn ducked out again, but they returned with large trash bags filled with clothes and sheets. Shannon plunked her load onto the floor. "That's the last of it."

Quinn cheered, took out his phone and played some music. His croaky singing voice sounded like murder—the murder of crows squawking in a summer breeze. He swung his hips to his ill-timed chorus singing, and I forgot about the comics for a moment and enjoyed the show.

"This is really awesome of you, Liam." Shannon startled me out of my Quinn-induced reverie. I nodded, taking out the hundredth comic from the box and arranging it by issue. She added, "I couldn't have stood the guy a day longer."

Quinn's singing halted. He pulled a pillow out of a box and tossed it at her. "Hey! You know you love me at your place."

"Nuh-uh. You promised no Pringles in bed."

"I was *grieving*. Besides, I didn't do it while you were in there."

"Yeah," Shannon drawled. "That makes it so much better."

Quinn leaped over his thick gray blankets and a bunch of clothes to engulf Shannon in a hug that made her burst into a shriek. She twisted in his grip and pushed him until suddenly Quinn was flat on his back, lying on his blankets. She pinned him down, and the guy roared in an uncensored laughter that seemed to make the rain on the windows glow with silver light. As if his laugh were magic, the true meaning of a silver lining.

"I am gonna miss your hugs," she said as she clambered off him. "Guess Liam will be the one getting most of them now."

Quinn sat up and pushed to his feet, glancing over my way and grinning. "Yeah, and he really needs them too."

"Me?" I fervently shook my head. "I don't—"

Damp arms curled around me and the air left my lungs as—in one bound—Quinn crushed me to his warm chest.

"Yeah, you do," he whispered in my ear.

The unfamiliar sensation froze me for a second. I pulled against Quinn, but then his warmth molded against me, supportive and comfortable.

Slowly, he released his grip, pulling back to shrug at me. "If you really hate it, I won't, of course."

I didn't really hate it. "There are worse roommates out there than ones that hug." I bent to pick up another comic with a slight tremble in my fingers. "Now when you said you had books, I thought you meant *real* ones."

"Uh-oh," Shannon said, an evil grin quirking her lip, "I wouldn't insult his comic stuff. He's quite the sensitive man-boy when it comes to them."

"Comic *stuff*, Shannon? Really?" Quinn folded him arms and pouted.

"See what I mean?" she said, brushing a blue strand of hair from her eyes.

I looked from Quinn to Shannon. They were such good friends and so . . . close. If I'd focused on finding friends instead of working non-stop, would I have had a friendship like this by now? Would it have made me a better writer for the party page? Would I have known Jack and Jill were such dicks?

Quinn said, "Our Liam here is thinking, Shan. You can tell by the clicking."

I dropped the pen I hadn't even realized I'd been holding, and drew my hand out of my pocket.

"What are you thinking about?" Shannon asked, and before I could stumble over an answer, she moved out of the room carrying a potted Aloe Vera.

If I hadn't peeked at Quinn, I might not have had to answer at all. But his not-so-subtle eyebrow raise forced me to answer.

"I . . ." I grabbed another comic and slipped it onto the correct shelf. "Who's your favorite character?" I asked him.

"I like Bruce Wayne and Clark Kent. I like them most without their costumes on."

"That's a bit too much information."

Quinn flushed. "I meant their superhero *costumes*. I like them with their clothes on."

I nodded and pushed up my glasses. "It's okay, Quinn. I'm not going to freak out, remember?" I picked up a comic and flipped through it. "I've never read comics much, but maybe I could take one to look at?"

"You can take as many as you like. Even"—Quinn plucked out a comic sealed in a Ziploc bag—"my most prized." He held it out, but when I reached for it, he pulled it back a fraction. "Just, please, no food or drink around it."

I jerked my head up. "Ohh, I *like* you."

Quinn's brow rose, and his gaze sparkled with a repressed laugh. "*That*'s the reason you like me?"

"Books should never be disrespected."

A comic featuring Booster Gold caught my eye. "This guy sort of looks like you. I think I have to read this one too."

"He gets shirtless in that issue quite a bit." He clapped a hand on my shoulder and said, just before he pushed away to find Shannon, "You'll like it. There's a lot to . . . *observe*."

CHAPTER SEVEN

Tuesday evening, I came home to the delicious smell of stew and Quinn draped over the couch chatting with Shannon over the phone. He wagged his eyebrows in hello and pointed to the stove. "Help yourself," he mouthed. He switched the phone to his other hand. Into the mouthpiece, he said, "No shit? Seriously?"

I peeled off my parka—

Wait. What was with the bandage peeking out from under Quinn's sleeve? I tried to get a better look as I shuffled into the kitchen, but I banged into the corner of the bar.

"Ouch," I yelped, quickly steering around the sharp corner and into the actual kitchen.

"Got to go, Shan. Lunch tomorrow? . . . Sweet."

I rubbed my side and took one of the clean bowls from the dish rack.

"You all right?" Quinn asked, coming up to the stove and stirring the stew with a ladle.

"Swell."

With a snort, Quinn grabbed my bowl and filled it with stew. "Eat up."

I took it to the table, grabbed a spoon and dug in. The hot, meaty gravy hit my tongue with an explosion of flavor and comfort. Quinn was perched on the end of the table, fiddling his thumbs.

I pointed my spoon toward him. "What happened to your wrist?"

Quinn yanked his sleeve further down. "Nothing much. Light sprain is all. Happens teaching self-defense sometimes. It'll be fine in a day or so." He slid off the table, grabbed his laptop from the glass coffee table in front of the couch and settled on the couch to work.

As soon as I'd licked my bowl clean, I rinsed it and quietly snuck into my bedroom. It was strange constantly sharing the same space with someone, and I wasn't yet sure where the line was drawn when it came to encroaching on Quinn's privacy.

I tucked myself into bed with my laptop and emailed a student named Garret, who'd been rescued by The Raven last year. After that, I sent Mom a quick update on my roommate, and then I swapped the laptop for my English Literature readings.

Alone in my room was fine. It was normal, and it . . . well, there was something comforting about knowing there was someone in the next room.

Dum-da-da-dum-dum came a knock at my door.

I straightened. "Yes?"

Quinn opened the door and let himself in, swinging his arms

into a clap. "See, the thing is," he said and jumped onto the bed, pinning one of my feet. I wedged it free. "You don't have a TV."

"It's not my thing," I said, slipping a bookmark into my book and resting it on the second pillow.

"I've been bored out of my mind the last few nights," he said as he laid himself on his side and propped his head up with his elbow.

"Don't you have studying to do?"

"I can't be studying all the time, I'd go nuts."

I glanced at my required reading. "You could invite someone over if you like. I won't disturb you."

"Don't have anyone I want to invite over right now."

"Not Shannon? Hunter?"

"Nope." He shook his head sadly. "Shannon is taking Hunter out to dinner tonight."

"Is there something wrong with that?" I asked.

"No. It's just . . . she tries too hard sometimes. Not that she'd ever listen to me when it comes to Hunter."

I thought back to the moment at Crazy Mocha Coffee. "She's very protective of him. I'm sure that's normal for a sibling."

Quinn plucked at the blankets close to my toes. "Yeah, sometimes." He pinched my foot. "Let's play some cards or something. Game?"

I hesitated a moment and then pointed toward the small bookshelf I had in the corner next to the dresser.

"Third shelf from the top. And Quinn?"

"Yeah?"

"I'm good at cards."

CHIEF BENEDICT LEANED BACK in his chair and gazed at each of us sitting around the oval table. I sat at the perfect angle—the Cathedral of Learning looked like an extension of his prominence.

I shifted on the hard seat, my fingers gripping my pen, poised to take more notes. After an hour in the room, surely we were close to winding down.

"Last delegations," Chief said, focusing on Jack, who sat next to Jill with crossed arms. He jerked a thumb behind him toward the cathedral. "Write a report on the reopening of the 32nd floor. The rest of you, BCA placements twenty-five through fifty come out the beginning of November. I'll hang a list on the noticeboard."

Chief stroked the spine of his frayed leather binder. "One last thing before you go." He cleared his throat. "I am pleased at the results I am getting from you. I'm proud of this team, and I look forward to reading more of your skilled work. Thank you."

Jill slumped further in his seat, and both he and Jack sent me a withering glance—one I happily reciprocated.

"Well? What are you all still sitting here for? Get back to work. Liam, hang on a moment."

I waited until the others left before I approached Chief Benedict. "Yes, chief?"

He stood from his chair, coming to a stand in front of me. "How's it going?"

"As well as can be expected. I am assuming you held me back for a reason?"

He let out an amused huff. "About your party page pieces . . ."

My fingers itched for my pen as I waited for him to continue.

Chief stroked his beard. "They're solid, and they'll do, but I think you might be missing the point."

I folded my arms. "And what point is that?"

"To diversify your style. To get you to jump into the shoes of others." The chief glanced over my shoulder at the thrum of the office behind us. "What you are giving me is the same in tone as your politics articles. I want to see you challenge yourself by pitching your writing to your target audience."

I had nothing to say to that, so I gave him a sharp nod. I

wasn't expecting his hand to clasp my shoulder, but when it did, the awful tightness in my throat made it difficult to swallow.

"I truly just want to help you become a better writer," he said. "That's all."

"Yes, sir. I want that position we talked about."

"You know it won't be the end of your career if you don't get it, right?"

I did know that. There would be other jobs out there for me, but I wanted the apprenticeship, and maybe . . . maybe there was a part that wondered what it would be like to have my father's approval. "I'm going to land the position."

The chief dropped his hand. "I like your focus, but be prepared for me to say you're not ready."

Dismissed, I went back to my desk and finished jotting down the names from past *Scribe* issues that had anything to do with The Raven.

Hannah looked over her desk at me and gave a shy smile as she picked up an eraser and fiddled with it.

"You seem like you want to say something," I said, leaning back in my chair to focus on her.

In this light, her hair looked less like mahogany and more like sixty-percent chocolate. She tucked a strand behind her ear as she cleared her throat. "Sunday's only a few days away now . . . "

I grabbed my pen and started clicking. "Yes, it is."

Click. Click. Click.

"Liam?" Hannah asked.

"Yeah, I still need to think. We work together. Things could get awkward—"

Two things interrupted me at the same time.

The first was Mitch—clad in a fitted brown T-shirt, jeans, and cowboy boots—strolling through the door and scanning the room for me.

The second was my phone ringing. I let it shrill two times as I waved to catch Mitch's attention before answering it. I mouthed an apology to Hannah, who shrugged and ducked her head.

"Liam Davis, *Scribe*."

"Hi, this is Garret. I'm calling about the email."

"Garret? Yes, yes. I am looking for any information I can get on The Raven." Just that morning, an anonymous thank-you letter arrived at *Scribe*, addressed to The Raven. He'd saved again, and at no small cost. The victim worried The Raven had a torn wing.

Hannah's head snapped up and she gave me a quizzical look. At the same time, Mitch slowed to a stop at my desk.

Garret breathed heavily down the line. "I don't remember much. I was in the hospital for a few days afterward."

"Anything you know might help me piece things together."

"You want to find him?"

"Yes."

Mitch looked curiously at my stapler, and more specifically at the eyes-and-mouth stickers decorating it. A Jack and Jill prank. Seeing I had no real friends, they'd stuck faces on all my office supplies—coffee cup, paper tray, tape holder. My office *friends*, they'd said.

It hadn't bothered me much.

Until Mitch jokingly pressed against the end of the stapler as if it could speak. I swallowed an angry lump.

Mitch would want to know why I'd done it, and when I explained, he might just think me as pathetic and laughable as the rest of campus sniggering over my party page columns.

"Why?" Garret asked, bringing me back to the call. "This guy saved me, I don't want to snitch and get him into trouble."

"I don't want that either."

I might have initially wanted to expose him just so I could feel better about myself and secure the features editor position, but my incentive changed the moment I read the threat at Hannah's desk.

The Raven's gonna lose his wings
We'll smile while he sings and sings
Then we'd love to watch him fly
Through a deep, dark, angry sky

I stared at the stack of *Scribe* magazines on the corner of my desk. From the swirls of colors, the haunting memory of Freddy's fingers surfaced. I shivered.

"I only really remember his shit-kickers," Garret said. "They were black and sort of fitting, and they sort of made me think the guy was gay. Which, hell, I know is a stereotype, but trust me *I* wouldn't have minded a jot."

"Thank you, Garret," I said before ending the call.

Mitch frowned. "Interesting call?"

I snapped out of my chair. "Yes. Come with me." I pulled my jacket off the back of my chair and slipped it on. "Let's go someplace we can talk."

Mitch followed after me. "So . . . what's up with all the stickers?"

"I'M GOING to get right to the point," I said, taking a seat outside with an excellent view of the spot where I'd banged into Hunter the first time. Mitch sat beside me and handed over half the sandwich we'd bought from the cafeteria to share. A light breeze rustled the leaves.

The sun peeking through the clouds highlighted the copper in Mitch's hair, which shone perfectly in the early shades of fall. He nibbled on his bread crust, staring toward a pair of squirrels scampering at the base of an oak. "I have Improv Theater soon, so to the point is good."

I bit into the sandwich, and a blob of mayonnaise splattered onto the thigh of my tan slacks. Wiping it off, I said, "Are you interested in dating Hunter?"

Mitch spluttered, and crumbs flew everywhere. The squirrels stopped and took notice. Mitch studied me, biting his bottom lip. "I want to," he finally said. "But . . . I mean, he's . . . wow, he's a charmer."

"So what bothers you?"

His cheeks bloomed the color of the leaves. "It wouldn't be right. I shouldn't."

Wouldn't be right? I could honestly say I didn't know what that meant, let alone how to respond. "Can you explain?"

"I mean, I . . . I have no idea how to date a guy, let alone one in a wheelchair!"

"Yes. That's a pickle." Hunter had made a bad decision employing *me* as his mole. How was I supposed to help when I barely knew how to date a girl, let alone a guy, let alone one in a wheelchair?

"It's just, you know," he said, "I question myself over everything. What if I say the wrong thing, like 'let's go for a walk' or something stupid and I offend him?"

"Okay, stop right there," I said, swiveling more in his direction. At least I could help on this point. "Granted I've only known Hunter a short while, but one thing I'm pretty sure about is that he's not easily offended. Besides, 'going for a walk' is an expression. He'll get that."

"I'm scared. I'll do something wrong."

"And what if you do something right?"

That had him thinking, and a smallish smile bracketed his mouth. "I do want to see him again. It's just—"

"Good. I'll tell him you said so."

"Along with everything else?" he asked, finally taking a proper bite of his sandwich.

"Yes." I leaned back and stared at the lightly-clouded sky. Just maybe Hunter was right; I had to make my own luck.

And I would.

I'd make real friends.

I'd wow chief with the best feature article.

And I'd write the best party page column *Scribe* had ever seen.

CHAPTER EIGHT

I had a third tea. The chamomile and honey running down my throat soothed me, and it sparked just the right energy in me to concentrate on the essay I had to write on the most influential villains in literature.

I slurped up the last of the tea, catching the gooey honey on my tongue, and got up from the table.

Quinn, lying on the couch with his knees up, peered over his book, *Muscular System*. "Sneaking off to your room now?"

"That was the plan," I said, setting my cup in the dishwasher. "Like every other evening."

He lowered the book to his chest. "Exactly. Like every

evening. Don't you want to spend one evening in the living room with me?"

"Why? You'd just be a distraction."

He grinned, and I was reminded of Bram Stoker's *Dracula*. "Oh would I?"

I wiped my hands on my jeans before picking up the laptop at the end of the table. "Yes, Quinn, you would. And I'd just distract you too."

His gaze skipped down the length of my dark flannel pajamas. "Somehow I think I can handle it. C'mon." He sat up and patted the spot in front of his feet. "Work here for a bit. Hard as it might be, I promise I'll do my best not to distract you."

I allowed a small smile at the waggle of his brows. Well now, I wanted real friends, didn't I? This was the perfect opportunity to work on that.

I stepped around the table toward the Quinn-dominated couch. The air was thick with warmth and I had the tingly heat in my cheeks to prove it.

Darting to the air-conditioning unit for the first time since the end of August, I turned it on. Cooler. That was better.

When I returned to the couch, Quinn raised his brow gently, as if to ask about the sudden detour. I ignored it and planted myself at the end of the couch, far too close to his navy-socked feet to be entirely comfortable. But it was a small price to pay in the name of friendship.

Quinn waited until I started my laptop before he resumed his reading. True to his word, he did his best not to distract me. His toes sometimes wiggled and slid against my thigh, but other than that, there was just the sound of my fingers clacking over the keyboard, his *chi-lip* sound as he turned a page, and our quiet breathing.

For half an hour, Quinn said nothing, and I barely made a dent in my essay.

Ten minutes later, I gave up, closing my laptop and laying it on the glass coffee table in front of the couch. Elbows on my knees, I scrubbed my face as I thought of something to say. We were roommates after all, yet I didn't know much about him.

I sneaked a peek at him from the corner of my eye and jumped when I found him looking at me.

"Gah!"

He shoved a bookmark into his book, shut it, and laid it next to my laptop. "What's up, Liam?" he asked, tucking his arms behind his head.

Obviously I hadn't adjusted the temperature low enough. The air in the room was positively smothering. Or maybe trying to make friends did that to someone.

My glasses were slipping with the sweat beading out of me. I pushed them up. It was a simple question, so it shouldn't have been a bother. And yet, somehow this time was much harder than any other time. "Do you want to play cards?"

I carefully watched every nuance of Quinn's reaction, the bobbling of his Adam's apple, the quiver of his lips, the slight angling of his head in my direction, the jiggle of his foot at my side.

Without realizing it, I'd held my breath, which was now very noticeable as I expelled it and gasped for more.

Quinn unlocked his hands from behind his head and pushed himself into a sitting position, pulling his feet nearer to him. "No," he said slowly. "I'd rather not lose again."

"Oh. Okay." Suddenly my bedroom seemed to be calling me. It promised that the air was cooler and I wouldn't have any problems concentrating on work. And work was better than cards, anyway.

I sprang off the couch.

But I didn't make it a step before Quinn grabbed my hips and tackled me onto the couch. To be more accurate, he landed on the couch, and I landed in his lap. His arms tightened around my waist. "Why on earth are you running away?" he growled into my ear.

"You didn't want to play cards!" I replied, twisting for freedom to no avail.

"No, I don't. One, because you'd just win again. And two, I just want an opportunity to chat. Shoot the shit. Share a little." He released his grip just enough to smooth his hands over my T-shirt and shift me to the couch cushion next to him. Quinn rubbed his forehead with the knuckle of his thumb. "You're not easy, Liam. You're always so serious. Blunt. Busy. Unaffected—except, strangely not just now. *Now* you actually felt something, didn't you?"

I swallowed a thick lump in my throat and kept my gaze on my arms, prickling with goosebumps. Jill was spot-on. I couldn't make a friend if my life depended on it. "I . . . yes. I felt something, okay? It was disappointment."

"Good," Quinn said, and the couch dipped as he swiveled more in my direction. "I like when you show your feelings. Otherwise, you're too much of a puzzle for me. We're . . . roommates. I want to understand what makes you tick."

He shrugged. "And, maybe you want to know a little more about me too?" He gestured to his textbook. "Like the fact I'm studying to be a physiotherapist. That I scrape by as a C student. That I absolutely hate onions." He squished up his nose and ran his hands over the edge of the couch. "That I think you have the most comfortable couch ever. That I can be quite a sarcastic son-of-a-bitch. That I still jerk off to the thought of my ex even though he cheated on me. That I love Shannon, but never in the way I know she really wishes I would. That I hate seeing Hunter, because every time I do, I want to fucking cry."

That was more information than roommates usually shared, wasn't it? I tried to formulate an appropriate answer.

As a reporter, I'd learned to tamper down my feelings so I

could focus on delivering facts. And I was good at it, because emotion didn't come easily to me.

I lowered my gaze from his, concentrating on his chin and firm lips instead. "I already knew you could be a sarcastic son-of-a-bitch."

Quinn leaned against the back of the couch, and when he turned his head toward me, his breath tickled against my temple. "And what about you? Do you ever relax? Jerk off? Because I just can't in my life imagine you doing that."

I pushed up my glasses again. "Of course I do. I schedule that in at shower time."

Quinn paused for a moment, his green eyes clouding in confusion. He bit his lip to smother a smile. His voice lowered. "Schedule?" He hummed. "That sounds far too practical to be any fun."

"It works for me."

"And do you have a girlfriend that you think about—"

"You know by now I don't have a girlfriend."

"Fine. Favorite model? Actress?"

"You are extremely curious about this."

He sat up, tucking one leg under him and folding his arms. His gaze could only be described as greedy. "Oh hell yes, I'm curious. It might help me solve this Liam puzzle."

I knew what he was trying to get at, but he was barking up the wrong tree. "I fantasize. Okay? Now, excuse me, but I have to get some work done. You've distracted me all evening."

"*I* distracted you? I was quiet as a button, man."

"It had nothing to do with you being quiet."

"Then, pray tell," he said with an arch of his brow, "how did I distract you?"

"I'll have to think about it." I leaned forward to grab my laptop, but I never made it because a cushion hit the side of my face.

"Christ." Quinn chuckled. "What do I have to do to get details out of you?"

I twisted toward him. His white T-shirt really wasn't thick enough. I could make out his muscles beneath it. "Is this the sort of stuff friends—I mean *roommates*—usually talk about? Because it seems like a strange discussion to me." I fiddled with the corners of the cushion.

"Yeah," Quinn said softly. "Friend thing. At least, that'd be . . . all right."

His sudden shyness had me rubbing my arms. I could—*would* —do this friend thing.

"Seeing Hunter really makes you want to cry?" I asked.

He looked guiltily at his knees and picked at a loose thread. "Yeah."

"That's it?" I arched my brow. "What do I have to do to get details out of *you*?"

A soft laugh. "It's just," he said, "I remember him before the chair, and"—he gestured toward his chest—"stuff gets stuck inside when I think of all the things he said he wanted to do that he can't anymore. And . . . and sometimes I'm relieved that I got lucky. That it never happened to me, and then I feel like crap."

Speechless, I just nodded. The silence held, but this tentative . . . openness we were having was drawing thinner and thinner. Afraid it would snap, afraid I would fail, I groped for something to share, something that might show him that this *friend* thing would be all right by me too.

I scratched the back of my head. "So lately, when I'm in the shower, I fantasize about winning the BCA competition for best article of the year."

Quinn blinked and looked at me, his gaze running over my lips as if expecting me to say something else. "The what now?"

I shrugged. "It's a competition I submitted three of my articles to. The results come out next month."

"Are you saying," Quinn rested his head on the back of the couch and stared toward the ceiling, the side of his mouth curling, "that you *literally* get off on work?"

I hadn't thought about it like that before. But, I guess—"Yes. Seems I do."

I stood, because I couldn't figure out what to do with myself. I needed to focus on something constructive so I wouldn't feel so —exposed.

Quinn didn't pull me back, but he touched the side of my knee. "You're something else, Liam," he said quietly. "And I'm going to figure out exactly what that something is."

CHAPTER NINE

My lashes fluttered away from my comic to meet the view of hummingbirds, and then Hunter in his wheelchair, arms crossed.

"I invite you here for coffee, and you just sit there and read?"

I glanced around the almost empty Crazy Mocha Coffee as I carefully set the comic on the table next to the tea I'd barely touched. "The only reason you invited me here was so you didn't have to wait for Mitch on your own. You are not alone, are you?"

He wheeled forward enough to snag the comic. "Booster Gold? You'd rather have his company than mine?"

"Booster will still be there when Mitch finally arrives and you give me my cue to leave." I sipped my tea, and my mind skipped from Booster to our campus vigilante. Where was he right now? Who was his daytime persona? Was it someone I'd recognize?

Hunter laid the comic on the table and wheeled closer to my side. He gripped my shoulder. "Dude, don't leave right away when he comes, okay? I invited you here because you're always so busy. If I didn't have a reason to meet, you'd have had something else to do. That's why I said I wanted you to wait until Mitch came."

"Oh." He wanted to spend time with me? "In that case"—I slipped Booster Gold into my messenger bag—"enough of him then. What about The Raven, the campus vigilante. Have you ever heard of him?"

With Hunter's hand still on me, I felt him stiffen, his fingers tight on my shoulder.

"I take that as a yes?" I pulled out my notebook and pen from my pocket. It wasn't that I'd changed my mind about leaving his identity a secret. I would. At least from the masses. But the thing was, every time I watched Hunter wheeling his chair, it reminded me how lucky I was and I wanted to thank The Raven in person.

That, and—to be entirely honest—I was curious. I itched to solve the Raven mystery almost as much as I itched to hear the BCA results.

"What about this vigilante?" Hunter pulled back from me and maneuvered to the opposite side of the table.

"Have you ever seen him?" I asked, scribbling down Hunter's first reaction. "Or heard about him?"

Hunter shook his head firmly and grabbed his coffee. "Nah. Just what we all hear in *Scribe*." He shrugged. "Have *you* ever seen him? Do you know who it is?"

Like with Quinn, I got the feeling he wasn't telling me everything. The question was: why not?

I took a long drink of tea. "He saved me from Freddy Krueger a month back."

"Freddy Krueger?"

"It was a nightmare and The Raven saved me from it."

"That doesn't make sense," he blurted. "You're not gay, and—" He shut up suddenly and swore.

I held my pen poised over my notebook and wondered why he was squeezing the life out of his wheelchair arms.

"Am I missing something here?" I asked.

"Ah, shit." He drained his coffee and then reached over for my tea as if he could drink his way out of the moment.

"Hunter?"

He set the tea down. "Fine. Look, I may have noticed a few things about this vigilante, like the fact that he only rescues gay guys. At least, up until you."

"Is that what you were hiding?"

"Look. It's embarrassing, but I sort of root for the guy, okay? I wish—" He cut himself off and ran a hand though his hair. "I just root for him."

I flipped back a few pages in my book to the list of guys who had been saved by The Raven. "All gay victims? Garret Tucker?"

"Gay."

"Dylan MacDonald?"

"Gay."

"Marcus Livingston?"

Hunter blushed at that name. "Oh yep, he's gay."

I listed all the names, and sure enough, Hunter responded "gay" to each one.

"All of them. See?" Hunter checked who was coming through the door. "Except for you."

I thought back to that night. How Freddy had attacked me right outside Mitch's apartment—"Your theory holds water."

Hunter raised a brow. "Something you're not telling me, sweetheart?"

"Mitch kissed me when I dropped him home."

Hunter scowled. "Right."

"He was quite inebriated, I doubt he remembers it. But

shortly after that, Freddy"—I couldn't help a shiver—"made his appearance."

Wheeling around to me again, Hunter threw an arm round my shoulders. "I'm sorry, man."

I looked at him hard and long before nodding. "Me too."

Something painful flickered in Hunter's eyes as he glanced to his legs. He quickly dismissed it, dropping his arms. "So, is Mitch a good kisser then?"

"I'm sure you'll find out for yourself."

"If he comes."

I checked my watch. Mitch should have been here twenty minutes ago. "I'm sure he has a good reason to be late."

Hunter laughed and thumped the arms of his chair. "I'm sure he has."

It seemed ages passed before Hunter tore his gaze away from the edge of the table and turned to me. He reached out and gently pried my pen from me. "Enough clicking. You don't have to say anything. It's okay. I'm okay. I'm here with you, right?" Dragging my notebook to him, he found a fresh page and started writing. "How about we work together on finding The Raven?"

"How'd you know I want to find him?"

"Because I do too." He jerked a thumb over his shoulder, gesturing to his camera. "I don't want to expose him, but I wouldn't mind getting some great shots of him in action. So, what do you say?"

"I say let's do it. Let's work on this together."

"Great." He slapped the table as if he carried a gavel, and then wheeled himself toward the exit. Looking over his shoulder, he beckoned me to catch up. "Every minute I spend sitting in here is like pouring more salt in the fucking wound."

"I THOUGHT YOU'D BE A SLOB," I said, peeking around the corner into Quinn's man-cave. Clothes lay strewn on the floor, the closed red curtains gave the room a ruby glow, and the air was thick and tepid. "Guess I was right about that."

Quinn shifted under his blankets, one big shivering lump.

He coughed, rough and raw, and feebly lifted a pillow and tossed it toward me.

The cream pillow made it only halfway, landing on Quinn's jeans that still clung to the leather belt threading through the loops.

I pushed up my glasses, rubbing at the bridge of my nose. "I wrote down your schedule in my calendar, and unless I got it wrong, you have a class at eight."

A muffled groan. "I'm not feeling well." He cleared his throat of what sounded like a tough bit of phlegm. I stepped back.

"Wait—you put my schedule into your calendar?" Quinn asked.

I nodded, although he couldn't see me the way he was hunched over. "Of course. If for any reason I need to get in touch with you, I'll have an idea where you are. For that matter, if you have any emergency contacts you'd like me to know about, I'm preparing a list."

Another coughing bout followed by a mumbled curse. "I have a paper due today. I'm not finished. God, my throat burns."

I glanced down at my watch. I should have rushed for class ten minutes ago. What was I meant to do with a sick roommate? Could he be left alone?

I glanced toward the door, to my literature lectures and my meeting with the chief.

What would a friend do? I wasn't willing to mess this possible friendship up over a trifling cold!

Quinn squirmed, snaking his arm out from the sheets to reach a bottle of water.

The bottle toppled over and out of his grasp.

With pitiable effort, Quinn lodged himself over the edge of the bed and snagged it.

Anyone who looked that pathetic probably needed some help.

I backed away from the room and moved to the couch, perching myself on the end of it as I rummaged through my messenger bag, took out my phone, and made a couple of calls.

When I was done, a pale-faced Quinn shuffled through the living room draped in his thick bedding. He gave me a cursory, runny-nosed nod, and slumped his way to the bathroom.

Cough! Cough!

Right. Sitting here wasn't helping him any.

I held my breath and darted into his room to grab his laptop.

I hurried back into the living room, plugged the laptop in, and opened it up. Of course it was password-protected. I stared at the ceiling as if it might provide some inspiration.

Instead, it provided the sobering fact that I still knew so little about Quinn. I couldn't even conjure an obvious password, like his favorite pet's name or his birthday. The laptop hummed, warming my thighs.

Quinn emerged freshly showered but still moving with that pitiful slump. He trudged to the armchair coddled in a blanket—no doubt a sweat-drenched blanket. I shifted a few inches to escape the path of his contaminated breathing.

"What are you doing with my laptop?" He rested his head like I just had and closed his eyes.

"What's your password?"

One eye peeled open. "I want to know why. But since I have nothing to hide, I'll give you a clue." He angled his head toward me and closed his eyes.

"You're sick, and you want to play games?"

"I'm sick, and if this is the only entertainment I'm going to get . . ."

I ran the tips of my fingers over the keyboard. "Okay. Clue."

"It's a comic book character."

I typed, hit Enter, and just like that I was in. "Thanks. Might want to make it a tougher clue next time."

"You got it already?"

"Sure. It was either Clark Kent or Bruce Wayne, both of whom you like without their costumes on."

Quinn laughter morphed into a bout of coughing, and I slid further down the couch.

"Where would I find your paper?" I asked, confronted with a mess of files on his desktop.

"In the right hand corner, just above the trash symbol."

I clicked into it. "That's no way to organize your work."

For the next few hours, I stayed in the living room, steadily inching toward the other end of the couch with every one of Quinn's coughs.

Arches of light stretched over the floors and onto Quinn dozing in the armchair. He snored lightly with his blocked nose, nuzzling his ear against the red-and-gold upholstery.

I fished out my notebook and pen, and let the words soak into the paper in the same heady, drowsy manner as the sun soaked into Quinn.

Ethereal. Calm. A golden king claiming his throne even in sleep. . . .

Sliding the notebook into my pocket, I read over Quinn's paper one last time. It had been mostly written, save for the conclusion, so reading it once had provided enough information for me to finish writing it for him. His main issue was poor grammar. I would have to sit him down sometime and introduce him to the comma.

Quinn stirred, his tongue clacking against the roof of his mouth as if parched. He blinked at me, his eyes unfocused, and said croakily, "Do I distract you today?"

A sound, something like an attempt to laugh, warbled from him.

"You seem to have a way of doing that, Quinn. Even when you're this sorry looking."

He frowned, and then shook his head as if to clear it.

"Your paper is ready to be sent in." I stood up and passed the laptop to him, stretching my arms out to maintain a good distance.

A tired smile tugged at his lips.

Ding-dong!

Finally!

I rushed to the intercom and buzzed Hunter and Shannon in. Two minutes later, they were rolling out of the elevator and into our apartment.

"Thanks for coming," I said, jamming myself against the wall to let them pass. "I have no clue what to do with him."

Both sets of blue eyes skipped from me to Quinn. Hunter chuckled, "Looks like we have a case of the man-flu, Shan."

Quinn raised an elegant middle finger.

Hunter rolled into the room, shoving his chair right up in front of Quinn—

"Travis!" Shannon grabbed his chair and pulled him back. "I don't want you to get sick."

Silence.

I was sure if I spoke, my voice would echo coldly like it did in the pre-Quinn days.

Trying not to get involved, I managed to slip and come to a crashing thump on the ground. I picked myself up. In the gap between Hunter and Shannon, Quinn quirked a brow my way.

"Sorry." Shannon stepped back from Hunter's chair abruptly.

Hunter didn't reply, pivoting his chair. The calm way he rolled across the room was belied by the flicker of a muscle in his jaw. Coming past me, he said, "I'll come back later. Keep doing whatever you are doing. Quinn will man-up soon enough."

"Hey!" Quinn managed in an awkward attempt to lighten the heavy air.

Hunter left, and Shannon just stood there with blue streaks of hair hanging over her shoulder and curtaining her face from view.

Quinn tugged her hand. "He'll be fine, Shan. He'll get over it."

"Yeah," she said, as I wondered where to put myself. In the kitchen where I could overhear them? Perhaps just disappear into my room? Stay put and say something to break the tension?

"Why do I keep doing that?" A hiccup rose out of Shannon and she took a steadying breath, her hands fisted at her sides. "Excuse me."

With long, steady strides, she marched to the front door and presumably chased after Hunter.

Lifting the blanket sunk onto his lap, Quinn covered his shoulders. "She finds it tough."

I stopped clicking my pen and snapped my gaze to his.

"She thinks it's her fault," he continued.

I perched on the arm of the couch and crossed my ankle over my knee. "What's her fault?"

Quinn gestured to the spot where Hunter had been. "She was supposed to pick him up from basketball practice that evening. She was late. . . ." He shifted suddenly, pushing himself into a wobbly stand. "I need to piss and, since you haven't offered, make myself some honey tea."

I stood abruptly, edging around the coffee table and keeping my distance. "Okay. Just sit on the toilet. I don't trust your aim in this state."

THREE DAYS AND A REMARKABLY-IMPROVED-QUINN LATER, it was my turn.

I dragged myself out of bed and into the shower. No matter how hot I turned the dial, the water wasn't hot enough.

With studded breaths, I hobbled back into my room and jerked on my linen pants and a long-sleeved T-shirt, the difference between a cat and a comma showcased on the front.

Perhaps Quinn might find it informative.

A wave of dizziness washed over me and I fought through it. I would not get sick. Not today. It would have to wait for the weekend.

The hairdryer seemed only to pump cool air, so I switched to scrubbing with a towel.

My phone beeped, and I checked the calendar update. I had to attend three classes and the weekly *Scribe* meeting. A glance at my watch said I was going to be late.

Shrugging my bag over my shoulder, I straggled into the kitchen, where Quinn was standing in his flannel pajama pants, tank-top, and worn gray slippers with his back against the counter listening to the radio as he shoveled cereal into his mouth.

"Morning," he said, sliding to the side as I filled a glass with water to soothe my dry throat. I took a sip and winced. Swallowing would not be fun today.

"You're looking a little flushed this morning," Quinn said, scraping the bowl clean.

I convulsed in another shiver and resettled my bag strap higher on my shoulder. "Flushed? It's freezing in here." I grabbed an orange from the fruit bowl. Behind me came the clatter of dishes. "Right," I said. "Bye."

A hand gripped my elbow, and Quinn coaxed me around. I dropped the orange to the counter and yielded, chasing after the warmth of that touch.

Quinn's mouth firmed into a thin line as he pressed a palm to my forehead. His gaze dropped to mine. "Yeah, you're not going anywhere."

"I'll be okay. I can hold off whatever this is until tomorrow."

Quinn pulled at my bag strap and my load lightened. Quinn chucked it over his shoulder and steered me around. "Back to bed."

"I really need to get to class—"

"You really need to get to bed. No arguing. Keep walking, or I will carry you there."

I feebly attempted to brush him off, but the fever took over, deciding Quinn's plans of snuggling back into bed were far superior to mine.

"Maybe just for an hour," I conceded. I would pump down a few painkillers and when they kicked in, I would make it to my second class.

Quinn laughed as he peeled back my sheets.

I collapsed onto the bed and let him tuck me in. He molded the covers around me, firmly pressing them to my sides, and then ducked out of my room only to return with more blankets.

They smelled faintly of Quinn. Quinn right after a shower, a mix of Axe and cashmere shampoo. "Have you washed these since you got sick?"

"Of course you'd ask that." He pinched my foot on his way out. "Yesterday."

"You must have slept with them since then. They have your scent."

He paused at the door. "Does that bother you?"

"It might have a couple weeks ago, but your smell has grown on me. I'll tell you when I'm sick of it."

I thought that was it, that Quinn would go off and do whatever he had to do. But he didn't. Throughout the delirium of my fever, he brought me cups of hot tea, hot water bottles, and hot chicken broth.

After I'd sweated through the first bout, he pulled me out of bed with cool hands. "Time to take off that funny shirt of yours and hop into the shower."

I pinched the sweaty comma-cat T-shirt from my skin, a flutter of cool air skittering over my chest. "It's not just funny. It's true."

Grabbing a fistful of material at the back, I pried the thing off me and it sounded like Velcro being ripped apart. Positively nasty.

Quinn scrunched his nose. "Dump it on the bed and go wash."

The last of the fever followed his orders, and I came back to a freshly-made bed and comfortable clothes to climb into.

"So much for working," I told myself as I greedily climbed back into bed. I slapped a hand toward my bedside table, feeling for my phone. At least I'd give Hannah some notice that I wouldn't be at the meeting today.

"You're not the only one missing the meeting," Hannah said, lowering her voice. "I overheard Jill telling the chief that Jack had to visit his brother in the prison infirmary. Apparently he got hurt pretty badly. But don't worry about the politics page. Chief said something about asking you, but I'd be totally happy to help out. You just get yourself better."

I groaned again. Why did I have to be sick the week I had the opportunity to write something good? I murmured a goodbye, hung up and curled an arm over my forehead.

That's when Quinn poked his head around my door. "Just gonna hurry to the laundry room so I can dry these. When I come back, we're watching a movie."

True to his word, when returned he set his laptop on the end of the bed and turned on *Batman*.

Watching the vigilantes reap justice had me dreaming of my own vigilante. I sank against the mountain of pillows at my back and pulled the blankets up to my chin.

That cold itch was coming back. "I'm glad for The Raven," I suddenly said. "For that night. He saved me. I want to do the same for him."

"If he wears a hood to protect his identity, I'd say he doesn't want to be found."

I shivered, twisting onto my side, my arms and feet stretching toward Quinn's side of the bed, searching for warmth. He sensed the change and shuffled closer, gently tucking the blankets tightly to my sides.

Through chattering teeth, I asked, "Was this what I should have done when you were sick?"

His profile, layered in colored light from the small screen, tilted toward me. "Nah, you did just fine."

I shut my eyes, straining to feel more warmth than just those words. "Two more questions, Quinn. Did you have any pets? And, when is your birthday?"

CHAPTER TEN

Beeswax and booze and fake blood. Lots of fake blood. A mixture of wealth and boredom decorated the mansion.

I took a deep breath, rearranging the cowl on the knight costume Quinn had thought all three of us guys should wear. I wasn't sure where he was going with the idea, or if the store had run out of all other costumes, but there we were in helmets, cowls, black shirts, tunics, maroon belts to match our leggings, and boots with a good one-inch heel.

It was far more comfortable than I'd have thought.

"What are we waiting for?" Hunter asked and rolled to the doorbell. He buzzed, and the door swung in. Nobody greeted us in the foyer, though the hollow breathing of someone standing behind the door indicated we were not alone.

A creepy coating of dust and cobwebs covered the surfaces and signposts pointing toward the party. Shannon, who dressed up as Zsadist—some warrior-vampire character I'd never heard of—drew out a fake dagger she'd slipped into her shit-kickers. "Fear fucking not," she said, scooting to the front. "I'll lead the way."

Children's voices started singing, interrupted by a scream that echoed through the dark hall. I inched toward Quinn with as much subtlety as I could muster. Logically, I knew there was nothing to be frightened about—

More screams and quickly-moving shadows. My mind filled with images of Freddy Krueger lurking in a bedroom doorway, waiting to jump out. My step faltered and I rippled with a shudder.

"Are you sure you want to be here, Liam?" Quinn's voice crackled, as if undecided whether to whisper or speak normally.

I straightened and veered away from Quinn to prove I could handle the rest of the night just fine.

"Because I can take you home," he added quietly as he took off his helmet. He ran a hand through his hair and tucked the helmet under his other arm. "It's okay if you don't want to be here."

"I have a column to write." Absently, I patted the synthetic pouch hooked onto my belt that carried my notebook and pen. "That's my priority. The whole reason I'm here."

"No other reason to be at a party, is there?" I didn't fail to notice the sarcasm.

We turned a corner and the hall widened into a large room with a dark mahogany staircase snaking up to the next level.

Pounding footsteps came behind us. A zombie football team charged down the hall. "Race you up!" one of them yelled.

They burst past us on either side, forcing Quinn and I to inch nearer. His arm pressed against mine as the convoy streamed around us and dodged Hunter and Shannon at the bottom of the stairs.

"Zombies?" I shook my head. "Seem more like roadrunners to me."

A grin twitched Quinn's lips but it faltered again as Shannon called out. "No damn elevator. Give us a hand?"

Quinn passed me his silver helmet and strutted to Hunter, hands on his hips, swagger in his tone. "Looks like it's the white knight to the rescue."

Hunter snorted and wrapped his arms around Quinn. "You're maroon, bro. And it's not your best color."

Quinn hooked one arm around Hunter's back and the other under Hunter's knees, and carefully lifted him. With a cheeky smile, Quinn dipped Hunter. His gaze lifted to mine for a second before he bumped his nose against Hunter's. "One kiss, my sweet, bonny lad. I'm after a prize tonight—"

Hunter clapped him over the back the head. "Just get me upstairs. Christ."

Music vibrated through the ceiling, making the chandelier jingle. I stepped out from under it and helped Shannon with Hunter's chair, trying to avoid the gobs of fake, sticky-looking blood that dripped down the stair rail.

At the top of the stairs we set the chair down, and Quinn lowered Hunter into it. As soon as he was seated, he wheeled off toward the open double doors and the pulsating crowds within. "Come, Liam," he called over his shoulder. "I'm going to help you find the perfect bloody angle tonight."

"Coming," I said and, stepping in front of Quinn, lifted the helmet and set it down on his head. He gave me a startled look that quickly melted into a smile and a wink.

"Thanks."

I gave a sharp nod, abruptly turned, and ran off to find the "perfect bloody angle."

I really wanted to explore how the customs and traditions of Halloween manifested in the party, but Hunter vetoed.

"How about you find three case studies of drunken students"—he pointed to some hags in the corner, drinking out of a cauldron—"and make up scarily disgusting hangover remedies for each?"

"How about a column on the dangers of candy-poisoning?" For the tenth—twentieth?—time, I glanced to the middle of the room where Quinn was dancing. It was almost a game the way we scoured the crowds for one another.

This time he was grooving with one of the football zombies. His head lifted and our gazes collided once more. A strange, static energy pulsed in the air as he continued to stare at me.

The zombie twisted Quinn around and the connection broke. I blinked hard a couple times. Quinn really should stop grinding with that guy; he might get infected and turn into a zombie roadrunner.

I shook off the thought, but before I dragged my gaze away, the zombie wrapped his arms around Quinn's neck, bringing his blood-stained mouth toward that smooth, soft part of skin just under the ear—

And there went the love bite! I swallowed tightly.

What was the protocol here? Was Quinn hooking up with this guy? Did it mean I had to find my own way home?

Hunter slapped my ass with a solid bite to it. I jerked in his direction. "Stop ogling Quinn," he said, shaking his head and grinning.

Ogling? No. "I was merely trying to determine how I should get home tonight, since he was our ride."

"Whatever you say. And Shannon will take us back. No worries. Now . . ." Hunter choked on his words. His jaw hardened and he cast his gaze sideways, toward a hockey player with a plastic chainsaw pouring himself some punch.

It took me a few seconds before I figured out his reaction.

There by the door, dressed as a pirate with smudgy eyeliner and a bandana, stood Mitch, talking with Jack of all people. At least Mitch didn't look happy about the discussion. That said something for good taste.

"Fuck. I need a drink," Hunter said, and I escorted him to the fruity punch. He poured us both one. The plastic cup was sticky, but the rest of it was quite okay. Fruity and easy on the taste buds.

"You know what?" I slurped down the last of the drink. "I think your angle could work."

Mitch's idea for an angle wasn't what I'd have gone for myself, but I could handle it for one column if it took Hunter's mind off Mitch.

Setting my cup on the table behind me, I fished in my pouch and pulled out my notebook and pen, resisting the urge to search for Quinn on the dance floor again. "Talk me through the idea . . ."

Forty minutes (and only two glances at Quinn) later, I had all the grizzly, alcohol-drenched details I needed.

"This will work just fine," I said, draining another punch.

I choked on the liquid as a gap in the dancing crowds revealed Mitch across the room, leaning against the wall with his arms crossed. His casual smile faded as he took us both in. He pushed off the wall with his shoulders and stepped forward.

Hunter's wheels squeaked over the wooden floor as he spun his chair around. The tightness of his jaw made it clear he wasn't interested in having a confrontation tonight.

Mitch took another step forward and stopped, watching as Hunter wheeled away. I gave him a shrug and bounded after Hunter, rolling through a set of double doors.

I caught up with him on a cozy balcony that overlooked the back garden, a trellis of jasmine spilling over the side to the lawn below. In the distance, a silhouette of the Cathedral of Learning dominated the skyline.

I folded my arms. "I suppose I should ask if you're okay?"

Hunter rested his head against the back of his chair, staring at the moonlit sky. "Yeah, I think I'm going to call it a night and get Shannon to drive me back."

I patted my pouch that held my notebook full of description ready to be molded into something readable. "I'm ready too."

When the coast was clear of Mitch, we snuck back into the party. Hunter beelined for Shannon, who was dancing with a witch from my English Literature class. I followed at a distance, scanning the dance floor—

A hideous green goblin with pointy ears and long, sharp fingers pushed into my side. I shivered at the touch, and then again at the voice.

"Fucking Davis."

Marc Jillson.

"Here to write a report on the University of Halloween?" Jill sniggered. He reeked of alcohol and something sickeningly sweet. I switched to breathing through my mouth.

Jill dragged one of his long fingernails down my neck, and it was just sharp enough that it would leave a scratch mark. "Let's see how many people laugh at your next party page. Did you read the comments in the opinions page, taking the piss out of you? I almost felt sorry for you."

I brushed Jill's fake fingers off me. I had just enough punch in me to not feel intimidated, though not enough to stop me from being curious. There'd been comments about me? I needed to look over last week's *Scribe* again.

"Haven't read them, have you?" Jill's lip twitched. "Well let me summarize. They think you've got a stick up your ass, like you don't even know how to party."

Over Jill's shoulder, Hunter was snagging Shannon and waving at me to get going.

I looked between him and Jill and back again. Hunter raised his brow. *Coming or not?*

That was the question.

I could go with him and be in bed before midnight, maybe even get an outline typed up. Or I could stay at this party and prove Jill wrong. If I wanted to, I could party. How hard could it be? It was just drinking and dancing. Anyone could do it.

I caught Hunter's gaze and shook my head. He saluted me goodbye.

That was the moment Quinn strode up to Shannon. He said something, and then scoured the crowds. When he caught sight of me, he mouthed something and held up a finger, which I assumed meant he'd be back in a minute.

Jill bumped rudely past me and bled into the crowd, calling out to Jack to wait up.

Left standing in the middle of the room in a sea of swarming monsters, I decided a drink might be a good start to proving just how much I could party.

Without anyone to talk to, I easily downed three cups of punch. I was starting on my fourth when Quinn returned.

The zombie he'd been dancing with clung onto his arm, but Quinn searched the crowds until he spotted me. Then, towing his zombie along, he wove through a crowd of dancing elves and closed the distance between us.

His eyes were on me, but mine wavered quickly to the zombie. He wore rags and painted-on blood, but his form was solid and he obviously looked after himself.

I took another large gulp of punch.

"Shannon's coming back after she drops Hunter off," Quinn said, stopping in front of me. His gaze dipped to my cup. "Punch, Liam? You know it's spiked, right?" He took a sniff of the bowl. "*Really* spiked."

"I *can* drink, you know," I said more sharply than I'd intended. I drained the remainder of the cup and wiped my sticky hands on my leggings. "I can dance as well."

Framed by thick, dark lashes, his eyes gleamed like I'd just told him I'd been to the moon. He tipped his helmet back and folded his arms. He nibbled on his bottom lip before he smirked and said, "I'd *love* to see that."

Mr. Zombie brooded next to him and tugged on Quinn's arm. "Maybe we should dance some more too?"

My cup crackled as my grip tightened on it. If I didn't know better, I'd say this was a classic symptom of jealousy.

I chuckled at the thought, dismissing it as a case of the jitters from having Jill in the room watching me party. "You guys go do your thing. I'll dance after one more cup of this scrumptious *spiked* punch." Somehow, a hiccup escaped me.

Quinn drew closer. He plucked the cup from my hand and threw it in one of the bins under the table. "I promised I'd keep close to you at these parties. Keep you safe."

I shrugged, and a small wave of dizziness passed over me. "I've managed to stay safe on my own while you were off grinding away."

Quinn's brow furrowed. "Oh, stop it. I've been watching you and you know it."

Mr. Zombie rolled his eyes, let go of Quinn's arm, and stalked off into the dancing crowd. Quinn didn't even acknowledge him, just kept staring at me.

I hunched my shoulders and wrapped my arms around my chest at the jolts of electricity that seemed to be thrumming though me. I'd never had more than two cocktails; tonight was a foreign experience for me. The alcohol combined with Quinn's unrelenting stare . . . well, I got how it could be addictive.

"Your Zombie ran off," I said, trying to push my glasses up but only prodding the lens. "You should chase after him. Don't worry about me, I'm actually feeling really confident." I gestured to the punch bowl. "It's like magic. No Krueger can scare me now."

Even as I said it a wave of dizziness clouded my mind. It didn't help my glasses were smudged. I took them off, but I had no good material on me for wiping them. The shirt I wore was not cotton like Quinn's looked to be . . .

"Tell me, Liam," Quinn said, his voice coaxing and soft as it brushed against the side of my face. "Why do you care so much about me and the zombie?" He lifted his hand and his fingers drew across my jaw and under my chin. "I know you've been watching me as much as I've been watching you most of the evening."

"I spent just as much time focusing on Hunter and my column, thank you."

"You don't deny it, then?"

Why would I? "Of course I was watching you with the zombie. I was trying to figure out what the protocol was. Whether I should let you go home first to give you guys some time in the apartment alone. Whether in the morning if the zombie comes out of your room hungry, I should offer him breakfast or shoo him out for you. I've never really been in this situation before, and quite frankly, I'm lost."

Quinn dropped his fingers, and cool air kissed my skin in their place. I focused on my smudgy glasses between us as the room started a slow spin. *Get your glasses back on!*

I reached out and tugged on Quinn's shirt, scraping my knuckles over his stomach as I used his T-shirt material to wipe my lenses. He startled and his tiny gasp tugged on a few strands of my hair. "Christ, how much have you had to drink?"

I pulled back a bit too fast and stumbled. Quinn's large warm hands gripped my shoulders and kept me from toppling over. "A bit too much, it seems," I answered him.

"Come on," Quinn said, looping an arm around mine and leading me toward the balcony. "Let's get you some fresh air."

The air helped a little, but it didn't stop the feeling of being suffocated by thick haziness. The warm night air made me want to spill all my words into it, liberate all the trapped words that weighed me down and pleaded for escape.

A part of me wanted to cry, but for no reason whatsoever.

Quinn stood next to me, bent over the railing with his arms

folded against it. I tried doing the same but the jasmine tangled me. Quinn laughed and straightened, tugging me closer to him and away from the trellis.

Hot in my helmet, I yanked it off and tossed it to Quinn. He caught it and set it down next to his in the balcony corner.

"How are you feeling?" he asked as he leaned back.

My mouth felt heavier than usual, like it couldn't be bothered to form words longer than a syllable. But I forced the words out. "Unusually good."

He gave me his signature raise of the brow.

"And," I continued, "I'm relieved that zombie guy is not an issue anymore."

Quinn bit his lip and faced the cathedral in the distance. "See, it's when you say things like that, I just . . ." He sighed. "Never mind, it's pointless talking about this now."

I touched Quinn's arm. Firmly as I could, I turned him toward me. "I'm not oblivious, you know."

"To what?"

"You, hinting at my undiscovered sexual orientation. You're not that subtle."

"So it's already discovered then?"

I hiccupped and half-shrugged. "Kiss me and we'll find out."

Quinn darted his tongue across his bottom lip. "Kiss you?" he repeated.

"Yes. It's quite simple. We touch lips, our tongues lock for a bit . . . I see if I feel anything and we settle this."

He laughed and shook his head, quickly moving toward our helmets and picking them up. "You're drunk. The only thing that's going to be settled tonight is you. In your bed."

I stepped away from him, raising a hand to stop him from dragging me home. "I can't go back yet. Jack and Jill are here, and I'm going to party."

"Jack and Jill. Yeah," Quinn drawled, rubbing on his ear. "I don't even know what to say to that."

"They work with me. They . . . they think I'm a loser who never should have scored the party page. They are probably right, but they are annoying enough I want to prove otherwise."

Quinn narrowed his eyes toward the double doors leading back inside. "Jack and Jill, you say?"

"That's why I need to stay. So how about a compromise?"

He gave a small, snorted chuckle. "Guess if you can still use big words, you can't be too far gone."

"Oh, I think I'm pretty far gone," I said, stepping up to him and planting a hand on his upper arm. "But before you take me home, I want to dance. . . ."

Turned out there was a snag in my plan.

I couldn't dance.

I tried again to mimic Quinn's moves as he danced beside me with a wizard. I jerked my hips side-to-side and knocked the witch I was dancing with. She cursed me. Well, cursed *at* me and pushed me backward until I landed on my ass. Certainly it felt like a curse.

Jack and Jill laughed at the edges of the crowd, pointing and sniggering through their tears. Quinn stopped dancing and crouched next to me.

"Who the fuck do you think you are?" he asked Jack and Jill as he slipped an arm around my waist and helped me up. My uneven footing had me pulling on Quinn's sleeve for balance.

Jill muttered, and suddenly Quinn left my side. In what felt like slow motion, I watched Quinn shove him.

Jill teetered on his heels for a moment before losing the fight with gravity and slamming onto the floor.

Colorful cussing followed Quinn as he charged back to me, hooked his arm around mine and lead me out of the mansion. Stormy shadows clung to him the entire drive home.

When he parked the car, he thumped the steering wheel and continued to stare out onto the road.

"Jill's a jackass," I said. I concentrated on Quinn's mouth as a focal point to minimize my dizziness and churning queasiness.

Quinn's shoulders dropped as if releasing the tension from the party. He leaned back against the headrest for a moment and sighed. "Let's get you inside. I have to go back so Shannon can get home."

"Shannon. Yes, I forgot." I sounded as disappointed as I felt. But I couldn't be sure why exactly. Tomorrow I'd have to look into it.

Quinn was already standing at my side of the car as I unbuckled my seatbelt. He opened the door and offered me his hand. Once I was firmly on ground, I pulled on his hand until he looked at me.

"There's going to be an investigation," I said, threading my cold fingers through his warm ones and stepping closer until we were against each other.

"Investigation?"

I nodded. "Involving kisses. It's imperative I settle this question of yours."

"You are so drunk," he whispered, coming close to my lips. "Adorable as hell, but still so far gone. I don't even think you'll remember this in the morning."

He gently untangled our hands and slid my glasses up my nose for me. "And, Liam, I think it's as much your question as it is mine."

I rummaged into my pouch for my pen and notebook. "Maybe. I'll take that into consideration as well."

I turned to the car and used the roof to rest my notebook so I wouldn't forget all these thoughts and questions—

Quinn plucked away my notebook and lifted me over his shoulder. His laughter vibrated through me as he carried me inside.

I hit his ass all the way up to the second floor and into our apartment, demanding he put me down at once. I even fished my cold hands under his shirt to convince him, but he merely slapped my ass with a stinging clap and took larger steps toward the bathroom, where he—finally—dropped me.

Standing vertically once more, I glared at him. "I'll kindly ask you to give me back my notebook."

He looked at my open hand and grinned. "Nope. You can have it once you've gotten yourself ready for bed." He shut the door and left me to relieve myself—much needed—and brush my teeth.

Once I was done, I struggled out of my knight costume and climbed into bed. Quinn popped his head around the door into my room. He seemed to dance his way in, but it had to be an alcohol-induced illusion. He set down my notebook and a large bottle of water onto my side table. "You'll be fine if I go out again?" he asked, shoving my legs over to sit on the side of the bed.

I shifted and shimmied down until my head was on the firm pillow. The room was spinning. "I've never been this intoxicated before."

"Right. I'll call her and tell her to catch a cab—"

"Don't," I said with a yawn. "You looked after me enough when I was really sick. This is nothing, I'll be fine."

It was only then I noticed he'd changed out of his costume too, except while I wore only boxer shorts, Quinn had on pants and a turquoise T-shirt. He also donned an amused expression and looked at me almost fondly. "Your phone is next to your bed," he said, the mattress springing up as he stood. "Call if you need anything."

"Mmm hmm." My eyelids fluttered shut.

Quinn chuckled and turned off the light before walking out. "Sweet dreams."

Before sleep clutched me in a suffocating hold, I mumbled, "I thought I wanted a cat. But you're so much better."

CHAPTER ELEVEN

B*rrrriiiing.*

I woke to the ear-splitting screech. I lurched toward my phone, twisting off the bed with a loud *thump!*

Groaning, I felt for the phone and brought it to my ear. "Liam here." I rubbed my head and sat up, peeling off the blankets that'd twisted around me.

"Dude, it's midday. Are you still asleep?"

A pulse throbbed in my head as I stood up. "Midday?" No, it couldn't have been more than eight—

A glance at my alarm-clock radio confirmed Hunter's announcement. I closed my eyes and shook my head. So much for my plan to be at the office wrapping up a first draft.

Seemed like I might need one of my disgusting hangover remedies first.

Hunter cackled down the line. "Damn. Sounds like you had quite the night. So do you know the news already?"

"What news?" I flung my blankets over the bed and semi-straightened them.

"It's all over Twitter, Facebook, and I caught the gossip on Tumblr: our vigilante made an appearance again."

I swapped the phone to my other ear and sat at the end of my bed, running my heel down the corner leg to satisfy an itch. "He did? What happened? When? Where?"

"That's the thing, it happened just a few blocks from the mansion. Our guy might have been there the whole night, right under our noses."

"Who got attacked?"

"No one knows. The victim isn't coming forward."

"So how does everyone know about it?"

"That's the thing." Hunter paused and I stiffened, waiting for the response. Somehow, I was nervous for our vigilante.

"The attacker got hurt. The vigilante broke his collarbone throwing him to the ground. He had to go to hospital. Now he's telling everyone the assault came out of the blue, that he wasn't hurting anyone."

"*What?*"

"It's a lie, of course. But if the victim doesn't speak up, it's looking really bad for The Raven."

Grabbing my notebook and pen, I asked, "Do we have any idea what time this happened?"

"Around two in the morning."

I'd been comatose by then. "What's the name of this guy?"

"It's ridiculous. He's calling himself The Night Warrior."

The Night Warrior? What did the guy think he was, a comic book hero?

"Look," Hunter continued, "I have a feeling this is going to cause some bad press for our vigilante. If we could find the victim and convince him to tell his side of the story, we might be able to derail the activists that want to make him pay for all the black eyes and bloody noses he's doled out."

"I can slip a public plea for information onto the opinions page."

We wrapped up the conversation quickly. Hunter needed to get to his basketball game, and my bladder felt as if it would burst.

I dashed to the bathroom, relieved myself, took a shower, and popped a couple of painkillers. With my towel wrapped round my waist, I darted back to my room.

Quinn sat on the straightened bedcovers. A tray holding a plate of omelet, toast, and what looked like freshly-squeezed orange juice rested on his lap.

He blinked, shifted quickly, and hurriedly refocused on the food. "Thought you'd be too hungover to get up."

"It smells delicious," I said. With Quinn's back to me, I made quick work of dropping the towel and slipping into my boxers and a clean but crumpled shirt.

"How are you feeling this morning?" Quinn asked tentatively.

I scrambled over the bed to my pillows and motioned for the tray. "Can I?"

"Sure." He passed it to me and watched me stuff a buttered piece of toast into my mouth.

I chased it with orange juice and, once I'd swallowed, spoke. "I can honestly say I've felt better."

Quinn smirked. "Was last night worth it?"

I recalled scraps of the night before. I remembered the punch. Dancing. Jack and Jill laughing. Quinn shoving Jill. And then Quinn carrying me into the apartment. "Yes. Just seeing Jill thrown to the ground was worth every stab of headache I'll have today." Thankfully, my painkillers seemed to be working effectively.

Quinn nabbed a piece of my toast and scooped some of the egg onto it. "Trust me, he deserved it."

"I don't remember it all. What else happened last night?"

That made Quinn grin, his ears rising slightly. With a teasing lilt to his voice, he ripped the crust of my toast off and said, "You wanted to kiss me."

I chewed the bit of toast in my mouth and swallowed. "Did I kiss you?"

He shook his head and waved the crust at me like he was waggling a finger. "No. But you *really* wanted to."

I leaned forward and bit the crust to just before his fingertip. With my mouth full, I said, "Quite obviously that was a drunken anomaly."

Quinn stared at the remaining pinch of crust between his fingers. "You're kidding, right?"

I shoveled one more forkful of egg into my mouth and rested the tray on the bed. My cellphone was ringing but I couldn't see it. Likely it had fallen behind the drawers when I tossed it and rushed to the bathroom. I scrabbled off the bed and felt for the phone on the carpet as I answered Quinn. "I've only kissed girls, so—no. Definite anomaly."

Ah ha! I lurched upright, triumphant, cellphone in hand. But before I could take the call, Quinn grabbed a fistful of my shirt and tugged me forward, between his legs.

I dropped the phone as Quinn's hand reached up behind my neck and drew me down. "Quinn? What on earth—"

He fell backward on the bed, bringing me with him. A roller-coaster thrill zipped through my body as I lost my balance and came crashing against his chest. Both Quinn's arms slipped around me, holding me firmly in place.

Quinn's deep green eyes stared intently at me. He brushed the tip of his nose against mine, tilted his head upwards, and kissed me.

The first sweep of his lips moved warm and softly. I gasped in surprise. Quinn's mouth sealed over mine, and his tongue twisted and pushed. He was an expert. I liked how he took control, led the entire dance of our tongues. All I did was follow along and enjoy the ride.

Quinn pulled back, resting his head against my mattress and grinned wickedly. "Still an anomaly, Liam?"

He was warm and comfortable to lie on, so I didn't bother moving. I linked my fingers and rested against his chest. "*Technically*, since kissing a guy is a deviation from who I normally kiss, the answer is yes."

Quinn roared out with laughter. "God, you're impossible." He slapped me on the ass and rolled me over. We nearly knocked over the breakfast tray, but Quinn steadied it and climbed off me. "I've got to get to my self-defense class. You can think about things, and we can chat over dinner tonight if you want."

I propped myself up on my elbows. "How do I join one of these classes?"

"Shannon and I are starting a beginner's course. Seven o'clock Wednesdays at the Rainbow Rec Center." He stepped back slowly toward the door. His face glowed, as if the idea of me learning self-defense pleased him. Perhaps he thought it would free up his weekend evenings, but that seemed fair enough to me. "You can come along then if you like."

I pushed myself into a sitting position. My lips still tingled and tasted of Quinn. I ran a tongue over my bottom lip as I watched him slink further toward the door. "Good call with that kiss, Quinn."

He paused, squinting at me like he wasn't quite sure what to say. He scratched his ear. "You don't need time to think about it? Fret? Go and pretend it never happened?"

I pushed myself off the bed. The warm carpet under my toes rubbed the soles of my feet nicely. I slid over to the jeans that lay in a heap in the corner of the room. "Pretend it never happened? Why would I do that?" I pulled on the jeans and found the phone I'd dropped on the bed. "Now I have some investigating to do. I think I'll call Hannah and ask her out after all."

Quinn opened his mouth to say something, but shut it immediately. His eyes lost their glimmer, dulling into a dark green. He stormed out of my room, murmuring as he went.

I rang Hannah and left a message. "Hannah, hi. Look, about us dating . . . I'm not yet sure that's a great idea. Can we have a trial date and see how things go?"

A minute later, the front door clicked shut, and Quinn was gone.

"A TRIAL DATE, LIAM?" Hannah said as I slumped into my chair on Monday morning and opened my laptop.

I looked over at her tapping a red pen to her chin. "I realize it's not the most romantic of propositions. But I feel we are both practical rather than sentimental at heart."

She bit the top of her pen and processed my words. In a soft voice, she replied, "Lotte warned me this will likely never go anywhere. If you didn't jump at the first offer, you never will, she said. I'm beginning to think she's right."

I opened my drawer, rummaged through pens and paper clips to the snacks I kept at the back. Pulling out one of the chocolate mints I knew she loved, I sent her a smile and handed one over. A peace offering of sorts.

She laughed as she picked it up and started unwrapping. "What's this?"

"That's me trying to say that I understand if you don't want to go on a date."

Holding the mint to her lips, she paused. "The thing is, Lotte rules her life with her heart and so far it's brought nothing but drama and heartache." She nibbled at the edge of the mint. "Pragmatism works for me. Let's do dinner, make out some, and see what happens. How does Friday work for you?"

I brought up my calendar. Friday, the results of the first round of BCA placements. "I might have a party to attend afterward, but I think it could work."

We shared a smile, jotted the date into our calendars, and got to work on our respective columns.

It was midday, after a short meeting with Chief Benedict, when Jill shuffled through the *Scribe* doors. Normally, I'd see him across the room and duck my head to concentrate on my work, ignoring the guy completely. But today, I stared at him transfixed. Curious.

Suspicious.

He shifted awkwardly toward his desk in the far corner of the room, keeping his gaze cast toward the threadbare carpet and his Converse. But what glued my attention to him most was the way he cradled his left arm—

He glanced up, quickly scouring the room—probably searching for Jack—and our gazes locked. I wanted to pull away and avoid the snarky comment that would likely come during our staff meeting, but the dark-blue bruise around his eye held me there.

What had happened to Jill?

What had Jill done to deserve it?

Hunter's words echoed in my mind. *The vigilante broke his collarbone throwing him to the ground. He had to go to hospital. Now he's telling everyone the assault came out of the blue . . .*

Could it be so simple? Could Jill have earned vigilante payback by attacking some guy for being gay?

Instead of sneering like he normally would have, Jill tore his face from my view and sank behind his desk. Across from him, Jack's working space was empty. He stared at his friend's desk and bowed his head, likely wishing he had a confidante that would agree with what he'd done and have his back.

A sudden urge overcame me. I picked up my office-friend stapler and imagined myself leaving it on the empty desk and finding out if Jill was The Night Warrior guy threatening The Raven. Except, even if I found out it *was* Jill, it wouldn't yield anything helpful if he didn't admit the truth. And why would he do that?

No, I needed to talk to Jack and find out who Jill had been with at two in the morning. If I could convince his victim to acknowledge the vigilante was helping him, maybe The Raven could continue protecting people like Hunter.

People like me.

CHAPTER TWELVE

Shannon's clear and steady voice filled the gym. "Be aware of your surroundings," she said, her solemn gaze skimming over me and the ten other students forming a semi-circle around her.

"No walking like you're free lunch." She hunched her shoulders, dropped her gaze to the floor, and slipped her hands into the pockets of her black cargo pants. She took a few steps. "The very first step in self-defense is to carry yourself *confidently*."

She spun around, this time holding her shoulders back, head up, hands unrestricted at her sides.

The double doors at the back of the room opened with a groan and heavy footsteps padded over the wooden floors before squelching over foam mats.

"Quinn," Shannon said, a grin quirking her lips for the first time since the lesson started. "About time you got your butt in here."

"Got caught up with my professor," came the thick voice I hadn't heard in a couple of days. I'd been living in the *Scribe* offices, late every night, finishing my Halloween special.

I glanced over my shoulder. Quinn strode toward Shannon, the fluorescent lights making his bleached hair and clubbed ears more prominent. His gaze scrolled over us, settling on mine. The moment marred his casual grace, and he hesitated mid-step.

I expected a smile or a wink, but after a second of blankly staring, he refocused on Shannon. On automatic, I pushed up my glasses but—thinking logically—I removed them and jogged them to the bench at the side of the room.

". . . strong body posture and eye contact," Shannon said as I slipped next to a slim fellow named Cheddar who sported an earring and a double-dimpled grin.

Quinn, now up front with Shannon, nodded. "The aim in self-defense is to get out of a situation. It's not about fighting to win; it's about fighting to *run*." He raised his brows toward Shannon and the rest of us. "We should all be big fans of running here. It can save your life. What we will show you over the next six weeks are techniques that can help you get to the point where you have a chance to run."

Shannon sprung a surprise attack on Quinn, pulling out a plastic knife from her pocket and lunging toward him. Quinn responded quickly, pivoting out of her aim and grabbing control of her knife-wielding arm. He yanked her closer and demonstrated kneeing her in the crotch and applying force to her arm until he could take control of the weapon.

A shiver climbed slowly and steadily up my spine until it released in a shudder. They made it seem so easy, yet when Freddy had attacked me, there hadn't been time to think. I blinked back the image of those sharp, glittering fingers. *Let's see how you like this up—*

And then The Raven appeared, swooping in out of the blue.

I tried to grab my pen but I only brushed my hand over loose, pocketless sweatpants. Instead, I balled my hands and focused my attention on Shannon.

"There are four distances of attack that we will look at: kicking distance, punching distance, grabbing distance and what to do if you are pinned on the floor."

After Quinn and Shannon demonstrated a few defensive moves, they paired us all up to practice.

My partner Genna, a Hispanic woman with a nervous smile and painted eyes, didn't hesitate to launch herself at me. I fumbled a block. After we righted ourselves, Shannon touched my arm.

"Mind if I give you a few pointers?"

"Go right ahead."

She showed me how to angle my hand so I wouldn't be likely to sprain or break my wrist in an attack. "Keep your fingers angled toward your attacker, you want them to hit their eyes."

Over her shoulder, Quinn and Cheddar were chuckling at something. Quinn drew Cheddar close, showing him how to grab an attacker's neck and bend him forward. I mimicked the move on my partner, getting a cheer from Shannon.

"Good," she said, sincere and—relieved?

How much did teaching these classes remind her of Hunter? I was under no illusion that she taught them for any other reason than wishing her brother had been able to protect himself.

"Keep practicing," she murmured and moved on, freeing my vision of Quinn and Cheddar yakking easily as they blocked and attacked.

Quinn's gaze flickered in my direction for a brief moment, and then he laughed loudly at something Cheddar said.

"All right," Shannon called out. "Swap partners. Get a feel for how someone else attacks and how to respond. Remember, confidence."

I thanked Genna and picked a path to Quinn. "Okay, let's do this," I said, planting myself front of him.

He blinked down at me, his brow creasing slightly in the middle. For a moment he said nothing, just stared. And then a professional, relaxed Quinn said, "Feet shoulder-width apart."

His hand landed on my upper arm and his fingers slid down my sleeve as he coaxed me forward. "Lean slightly inward. Keeping your balance is essential."

"It's been a busy few days," I said, practicing throwing a palm-punch to his face. My fingertips brushed over his nose, cheek, and the side of his eye. His eyelashes scraped over the pad of my thumb as he blinked. "Hope you haven't been making dinner expecting I would come."

No answer.

"If you have, I'm sure it made for good lunches."

Quinn stepped closer, slowly sliding his hand around the back of my neck. His palm was warm where he pushed me down. "Try it," he said.

It was the same move I'd watched him show Cheddar, the one I'd practiced on Genna a few times already. I copied step-by-step, catching the tips of Quinn's hair on the length of my fingers as I steered him down.

When he came back up, I waited for his comment. Again, nothing.

It was my turn to frown. I started to describe how well I executed that maneuver, when he suddenly spoke. His words were puffs of air against my cheek as he locked his arms tightly around me. "You look different without your glasses on."

Per Shannon's earlier instruction, I shifted into his embrace instead of against it, pressing quickly against him and steering my thigh to his crotch in a would-be kick. I smirked. "You look different without my glasses on too."

This was the part where Quinn was supposed to show how my moves affected his balance and stumble backward in submission.

He didn't. He tightened his arms instead until I was cocooned in warmth, the light smell of Axe mingled with sweat filling my nose. He said quietly into my hair, "Did you ever get that date?"

"Yes." I pushed until our bodies were flush. "Friday."

This time when I lifted my thigh to his groin, I knocked him enough off balance that he didn't have to feign stumbling. He caught himself, straightened quickly, and acknowledged the move by cocking his head.

"I got myself a date too," he said.

He had? "Who with?"

Quinn jerked his thumb toward Cheddar.

"The cheese?"

Lips stretched into a satisfied smile as he crossed his arms. "My favorite."

"To each his own, obviously."

"It won't bother you?"

"We've been over this, Quinn. No freaking out, I promise."

"Not that. I mean—"

"Oh," I said. Was he worried I would take it the wrong way because of our kiss the other day? I quickly shook my head. "I'm not jealous or anything if that's what you're asking. I mean, the kiss was great, Quinn. It opened my eyes to new possibilities that I need to investigate further. But I can promise you, I'm not going to act weird around you or suffer under a pathetic crush."

Quinn's cheeks bloomed with color and he scratched the back of his head. "Right. No pathetic crush. Good."

Shannon's voice sliced through the conversation. "And switch partners again."

"Can I catch a ride home with you after class?" I asked, noting that Cheddar was eyeing us. Guess I knew my next partner.

Quinn sighed and motioned for Genna to pair up with him. "Sure, Liam. Sure."

CHAPTER THIRTEEN

Hunter rolled through *Scribe*'s office doors, wearing a white tank-top that made his arms look as beefy and intimidating as Booster Gold's. "Which one of these geeks do you think is The Night Warrior?" he asked, with a sideways grin.

"Guy in the corner," I said, beelining to the back of the room where a crowd had gathered around the noticeboard to see the first set of BCA results. Obviously, I hoped to place first through twenty-fifth, but it was possible not all three articles pulled high rank.

"With the bags under his eyes, wearing a rugged red shirt?"

"The one with a permanent sneer on his face."

Hunter clapped the back of my brown pants. "Give me five minutes with him."

He wheeled toward Jill, who sat alone staring blankly at Jack's empty desk.

I rounded the dissipating crowd and slunk through a gap to the board. Hannah bumped her shoulder against mine.

"Thirty-second place for my report on guns on campus." Her breath came out in excited puffs close to my cheek, and her smile lit her eyes.

I recalled the article. "It was a thorough and thoughtful article. I'd have thought it'd place higher."

Her smile faltered. "Do you know how many reports are submitted to the BCA?"

"About 3000 on average."

"That wasn't what I meant. I meant . . ." she sighed. "Thirtieth is pretty good."

Thirtieth put her in the ninety-ninth percentile. I laid a clumsy hand on her shoulder. "You're right. I should have said congratulations. I think you are very talented, Hannah. I just wanted more for you."

Her lips quirked into a smile. "Better," she said, backing away. "I hope you're satisfied too. I've got to get to class." She bit her bottom lip. "See you tonight then?"

"Yes. Let's meet at the theater. Seven-thirty."

"Okay, I'll be there." With that, she spun on her heel, clutched her messenger bag tighter to her side, and wove toward the exit.

I fingered a line down the list until I hit my name. I let out a relieved breath when I caught the title of the article that won twenty-eighth place. *The Ghosts of College Past, Present, and Yet to Come.*

If that got me twenty-eighth place, then I had a right to be excited about the final placements. I turned from the board, making my way toward Hunter.

Chief Benedict stood, leaning against his office door, staring toward the BCA list. His gaze panned toward me and he nodded his head in congratulations.

The article he'd submitted on my behalf had done well, which was great. But I still didn't believe it to be my best work. When the top placements came out, I would prove it to the chief as well.

Hunter's voice reached my ears. "Dude, calm down. It was just a joke."

"Well fuck you," Jill said, gathering his crap from the table and stuffing it awkwardly into his bag with his left hand. "Nobody beat me up. I can handle myself! I *can*."

"Aren't we getting a bit touchy?" Hunter asked, unfazed—almost amused—by Jill's cutting sneer.

I stopped closer to Jack's desk and pivoted toward the window, staring at the two from the corner of my eye.

Jill flushed. "*Touchy?* I'm not—"

"Yep, you are. It's a good thing Liam isn't your friend, else I'd have to question his judgment."

I startled at my name and blinked toward Hunter casually drumming his fingers on the arms of his chair.

"Liam?" Jill spat. "You know him?"

"More than that, I *like* him."

Those three words functioned like a warm blanket on a cold day. I approached Hunter's side, resting a hand on the back of his chair. Jill wasn't going to confess. "Let's get lunch," I said.

We left Jill guffawing, and grabbed some sandwiches to eat at the park. We planted ourselves at the exact spot near the trees where I'd spoken with Mitch. Hunter reluctantly donned a sweater.

"I think the guy needs to be laid over a knee and given a good spanking," Hunter said, "but I don't think he's The Night Warrior." He motioned toward my face. "Crumb."

I blinked away the image of Jill ass-up and swiped a hand over my mouth. "Not him? But—"

"Look, he checked me out, okay? You know," Hunter slowly stroked his gaze over me from head to foot, lingering a moment at my crotch. "He's gay. My bet, the victim."

Jill? The victim?

"He was acting defensive back there," Hunter continued.

"Then he can identify who attacked him!"

"I don't think he's going to come forward about it any time soon. He's angry, embarrassed."

"Then what should we do?"

Hunter cocked his head and grinned. "Leave it to me—I have a way with stubborn men."

"Didn't seem to work with Mitch," I pointed out.

He hurled his sandwich wrapper at my stomach. "You really say what you think, don't you?"

"Because it's true."

Hunter laughed. "Yeah, but sometimes a little sugarcoating or downright fake forgetfulness goes a long way."

"You want me to forget this thing with you and Mitch?"

"Yeah. Because there is no me and Mitch."

"Making your own luck didn't help then?"

"Sure it did. Mitch wasn't the only one I was making my luck for. He wasn't even the main one."

I scrunched my sandwich wrapper around Hunter's, attempting to mask the warm feeling flooding me. I tried to thank him, but it struggled to come off my tongue so I nodded instead.

"Right," Hunter said, rolling forward. "Let's go somewhere I can take my sweater off."

I DRESSED in a suit because it *was* a date, after all. The cuffs were stiff at my wrists, alternating between annoying and, well, pleasant when they tickled my skin lightly.

Quinn stomped around the kitchen, so I decided against blow-drying my hair in favor of giving him a quick greeting.

He stopped abruptly, the milk from his glass splashing on the floor. Placing the newly-emptied glass on the bench, he dropped a dishtowel onto the small puddle and swiped his foot over it, side to side. "Might want to lose the jacket," he said tightly, his gaze doing the same sweeping that Hunter demonstrated earlier.

"Really?" I asked, veering around him for a slice of bread to pop into the toaster. "Is that why you were checking me out?"

Quinn picked up the dishtowel with a thin laugh and tossed it into the sink. He suddenly appeared right beside me, prying the bread from my fingers. "Why eat if you're going out on a date?"

"We're just doing a movie. Then she wants to help out with ideas for my column."

"Your column? That's your idea of a date?"

"Well, yeah. We're going to Jell-O Fight Night just off Fifth. So right now"—I snatched back the bread and popped it in the toaster—"I'm hungry."

Zing!

The toaster spluttered and sparked and I jerked my arm back.

Quinn swore and pulled the plug from the socket. He twisted me toward him with a tight, panicked grip on my forearms, checking me over carefully. "Are you okay?"

I swallowed. Blinked. "Have I ever told you you're better than a cat?"

Quinn's lips contorted into a grin that he proceeded to smother and turn into a frown. His hands moved to my jacket and pinched at the V just above the first button. "Jell-O Fight Night? I thought you wanted some muscle at your side when you went to party?"

"Somehow Jell-O Fight Night doesn't sound all that intimidating. If you were a mop and a bucket, I might have taken you along."

"In case you change your mind, I'll be a phone-call away." His fingers slid to the buttons, undoing them one at a time.

I let him. I liked watching the slight shake of his hands as he drew his fingers over the material, knuckles scraping gently over the shirt underneath. I shivered at the loss of the touch when he pulled back. "Wear it undone."

"Thanks for the tip. When are you meeting the cheese tonight?"

He looked at me blankly for a moment, then twisted toward the fridge and opened it. "Yeah, Cheddar. He . . . uh—I mean, *we* —are meeting soon. What movie did you say you're going to?"

"It's that student documentary, *Played With. Lost.* At the campus theater."

"That's a coincidence," Quinn said, pulling out some lettuce and tomato and moving to the chopping board. "We were planning on seeing that too."

I tilted my head slowly. "This isn't you getting jealous, is it?"

He laughed so loudly I had to rub my ears a little. "Nah, just a coincidence. And . . . since neither of us have any pathetic crushes on one another, you won't mind if we're there too, right?"

I rested against the bench and passed him the bread when he gestured for it. "Right. I just didn't pick you for the documentary type," I said. "You or the cheese. But since you are, would you mind giving me a lift?"

Quinn prepared sandwiches, cutting them neatly down the middle. "You know who might mind? Cheddar. Let me just give him a call and see how he *feels* about it." He passed me the plate of prepared sandwiches and darted off to his room.

I stared down at the plate, a solid weight in my hand, just as Quinn was a solid weight in the apartment. *I could get used to this.* With a smile, I moved to the table and ate.

I SAT close to the front of the small, almost empty theater with Hannah, who was a bouquet of smiles and laughter next to me. Behind us somewhere were Quinn and Cheddar, but I gave them their privacy by not looking back.

About halfway through the documentary, I slipped my hand over the arm separating our chairs, and nudged Hannah's pinkie. I whispered, "Maybe we should—"

Hannah pressed her hand against mine, threading our fingers together. Clammy and stiff, but warm too. Reassuring, somehow.

Well, yes, the kiss with Quinn had been better. Comforting and spiced with little electric thrills. But holding hands was hardly a fair comparison. I'd never done that with Quinn. Maybe kissing Hannah would be just as good.

Colored light from the screen flickered over Hannah's face, softening the sharp profile of her nose and highlighting her full lips, stretched into a nervous smile. She peeked at me from the corner of her eye. "What?" she mouthed.

Again, I whispered in her ear, "May I kiss you a second?"

She faced me, teasing her bottom lip with her front teeth. Cute as a bunny, to pen a fitting phrase. Yes, cute flushed cheeks, sweet smile, nice eyes . . .

I cupped the side of her face and leaned in to kiss her. Her lips moved shyly against mine, but her breath puffing out was warm and smelled like cherry-flavored bubblegum.

Pleasant. Fine. Okay.

Where was the static? The strange moment where I skipped a breath? The promise of cocooning warmth that came from a bigger body?

I tried the kiss again, searching for something else perhaps I'd missed the first time. I threaded my fingers through the back of her soft hair, loosening it from the hair-tie. She danced delicate fingers up my arm to rest lightly on the curve of my neck.

Our mouths locked awkwardly and a slither of tongue over my bottom lip just made it feel wet.

"Hmmm," I murmured. A sudden silence in the documentary emphasized the sound.

She squeezed my hand and drew hers away. "Let's give it to the end of the night to be sure."

"Maybe it's the angle," I said. The time? The heat? The fullness from Quinn's sandwiches? The need to urinate?

"Or not," she said with an apathetic shrug and smile. To the point. Factual.

"Or not," I agreed.

I excused myself and sidled out of the row, passing the only other person in there besides my party and Quinn's.

I'd just finished relieving myself in the bathroom when the door swung in. I caught the action in the reflection of the mirrors to my left, and was buttoning up as Quinn sauntered in. At first he must have been looking at me, but then his gaze met mine in the mirror.

There was something almost predatory as he kicked his way across the room.

With a slight shiver, I turned to the sink and pressed down on the faucet. Antiseptic soap scented the air. "How do you like the film?"

Quinn stood behind me, keeping eye contact through the mirrors. "I don't."

I shrugged. "I wish I could comment more constructively, but I've been oblivious to the screen. This dating thing is more challenging than I thought. It's like an equation I'm not schooled enough to solve. The angles, the timing, the—"

"Fact she's female?"

I nodded. "Maybe that, too. I tried to kiss her but all I could think about was how much better it was with you. How I could feel it in my toes. How even just remembering makes me itchy."

Quinn stepped closer, his chest rising as he took in a deep breath.

I asked, "Do you mind giving us both a lift to Fifth?"

His chest deflated, and his gaze darted from the mirror to the urinals. He started running a hand through his hair.

"Looks good," I told him, drying my hands.

"Cheddar thinks so too."

"Then the cheese has taste."

Quinn almost grinned, but something held him back. Maybe the fact he needed to piss and hadn't yet because I was standing around. Some men were shy that way.

"I'll leave you to it, then," I said, slipping past him to the door. "Are we good for the lift?"

"It'll be a tight fit. Cheddar's coming home with me."

"I'm taking that as a yes."

JELL-O FIGHT NIGHT.

Well wasn't this a pretty sight?

A ten-foot, rectangular paddle pool lay lengthwise in an empty living room. Tens of students surrounded the pool at a wide berth, watching two women in jeans and T-shirts wrestling in ankle-deep putrid green Jell-O.

The party smelled of beer, citrus, and cheap thrills.

Hannah pressed closer to my side, scoured the scene, and shook her head. "I need a drink."

Alone in a crowd of cheering guys, I reached for my notebook and pen.

A guy in a tank-top and running shoes hollered from the corner of the room. "If your number is called out, please make your way to the pool. Seventeen and twenty-three, you're up."

My gaze veered from my notebook to the fifty-seven that'd been stamped on my hand, apparently for entry to the curved fishbowl of numbers.

Well. They could forget that. No way in a hundred years would I expose myself to such crass ridicule.

Was this the type of thing Jack and Jill found fun? No wonder my columns were a disappointment if *this* was the type of cut-rate angle readers sought.

Flyers were pressed against my chest and I clutched the pile on reflex.

"Take one, pass it on," someone said. I awkwardly shifted them to Mr. Buzz-Cut next to me and resumed note taking.

Hannah pushed her way back through the thickening crowds, her hair loose, spilling over her shoulders and snagging on horny guys as she squeezed free.

She handed me a large, plastic shot glass of red Jell-O. "I tried them all. This is the best flavor."

Tried them all? I glanced at her semi-diluted pupils, jamming my notebook and pen under my arm while I took the shot glass and sniffed. "How many flavors were there?"

"Five."

The raspberry shot burned my throat. "Five?" I spluttered. "Why would you do that?"

"Look, I know this isn't going to work out between us, so I just want to be drunk when I hear you say it."

Her cheeks flushed and she downed the other shot, a squirt of liquid dribbling down her chin and plopping onto her turquoise shirt. Hurriedly, she wiped her mouth clean. "Guess I'm drunk enough to hear it now. Go."

Cheers roared around us, and in a quick glance through the narrow gaps between heads, I caught sight of a tangled trio in the pool. Some intoxicated guy had thrown himself into the mix.

I set my empty shot glass down on a nearby windowsill, rubbed my brow, and aligned my glasses proper. "I was curious if it would work out with us, but you're right. I'm not romantically inclined toward you."

"Right," she said, setting her glass down too. "Yeah. Me neither."

"You're still the girl I want to share my mints with at *Scribe,* though. And I hope—" My voice faltered and a nervous shiver had me shifting my weight. "I mean, when we're not too busy, I'd like to go to the movies with you again. Or eat lunch, or—" I laughed at myself for the sudden fear that gripped my stomach. What if she said no? "I'd like to replace my office friends with real ones."

The host yelled, "Numbers fifty-eight and sixty! You're up."

Hannah glanced at the back of her hand as she wiped her palms over the thighs of her jeans. "Fifty-eight. That's me."

She veered toward the center of the room, threading though the sweaty, anticipatory crowd.

I snagged her sleeve, and she looked at me over her shoulder. "Don't do it."

She shrugged. "I've never done anything just for the heck of it, Liam. I want to have a life. At least, I want to try new things before I dismiss them."

I frowned. There was certain logic to that.

"Besides," she said, backing toward the kiddie pool, "you can use me as your angle. You could call it *Letting Loose after Lectures*."

She pulled off the small beaded bag she wore and stripped to her undershirt. "That's all you're getting from me, guys," she said, kicking off her shoes and chucking them into a pile at the side of the Jell-O pool.

I opened my notebook again and scribbled some more, although this time my pen didn't move as swiftly and I kept shifting positions, searching for something comfortable.

Hannah was pitted against a bear of a guy who'd been pushed into the pool by his chuckling friends. With a thick crop of brown hair and a light beard, he rested his hands on his hips and blinked thick lashes toward his opponent. He threw his friends a hard look and leaned his hulking frame forward.

"Sorry about this," he said warmly. Then to Trainers Guy, "This is hardly a fair fight."

"Luck of the draw," came the shrugged answer.

"But she's *half* my size."

Not quite true. She was two heads shorter than he was, but that put her in the range of normal and him in the league of giants.

Hannah straightened and snapped her gaze to his. "That's presumptuous."

He quirked a brow at her. "What's presumptuous?"

In answer, Hannah deftly grabbed the loops at the waist of his jeans and hauled him forward.

He budged a fraction in the thick Jell-O, while Hannah slid violently forward. A muffled groan escaped her from where she had face-planted into his chest. "So it's all muscle, then."

Giant Guy grinned, his cheeks dimpling deeply. "And I don't want to use it against you. So how about falling to the pit for three seconds, eh?"

Hannah scowled and shook her head. Her gaze sought mine and she said, "I want you recording this, Liam. Every detail. Every plea to let him go."

Amongst the murmuring chatter of the crowd, I re-gripped my pen.

Giant Guy snorted. "You're funny."

"Let's see who ends up laughing," Hannah said, and sank her fingers into his armpits and wriggled.

"Ga-ha, stop it!" Giant Guy rolled his arms back, the swing of his arms sending him off balance and launching a half-stride slip.

Hannah doubled her effort.

Whallomp!

Giant Guy over-corrected and ended up on his ass, pulling Hannah with him.

She wasted no time to straddle him and continue attacking his armpits with rigorous tickles.

"Stop, stop," he cried out between tears of uncontrolled laughter.

"Fall back into the pit for three seconds," Hannah said,

pushing herself hard against him in an effort to force him back. "Then I'll stop."

He gave a pathetic attempt to shove her off, but it exposed his armpits more, and he ended up surrendering quickly, much to the amusement of his friends and the crowd.

In her eagerness to get out of the pool, Hannah slipped and crashed once more into the slippery giant. His arms circled her waist, steadying her. "Careful now, my pride's been shot enough tonight. Can't have you tackling me to the ground twice."

She laughed, looking up at him. He smiled down at her, his eyes crinkled.

I carefully ripped out a piece of paper from the middle of my notebook. When they clambered out of the pool, I handed it and my pen to Giant Guy.

"What's this for?" he asked, grabbing it with slimy fingers as Hannah awkwardly jerked putting her shirt back on.

"That's what attraction looks like." I gestured to the paper. "For you to give your number to Hannah."

He raised his meaty brow. "And you are?"

"Liam Davis. Reporter for *Scribe*."

"Just give it here," Hannah said, snatching the pen and scribbling something on the paper. She curled a finger around one of his belt loops and, when he came forward, slipped the paper into his pocket. "In case you ever fancy eating Jell-O with me again."

"I didn't really eat any Jell-O, you know," he said, grinning as he slipped a finger inside his pocket.

Hannah laughed. "Yeah, you ate it all right."

With style and grace, and a playful smile, she took my arm and steered us out of there.

As we crossed the threshold into the cool night air, a flyer stuck on my shoe. I shook it free and the yellow paper fluttered down a few steps toward the path. Written in large letters across the top was *Have You Seen The Raven?*

I picked it up, Hannah leaning against my shoulder to read it too.

"Someone really doesn't like The Raven," she said as I scanned the flyer again and looked back at the lit Victorian house behind us. Hannah was right.

I folded the flyer and stuffed it in my other pocket. We ambled to the corner of Fifth and Walnut.

"Thanks for the evening," she said.

"You put yourself out there," I said, hailing her a taxi. "Seemed like it worked for you."

"Yeah." She curled an arm around my neck and, with vodka Jell-O breath, she pecked the side of my cheek. "Jack and Jill are such dicks," she said, "Of course I'm your real friend, Liam."

CHAPTER FOURTEEN

The light in Quinn's room leaked from the slit at the bottom of the door. I slipped out of my coat and suit jacket, and toed off my shoes.

I rubbed at a splotch of dried, crusty Jell-O on my thigh. It wasn't the best idea to turn up to the Jell-O party in my suit. But never mind. I'd stick them in the wash.

Movement came from Quinn's room, and I sidled closer to the wall that he shared with the living room. I only heard silence, so maybe Cheddar had left already? That, or they had very quiet intercourse.

I swallowed the sudden dryness in my throat, and almost immediately followed it up by banging on Quinn's door.

"Liam?" Quinn asked, pulling the door open.

One glance told me he was alone in the room, and I shifted my gaze back to him. His worried frown quickly disappeared, and he casually leaned against the doorjamb in nothing more than a pair of sweatpants.

Goose bumps didn't scatter over his skin like the last time I'd seen him shirtless, but his nipples were stiff and redder than I remembered, though it could've been the light.

A finger curled around my chin and lifted it. "My face is up here," Quinn said with an amused smile.

"Are you serious about Cheddar?"

"Why?"

"I might be gay," I said.

"You just figured that out, smart guy?"

"I need more proof to ascertain it's true." I walked forward, pressing my palm against his warm chest. His hairs prickled my skin and sent electric beads of excitement up to my elbow. "Cheddar?"

A delicate blush streaked Quinn's cheeks and his boxed ears lifted a fraction. His large hand cuffed mine, pressing firmly, as if to keep me right where I was.

"Cheddar's a friend of mine," he said quietly, his green gaze burrowing into mine and sending all the blood I could spare right to my groin. "A friend who played decoy tonight."

"Decoy?" I asked, my body leaning toward him.

He bent forward, holding his nose just far enough from mine that it felt as if our noses were touching, even though they weren't. "I really hated that documentary."

"So you do have a pathetic crush on me."

His mouth closed on mine, and with a quick spin of my body, Quinn pinned me to the doorframe, one hand cupping the back of my head, cushioning it from the wood.

Our breathing quickened. Warm, delicate puffs escaped between the meshing of soft lips and nipping teeth, and each time his tongue touched mine, my blood seemed to sing and I shivered. My cock ached like it never had without my hand on it.

A rasp of Quinn's stubble moved from my cheek down the side of my neck as he tasted the skin below my ear. His tongue flicked, and the air quickly cooled the spot. I threaded my fingers in his hair, slightly stiffened at the tips with product. I squeezed, pushing him and his lips toward that spot again.

This time he moaned as he tasted me and sucked hard until it stung. I let out something between a groan and a pant.

"Touch me," I said, cocking my hips and thrusting my crotch against his. The bulge of his hard cock had mine pulsing.

My hands trailed over his shoulders to his chest and I squeezed his nipples. "I need your hands down my pants now."

"Fuck that's so hot." Quinn stole my lips once more and his fingertips worked the buttons of my fly, his knuckles brushing over my length in a way that had me clutching at his back for him to hurry.

He chuckled and spoke in my ear as his slightly cool fingertips darted into the waistband of my boxer-briefs and drew an agonizing line from one side of my hips to the other, crossing over the head of my cock to finish.

"I want you to remember this."

I thrust toward him again. "I have a good memory. I doubt I'll be forgetting any time soon. Grab me. Jerk me."

His groan rumbled at my ear, and his stubble came hard and rough against my neck as he drew his chin from my ear to my shoulder. He had to know it felt good. Had to know how much it made me want to spill in my pants.

His hand fished into my briefs and took hold of me firmly, just like I wanted him to. He pumped slowly, the throbs tightening my whole body. I rested my forehead against his smooth, slightly freckled shoulder. "Yes, like that."

The light from his room made a silhouette of Quinn's stiff cock tenting his sweatpants. "I want to touch you too," I said, my breath hitching as Quinn circled my pre-cum around the head of my cock with his thumb.

A hummed "yeah" brushed through my hair.

"Tell me what to do. I haven't touched a man before."

He didn't lift his hand off me, but slowed his movements as he shifted, taking my hand and pressing it against the taut material and his even tauter cock. "Touch me like you do to yourself, in the shower."

He squeezed me and along with the pleasure, I took the encouragement, peeling back his sweatpants and underwear until Quinn's cock sprang free. I closed my hand around it. Thicker than mine, though not quite as long. Warm, with such silky skin at his head. I jerked him to the rhythm he was working me, getting used to the new, hard weight.

I circled his pre-cum and flicked my fingertip lightly over the slit at the top, where it was most sensitive on me. He twitched and groaned, lips seeking mine and jamming them into an ardent kiss.

Our hands worked faster, thumbs banging against each other in our greed.

What would Quinn's velvet length feel like rubbing hard against mine? "I want our cocks together," I said. "Fuck me."

Quinn let go of me and pried my hand from him too. He widened his legs and leaned forward, taking both our lengths in his large hand.

I whimpered at the electrical currents that zapped through me at that touch, at the deep stare Quinn gave me. He pumped a few more times, my climax building rapidly. And then his head fell back, lips parted in a moan—

I stiffened, my release coming to a sudden, urgent end. Quinn jerked us twice more and braced with me as spurts of our hot come shot over his chest and abdomen, mingling and dribbling a crooked path over his skin.

Quinn slowly released our cocks, tucking mine away and then his own as he caught his breath.

I pushed away from the doorframe, my back definitely feeling the effects of the hard wood. Tentatively, I fingered our come on Quinn's chest. "That clears some things up. I must be gay."

Laughing gently, he fell back a few steps into his room. He picked up a T-shirt off the floor and wiped himself with it. He looked up at me with a slightly raised brow and a quirked lip. It almost came off as a leer. "If you need to prove it again, you know where my bedroom is."

"Thank you for the offer." I buttoned my pants. "Will it be awkward now?"

He gripped his shirt. "No. We won't let it be."

"Good. I like you as my friend."

Quinn's mouth opened, as if he wanted to say something more, and then he shut it again. "Sure. Me too."

I turned and left. "Good night, then," I said, and made a path to the bathroom. I looked just the same as I always did when I looked in the mirror. To myself, I said, "You learn something new every day."

Then, teeth brushed and ready for bed, I went to my room and drafted an outline of *Letting Loose after Lectures* on my laptop before falling into a heady sleep.

I CLICKED MY PEN, narrowing my gaze on the notes scribbled before me. My office-friend stapler kept staring at me and I slid him out of view. Though it was late in the evening, *Scribe* was still thrumming with life. From the chief's open office door, I heard murmuring as he conversed with Jack. Something about one of his projects needing more expansion.

Words swam in my open notebook. A vortex of doubt regarding my final feature article swirled in my mind. It had to be pitched just perfectly to get the chief's approval. I knew the chief was fascinated by modern technology, and the way he divided his trash into garbage, compost, and recycling suggested he might be swayed to accept an environmental angle.

I dropped my pen and sank my tired body into the chair.

Across my desk, Hannah twirled a thick strand of hair around her finger. Giant Guy—who turned out to be called Roger Delaware—stood chatting with her. His dimpled smile and soft gaze as he looked at Hannah had my approval.

Hannah yanked on her hair and hurriedly let go, as if she'd just realized what she'd been doing. She straightened and cleared her throat. "I just don't know," she said, a quirk in her lips betraying her attempt at a tease. "Going out for a fancy dinner with a handsome hulk or curling up on my worn couch with my history assignment? Tough call."

Roger grinned. "If you put it like that, what was I thinking? Dinner with a beautiful smartass over doing my math assignments?"

A sweet, nervous laugh floated around them and Hannah lightly got to her feet, fisted Roger's shirt, and pulled him down. She kissed him quickly on the mouth and nodded toward the exit. "Let's get out of here."

Roger nodded mutely, but when Hannah twisted to leave, he snatched her hand and hauled her back. Cupping his hands on her face, he kissed her again, this time longer. When he pulled back, he was smiling and she looked like her bones had melted.

I lightly tossed my pen toward them, breaking their long, searching gaze. "While you may be tempted, there are still far too many people in here for you to attempt ravishing each other on the desk."

With a bright blush, Hannah laughed and—tugging Roger with her—left the building.

I stared from my notebook to my pen on the floor. I spun my chair slowly and peeled myself up to retrieve it. An article on the invasion of internet mass media? A look into student involvement in environmental protection?

Or—yes! What if it was something combined? How the internet and mass media support student involvement in environmental protection?

With a *whoop!* I swept up my pen. It almost felt hot in my hand with all the thoughts streaming toward it, begging to be written.

A step before my desk, the chief caught my eye, beckoning me over.

"Yes, chief?" I asked, stopping in front of him. He stood solidly in the doorway, arms folded.

"You were in here until late last night, are you planning to be again?"

I nodded my head. "I also have the feature article you requested me to write."

"Ah, that." His frown lightly dented his brow. "Let me stress again, writing it is not assurance you will get the features editor position."

I clicked my pen. "But if I wow you, I have a chance, right?"

"Right."

I stopped clicking. "Then my article will be in your email by no later than midnight, Friday, the fifth of December." I turned to leave, but a hand clamped down on my shoulder. I glanced back at the chief, his lips in a firm line.

"The office will be closed over Thanksgiving weekend."

"Oh." A shame, but as long as I organized myself, I could work from home, so it wasn't the end of the world. I slipped from his gentle grip. "Okay."

I worked another hour until it was only me, Jack, and the chief. At nine, Hunter texted. He'd just finished basketball practice and wanted to know if I was up for a drink. I texted back that I was still working, and fifteen minutes later, Hunter rolled through the doors.

"Shut that thing," he said, chin jerking in the direction of my laptop. "We're going for a drink."

"I can't, I have to plan this article—"

Hunter's chest puffed up as he folded his arms and directed me a hard look. "Can't or won't, Liam?"

I pushed up my glasses. "This article has to be perfect or my father won't let me work for him."

Hunter nudged his chair forward, pressed save, and shut my laptop. I just watched, twiddling my pen as he did it. "You're smart, there will be other people to work for."

Numbly, I nodded, but when Hunter slipped my laptop into its gray skin, I shook my head. "I don't think it's just about the position," I said quietly. Standing up, I packed the rest of my bag and followed Hunter to his van.

He drove with purpose and speed—in the *opposite* direction of home.

"Where are we going?" I asked, gripping my seat belt as we whipped around a corner.

"Cryptions. A bar on Liberty Avenue."

"Since we could get a drink on Ellsworth without the detour, I am guessing something else is at Cryptions. Perhaps a *someone* else?"

Hunter grinned, looking at me from the corner of his eye. "Mitch texted me. He said he's working there and wants to see me."

"And I am here because . . .?" I clung onto the arm of the door as Hunter swerved around a deep pothole.

"Because I like your company, you need a stiff drink, and I like having someone to yak with until Mitch gets a free moment."

The parking lot was busier than I thought it would be for a Tuesday. Inside, a thick crowd of mostly male students undulated to noisy music. I stuck close to Hunter as we threaded our way through the crowds. Thankfully, most were decent enough to make way for Hunter's chair, though Hunter's *You better fucking move* look was likely helping.

"What can I get you?" Hunter yelled over the noise as I squeezed into a free spot at a corner booth.

"Some peace and quiet would be nice. But seeing that's unlikely, a Coke will do."

A mid-twenty-something with a double nose-piercing leered at me. I quickly choked out, "And spike it with bourbon!"

Hunter chuckled and left, and I studiously avoided eye contact with anyone. Taking out my notebook, I sketched a few ideas for my environmental angle, and when my phone beeped, I took it out and read the new e-mail from Mom:

Liam,
I don't want to disturb you, love, but a couple of things:

1. *What are your plans for Thanksgiving? I have been asked to work that day, which would be great for getting in the good books with this new job, but I wanted to make sure that you'd be okay with it?*
2. *We have a new neighbor here. Every morning at seven he walks his Persian cat by our house and waves. I think I shall introduce myself to him.*

Look forward to hearing from you,
Mom

I quickly wrote back:

Mom,

1. *I have plans for the weekend, so no problem.*
2. *Introduce yourself. Tell me the details.*

Liam

Hunter bumped his chair against mine and snagged my notebook from the table. "I'm confiscating this until our bro-date is over." He slid it down one side of his chair. "Drinks are on the way."

I glanced toward the bar. Mitch was at the far end, wearing a net T-shirt and thick eyeliner; his skin glowed the same red as his hair in the orange lights above him. "Did you get to talk?"

"Not yet, he said he'd come over soon."

At that precise moment, as Mitch filled a glass with ice, he looked across the room toward us.

Hunter shot him a wink, and Mitch fumbled with the glass, ice scattering over the counter. "He's adorable," Hunter murmured. He focused back on me, his lips curving downward at the edges. "I had another chat with Jill today."

"You did?"

"Caught him hunched over a book at the base of a tree by the cathedral."

That explained why it was only Jack in the office today. "Bit cold for that, isn't it?"

"That's what I thought. It was almost as if he were waiting for someone. Anyway, not great news on that front."

"Did he tell you to fuck off?"

"Among other things. He's got a foul mouth for such a pretty boy."

"The foul part is right."

"Yeah, well." Hunter scrubbed the back of his head and casually locked his fingers together. "He's not ready to talk. It's more than the arm and fear that's hurting him, I think. Can't push that."

Mitch set our drinks down and scouted the booth for seats, but nothing was free.

Hunter slapped his lap. "You can sit here if you like."

Mitch grinned and made the corners of his eyes crinkle. "You'd like that, wouldn't you?"

I picked up my drink and sipped. Sweet and smoky.

Hunter snagged Mitch's fingers and drew him forward one step. "Yeah, and I'd like it even more if it came with an answer."

Mitch's Adam's apple bobbed. "What answer?"

"Why didn't you show up the other week?"

Mitch and I stared at his and Hunter's entwined fingers. Such a simple touch, yet it made their faces glow like the New York City skyline.

"I'm sorry. I"—he glanced uncomfortably at everyone around the table—"I'm really sorry."

Hunter played with Mitch's fingers, looking into his eyes. "Look, you can talk to me okay? I know things aren't ideal. I expect there to be issues. Just let me know what they are, okay?"

"Okay."

"Lean in, I have something else to tell you."

With a curious frown, Mitch leaned in. Hunter cupped a hand behind his neck and drew him closer still, as if to whisper in his ear. His lips brushed against Mitch's jaw, then swiftly to his mouth. Their kiss wasn't delicate in the least. Hunter locked him into a tongue party that had Mitch moaning and crumpling toward his lap.

With a murmured laugh, Hunter slapped Mitch's ass and pulled back. "More of that on Saturday, after a date. What do you say?"

Mitch gulped and nodded, touching his ass in wonder. "I mean, no, I can't."

Hunter stilled his hands on the arm of his chair and a strange desire to pat him came over me, but I reined it in.

"Wait, this is coming out wrong," Mitch said. "I'm leaving for home at the end of the week. My sister is getting married, and since Thanksgiving is next week, I'm taking the whole week off." He bit his bottom lip as he continued, but I got the feeling there wasn't much enthusiasm behind his next words. "Will you maybe come to the opening party of the 32nd floor of the Cathedral of Learning? With me? As a date?"

Hunter needled a finger into one of the netted holes of Mitch's T-shirt and drew him in again. "You betcha," he said with one last nip at his lips.

Mitch floated back to his position behind the bar, and Hunter drank his lemonade with the most enthusiasm I'd seen yet. I snuck a sip to make sure it hadn't been spiked. Nope, unless plain ol' good mood counted.

When we twisted and turned and rolled our way out of the bar, he asked about my work and the article I was intending to write for the chief.

"Sounds okay," he said, unlocking the van.

"Just okay?"

"I mean, I've read your work. You'll make it awesome."

Once we were settled and strapped into the van, Hunter rested his arms on the steering wheel and looked over at me. "I just—"

"What?"

He started the car and reversed. "You said you didn't think you were doing it just for the position at your dad's company."

He *had* heard me then. I'd just assumed it wasn't worth acknowledging. A slight twist in my gut had me swallowing hard. I liked that he listened.

"That's right," I said, counting each wave of light rolling over us from the lampposts we passed. "I never thought it bothered me, but I want him to recognize me. See me as someone worth getting to know. I think I've associated winning the spot at his company with a chance for him to do that."

The waves of light were coming slower now; Hunter must have lowered his speed.

"I get it," Hunter said, his thumbs tapping against the wheel as if he were deep in thought. "I'm sorry for dragging you away from your work tonight."

I rubbed my hands together, jamming them for warmth between my thighs. "I was probably too tired to produce anything of quality, anyway. Thanks for the distraction. Which reminds me"—I tugged at my seatbelt strap—"I'm gay, or—heavily leaning toward males."

The van lurched, throwing me forward a couple inches; the seatbelt locked hard across my chest.

"When did you figure that out?" Hunter asked, regaining his control and smoothly turning toward home.

"There were a few signals from the start, so I decided to test my theory out."

Hunter zipped onto College Street without indicating. I could just make out my apartment from here, its teal trimming a funky dark green in the night.

"Go on," Hunter said.

I picked at the belt across my chest while I described my findings. "Things felt better with Quinn than they ever have before, and since the weekend I've been looking at guys differently. I think I can now say I am empirically more sexually attracted to males than females."

Hunter raised one sharp eyebrow and gave a smirk that could land a mark in the dark. "Go back to the bit about Quinn."

"Speaking of," I said, gesturing out the window toward the path leading to my apartment. Standing opposite each other, arms widely gesturing as if in the middle of a row, were Shannon and Quinn.

Hunter slowed down just before our place, applied the brake, and leaned back in his seat, threading his fingers behind his head. "Well, you don't see that often," he murmured.

Even though we were double-parked only a car's length from my place, neither Shannon nor Quinn seemed to notice us.

Hunter used the main control to roll down my window. A cool breeze and Quinn's voice hit my face.

"I'm telling you because you're my best friend." Quinn kicked his heel into the grass at the edge of the path. Then softer, "But I should have told you sooner. Much sooner. I'm sorry for that."

Shannon's hair shook free of a loose hold. Her blue streaks shone brightly under the ornate lamppost nestled in front of a large willow lining the path. She was scrunching something in her hand, paper of some sort. "You . . ." she trailed off, stepping back, her shit-kickers clomping against the concrete.

She glanced to her side, and her gaze latched onto the van. Us. She sought Hunter, eyes glazed and saddened.

Tossing the paper at Quinn, she hurried up the street, quickly disappearing into thick shadows.

"What was that about?" Hunter mused as we watched Quinn chase after her in his pajama bottoms, unzipped parka, and unlaced boots.

I slipped out of the van. Shivering against another breeze, I darted to the path, chasing after the scuttling balled paper. I opened it, carefully flattening the paper against my thigh. The words jumped out at me, sharp and long like Freddy's fingers had been. It was the flyer from the Jell-O party. The one wanting any and every bit of information on The Raven. The one threatening to hurt him.

For a long, cold minute I stared at that paper until all of my thoughts crashed together and unified to give me an answer. *The* answer.

Calmly, I walked back to the van. To Hunter. I leaned against the door and looked over at him. "I figured it out," I said, sliding the paper onto the passenger seat. "I know who The Raven is."

"You just figured it out? Bang, just like that?"

"You sound surprised."

He tried to laugh, but his curiosity was too dominant. "Who is he then?"

I leaned in and told him. When he'd heard everything I had to say, he shook his head. "No. That can't be right." He was already starting the car. He dropped his gaze to his legs, and I shut the door. His head shook again, and he glanced at me one last time before hightailing out of there. "I would have known."

CHAPTER FIFTEEN

I dressed for bed and sat myself on the couch with my laptop, awaiting Quinn's return. I had scanned old articles that had anything to do with The Raven, and in combination with what victims had told me, I was certain I was right.

Quinn came in with a bang of the door, and kicked off his boots. He shrugged out of his jacket, letting it fall to the floor. He didn't bother to pick it up. The bottoms of his pajamas were soaked with mud and he peeled them off, hopping on one foot and muttering cuss words when they caught.

I swiveled on the end of the couch, shutting my laptop and setting it on the glass table.

The motion elicited a startled look from Quinn in my direction. His stiff shoulders relaxed a fraction, and he tossed his pajama bottoms on top of his abandoned jacket and moved toward me, wearing only his tightie-whities and a matching tank-top.

"Liam," he said, my name coming like a relieved sigh off his lips.

It was a warm sound that skittered over my skin, the same way the electrical current did between us when we got close. Part of me wanted to give in to the feeling, loosen with it as if it were a drug, but I was in better control of my facilities than to let that happen.

I pushed myself off the couch and faced him. Whatever my expression was, it was enough to make him stop mid-step. I didn't beat around the bush. "I know who The Raven is."

He braced his other foot to the floor. "You do?" But it came out less of a question, than a resignation.

"Yes, Quinn. I do."

He drew a pattern with his sweaty sock over the floor. A triangle, or a square. "What are you going to do?" He paused, and his voice grew softer, wearier. "Report him?"

"It would be a sure way to land the features editor position." I swallowed and searched his eyes. "But I'm not callous. Especially not when it comes to you. As far as I'm concerned, I don't know squat about The Raven. But—"

He lifted his head and angled it, reading me so intently all those tingles returned.

I shook them off. "But it has to stop, Quinn. One wrong move and it could be over. The end. I don't think either of us wants that happen."

He closed his eyes and nodded. "I'm trying. But it's not as easy to stop as you think."

"Try harder. I'll help where I can too, just like I was helped."

His Adam's apple jutted hard. "You—you don't seem surprised.

I guess I expected, if you ever found out, that you'd be more . . . well, surprised," he finished lamely.

"Once I put all the facts together, it just made sense. It was right under my nose the whole time"—I shrugged—"I should have seen it sooner."

"And you're not mad I didn't tell you?"

So he didn't tell me? No big deal. "Just because we're friends doesn't mean we've made promises to share all our secrets."

"Right. Thanks."

Our gazes held and he came forward, pushing a thick wall of tingles and goosebump soup with him. I wanted to submerge myself in it, wrap myself up in his strong arms, taste him all over again, but then I looked up. His eyes were ringed with shadows and tension, and I knew his calendar enough to know he had an early morning start tomorrow.

"Is there anything else, Liam?" he asked, a mixture of soft and tired. "Anything you might like to say to me tonight?"

I shook my head and veered around him toward my bedroom. "No. I think that's it."

"IF YOU FIND yourself pinned to the floor, there are a few things you can do."

I hurried in, five minutes late for my self-defense class. The mats squelched underfoot as I made my way to the semi-circle watching Quinn's instruction, detouring briefly to dump my bag and jacket on the bench.

A quick glance at today's participants told me Shannon wasn't teaching today.

"First throw him off balance," Quinn said. My gaze was drawn to him as he beckoned to Cheddar to come forward and straddle him. "Hold my wrists to the floor." Cheddar pressed down, locking him tightly. I shuffled around the others until I could see Quinn better. His serious gaze was focused intently on Cheddar.

"Draw your attacker in," he continued. "Likely any attackers are expecting you to shove them back, push them away, struggle. They'll be off guard if you do the opposite. Instead"—he slid his arms over his head, effectively closing the gap between him and Cheddar—"bring them closer. As soon as they've lost their center of balance, thrust your hips up, like this, at the same time as you sweep your hands in an arc to your legs, and shove your attacker to the side."

Quinn sprung to his feet and offered a hand to pull Cheddar up, who grinned like a kid. With a cursory glance around the semi-circle, Quinn stopped on me a long moment. "Partner up, and practice."

A quick calculation told me there were an odd number of students. I had an easy solution for that and, after removing my glasses and setting them next to my bag, I headed for Quinn.

"Let's do this," I said to a bland stare.

His jaw clenched, muscles rippling. "I have to annotate the others."

"Annotate them after you're done with me, then," I said, lowering myself to the mat.

Quinn stared down at me and swallowed. With a mutter and a grumpy expression, he straddled me, thighs gripping my sides tightly and hands firmly pressing my wrists to the mat.

"What's up?" I asked.

"What's up?" He shook his head and the blond tips of his hair glittered from the light above like a halo. His voice dropped to a whisper. "I'm frustrated."

"Why?"

"You're acting like nothing's happened between us!"

"We jerked each other off. I liked it." I shoved my hands up like he showed us; he collapsed with a warm, solid weight against me and our noses bumped. "I didn't realize it was mandatory to broadcast it the entire week."

His gaze dipped to my lips. He looked poised to say something about that, and then shook his head. Instead he said, "This is the part where you're meant to buck me off."

"Yes. I just don't want to."

"God, Liam. What are you doing to me?" His lips tilted toward mine and then he huffed out a groan and rolled himself off.

He lay on his back a while, rubbing the heel of his palm on his forehead. "I always fall for the wrong damn guy."

I frowned at that, and sat with my arms around my knees as he picked himself up off the floor and moved around the room, commenting on other partners. I tried to fish for his attention with long looks his way, but he wasn't biting. He didn't for the rest of the lesson.

Did it mean he needed more space? That I should find my own way home today?

After we finished, I grabbed my stuff, tucking my jacket tight to my neck and my hands deep into the relative warmth of my pockets. The streets were already dark outside, but at least there was a bright moon tonight.

Shadows from the trees made me jumpy, and I recalled our first self-defense lesson. I pulled my hands out of my pockets, straightened my shoulders and walked with purpose. Assertiveness.

It actually helped, even if it didn't expel the visions of Freddy looming in the shadows.

A horn beeped, and I jumped, spinning toward it—

Quinn, driving his beat-up Toyota. The car crawled along next to me as he beckoned me in.

Though relatively confident I could make it home safely, it *was* cold, and a quick drive was by far more preferable.

I slipped inside and buckled in. Despite offering me the ride home, Quinn didn't seem to be in the mood for talking. Broody and silent the entire way, Quinn maintained his bad mood even once we'd made it inside and peeled off our outer layers.

I watched him mope into the kitchen and pour himself a drink. Deciding to leave him some alone time, I snuck silently down the hall, grabbed a towel from the linen cupboard, and jumped into the shower.

Water hit my back, warm and firm, like a much-needed massage. I picked up the soap and scrubbed myself clean. A knock at the bathroom door had me rubbing a clear circle on the fogged plastic door. Was Quinn bursting so hard he couldn't wait? "Come in."

He did. Through the plastic, Quinn was mostly an outline, blurred with color. But he didn't stop at the toilet; he came right up to the door until I could see his features more than clearly.

Again, I wiped through the steam. "What do you want?"

"I want to be a bit more like you. Blunt and to the point." The shower door opened, and Quinn, in his boxers and tank-top, stepped inside. "I liked what we did together last week."

I moved back, offering him a shared part of the hot water. "I did too."

Water sprayed over his chin and shoulders, clinging his tank-top to his chest and matting a few of the hairs that peeked over the top.

The lust of his gaze running slowly down the length of my body heated me up more than the hot water, and on instinct, I touched myself, blood rushing to my groin.

Water soaked Quinn's sky-blue boxer-briefs, outlining his hardening length.

"Your point is certainly clear," I said through a tight throat, watching rivulets of water drip from my arm and onto Quinn's inner thigh.

He angled the showerhead so it hit the back wall, creating a makeshift waterfall. Carefully, he stepped in and pushed me toward it. It was like warm silk flowing down my back, while the rest of me was exposed to air that should have been cooler, but instead was heated by animalistic lust.

Quinn's fingers lifted my chin until we were focused on each other. "I'm not sure my point is clear yet," he said, angling his head. The tips of his wet hair tickled against my forehead as his hungry lips sucked on mine.

I slipped my arms around his shoulders, dipping under his tank-top then running a hand through the back of his hair, holding him there, forcing him to deepen the kiss.

His lips pulled back an inch but his forehead came to rest against mine. "I want to take you in my mouth."

My cock twitched at that, the head lightly tapping Quinn's hip at the edge of his wet cotton briefs and smooth skin. "Please," I said.

His breath whistled over my cheek and he kissed me again, lips moving softer this time, taking his time, *teasing*. Sensual.

My skin prickled as his lips drew crooked, explorative lines over my chest, pinching at my nipples and pulling them into his mouth. He lapped at my right nipple, the one surrounded by a smattering of dark freckles. His fingertips danced over them as he lightly bit, sending a shock of current to my already hard cock, making it leak and bob against Quinn again.

I gasped as his hands traveled down my sides and rounded my backside, one finger stroking my entrance. "Take me into your mouth!"

He murmured a laugh as he bent to his knees, his mouth sustaining its contact with my skin. "I want to hear you cry my name when you come."

His tented briefs brushed over my leg and the moan he let out skated over the tip of my cock. I tilted my hips toward him, nudging my head at his parted lips. His gaze flew up to mine as his wet, warm mouth enveloped me. I moaned, my head falling to my chest as my eyes shut with the intense pleasure of being firmly sucked deep into Quinn. I thrust lightly, the head of my cock squeezing down his throat and twisting gloriously.

I slammed my arms on either side of the wall as Quinn moved in time with my thrusts, as if he knew my song and could sing it to perfection. I wanted him to never stop.

Quinn's finger harmonized with my song of pleasure, nudging at my entrance with every outstroke. Water trickled down my ass and thigh and over Quinn's shoulder. My tempo increased. I wasn't sure which one I wanted more, to plunge down that deep, tight throat or to impale myself on his finger.

My orgasm built quickly, and I was panting harder and harder and—

"*Quinn!*" It burst out of me, and my pleasure swelled with each of his swallows. I sagged against the wall, a spray of water hitting my shoulder and fanning outward, lightly misting Quinn.

He carefully drew off me, palms running down the backs of my thighs. He held my gaze as he slipped his hand down his boxer-briefs and drew out his hard length. "Stay like that. Keep looking at me."

Sitting back on his haunches, he pumped himself hard and fast, as if already close to the end. His eyes shut briefly, but when he reopened them, they were locked on mine again. His body stiffened and he shot over my knee, my ankle, the floor.

He was suddenly trembling, so I moved to the side, re-angling the showerhead so he could get some warmth. "No, that wasn't what I—thank you," he said.

He peeled out of his clothes and for the next few minutes we focused on cleaning, taking turns to rinse off under the water.

Once we were out, towels tightly wrapped around our hips, I headed for the door only to have my wrist snagged. I turned back toward Quinn, who was staring intently.

He softened his grip but didn't let go. "I don't want you racing off to your bedroom, and I don't want to wait another week without mentioning this."

My gaze dropped to my wrist and back to him. "Are you saying you want a relationship, Quinn?"

He drew himself and that tingle-inducing shell he always seemed to wear right up close. He nipped my ear. "You bet your ass I am."

I MOVED TO HIS ROOM, snatching up my laptop on the way. His bed hadn't been made and, climbing into it, I kept an eye out for the likelihood I'd be exfoliated by Pringle shards. Seemed a low possibility. The bedding might have been tangled, but it also smelled faintly of washing powder.

Sitting back against the headboard with the pillow jammed behind me and my naked legs stretched out, I burrowed the right leg against Quinn's body and opened up my laptop.

Quinn pecked my elbow, rasping the edges of his teeth lightly over my skin. "Of course you'd bring your work in here."

He delicately nipped my elbow again, and then watched as I checked my mails. My mom had written promising next year she'd make up for having to work.

I hit *reply* and typed back that it wasn't a problem, and then I described in detail my ideas for "the article" that had to "wow" the chief. Mostly it was to cement the ideas for myself, but I knew my mother liked it when I went off on detailed tangents. She said it was always a privilege when she was allowed inside my head.

I wrapped up twenty minutes later, asking her a question at the end about how her new job was going. Quinn watched, his breath funneling under the sheets and over my hip.

I dragged the mouse symbol to the "send" button, and hesitated. A quick glance at Quinn's blond tufts and clubbed ear nuzzled close to my side, and I added a P.S.

A soft chuckle came from Quinn, and the mattress bowed as

he shifted himself into a sitting position. "'P.S. I'm gay?'" he read aloud.

I pressed send as I nodded, and then opened a fresh document for brainstorming. "Thought telling her might be appreciated."

Quinn nudged my leg and I glanced at him as he picked at the seams of his bedcover. Slowly, he raised his head. "So, was I clear enough back there in the bathroom?"

My fingers stilled over the keyboard. "Yes, you want a relationship."

"And?"

I clicked opened my calendar, and looked over the dates and appointments and deadlines. "Can I give you my thoughts after I've submitted my features article?"

"You don't have thoughts right now?"

"Of course," I said, resting my head back against the wood, "but they are . . . overwhelmed. I'd like to sort them first and find the right answer, and at the moment, I'm too distracted with this article I have to wow the chief with."

Quinn twisted onto his knees, sheets falling to reveal his stunning nakedness. "Sometimes there is no logical answer. Sometimes it's just a feeling. Stop thinking up here—and start thinking *here*."

He touched my chest, and I frowned at his fingers, staring at the bitten-off nails a long moment before I spoke. "What if I will never be like you, Quinn? What if I don't always yell and laugh and cry and cheer at things you or others might?"

He dropped his fingers to the edge of the pillow under me.

"Maybe," I said, drawing the laptop closer and jotting in the date, "we should *both* think about things."

His nod was slow and measured.

"Do you want me to leave?" I asked, gesturing toward the bed and the door.

"No." He planted a kiss on the side of my lips. "I still want you to sleep next to me. And would you think about something else if I asked?"

"Of course."

"Would you come home with me, Shannon, and Hunter for Thanksgiving?"

CHAPTER SIXTEEN

Heavy. My limbs felt heavy as I made my way into *Scribe* that Friday. Each step toward the office felt like I had weights around my ankles. I chalked it up to a case of extreme nervousness, but that didn't help the matter. Logically, I knew my articles were of the utmost quality and that I had to place in the top twenty-five of the BCA competition, but . . . but—

What?

There was no reason to allow this heavy feeling to consume me. I shook my head as if it would help lighten me, but it only sent a wriggly, tickly feeling to my stomach.

My pocket buzzed. A text from Hunter. He wanted to meet for coffee at Crazy Mocha Coffee that afternoon.

Okay, I wrote back. By then I might be able to eat something. I couldn't eat this morning—Quinn had pressed a spoon of oatmeal to my lips but they wouldn't budge. Even the kiss he gave me afterward, licking away the smudge of mushed oats, left me empty of our usual thrills. All I'd wanted was to lean my head on his shoulder, for him to take the heavy feeling away.

I stepped out of the stairwell. In front of me were the frosted glass doors separating me from the buzzing, literary-charged atmosphere that encompassed most of my life—and the BCA results.

If I placed in the top ten, along with winning a feature article, surely the chief would be hard-pressed not to promote me to features editor? As soon as I had his word, I'd have a reason to mail my father again. He'd sit up and pay attention then—or at least keep me on his radar over the next couple years.

I pressed my clammy hand to the textured glass, rolled my shoulders back, and opened the door to the next stage in my life.

The board loomed at the back of the room, a halo of white notices around the navy-framed results.

One step in. To my right, in the corner of the room, Jack leaned back in his chair, swiveling as he chatted to a copper-haired girl I'd never seen before.

"So," she said in a playful voice, "are you going to invite me to the cathedral party or not? It's supposed to be the party of the year, and I could *really* make it the party of your year."

"Sorry, babe, not this time. I'm only there to work. But maybe next time."

Five steps in. To my left, photocopiers murmured and beeped, and ahead the chief was bent over the sports reporter's desk, tapping Nick's fingers away to type into the laptop.

"An intro something like this . . ."

Ten steps in. Hannah was frowning as she grumbled into the telephone, doodling on a loose piece of notepad.

Twelve steps in. Someone cut in front of me. His Mohawk

casually lifted before he returned to studying the stack of old *Scribe* magazines he carried.

Fourteen steps in. I was one step away from the board. A few people stood checking it in front of me, and I tapped my foot, unable to hold back the impatience. I glanced back to Hannah and raised a hand. She nodded and then turned into the phone once more. The doors at the back opened. I pivoted. Jill was coming in, fumbling with the flap on his satchel. He let it go with a frustrated slap and stepped toward his corner desk—

And froze. His body seemed to tighten as if he'd been magically turned into a statue. I followed his gaze to Jack's hand climbing up Copper Girl's arm to her cheek.

Jill snapped into action, twisting away from the sight, and left the office.

Jack scowled as he stared over Copper Girl's shoulder at the fogged doors. There was definitely something going on between the two of them, and my initial thoughts were: lover's quarrel. Then I adjusted them to: unrequited love.

Maybe that was the reason Jill didn't want to speak up about that night. Maybe he didn't want it known that he was interested in his best friend. Perhaps The Night Warrior had seen him try something on Jack and when Jack retreated, leaving Jill humiliated, The Night Warrior had his victim just the way he wanted him. Vulnerable. Easy lunch.

Jill would hate anything that made him appear weak or outcast to his peers. It would affect his having a "life."

Finally the board was free. I nudged my glasses upward and read the list from the bottom up. The heaviness affected my finger too, increasing with every inch I had to lift.

I stole higher and higher, my stomach twisting again, a panicked flare gurgling out of me when I reached the last few places.

My name. It wasn't there. It wasn't . . .

"That can't be right," I said, scanning through the list again. I must have overlooked it—

Nothing?

I blinked at the paper over and over as if somehow my name would suddenly appear. I scratched the back of my neck, my glasses popping forward with my frown. I rubbed a knuckle against my brow, and slowly picked my way to the chief. Hannah sent me a sympathetic smile as I passed. How long had she already known?

The tight lump in my throat hurt to swallow, but I swallowed nevertheless before moving into the chief's office.

He wasn't in there, but I'd seen him talking to the sports reporter. He'd be here soon. The chair dug into me and the seat was still cool after ten minutes of sitting on it. I fumbled with the pen in my pocket, but it was a lazy, irresolute touching. I couldn't even summon the energy to click.

The air stirred as I waited for the chief to round the desk.

He did, slowly. "Liam," he said as if he'd been expecting me to pop in. "How are you doing?"

He sank into his chair and stroked his beard, gaze leveled to mine.

"There must have been some mistake," I heard myself saying. "My articles should have placed."

"It's a blow, I understand. But you did well with one of your three submissions."

"Twenty-eighth? It's a good ranking for *that* piece, but—"

"*That* piece, Liam, is good, and it is what your peers want to read. I'm sorry you didn't do as well as you wanted to, but that is the nature of competition. From what I've seen developing in your party page columns, I'm very sure you'll do even better next year. Look at this as a learning curve, not a curve ball."

I let go of my pen, withdrawing my hand from my pocket, and stood. The chief had certainly made his point. Perhaps I should be thanking him for submitting the story that placed at all, but I couldn't. Every swallow was bitter and painful.

Chief Benedict sighed and smiled, soft and empathizing. "Look, Liam, It might not seem like it now, I'm just trying to help nurture your potential."

My glasses kept sliding down my nose, and I pushed them up again as I stood. "I'll still wow you with my feature article, chief."

CRAZY MOCHA COFFEE. Two o'clock, and half full. I sat at our usual table and lethargically leafed through a Booster Gold I'd had carefully tucked in the back pocket of my bag.

Hunter rolled in at quarter past, a smug smile on his face. "Get me a latte. I think it's your turn to shout."

When I came back, two coffees in tow, he slapped the comic shut. "That's a good one," he said with a wink.

I nodded and slumped onto the chair.

He took a sip, placed his cup on the table, and reached for his camera. "What party is up for tonight? I was thinking, maybe you want me to take some pictures that you could add to your column? If you want."

My column. Oh, the party page. I couldn't remember what party I was supposed to go to tonight. It was on my calendar. I'd check it later. I gave Hunter a short nod and dipped my finger into the foam of my coffee, swirling it around.

"That's it?" Hunter asked, cocking his head at me. "I thought I'd get more than a nod." He flipped off the lens cap. "Say cheesy balls. . . . Still a no? Okay, then cheesecake."

Snap! Snap!

"I'm good, you know," he said from behind his camera. "This could add some cutting edge to the whole overall impact of your column."

That sore lump rose in my throat again.

"And that's exactly what my work needs to be enjoyable, isn't it?"

Hunter drew back, lowering his camera. "Whoa, man. It's just an idea. I've been searching for something to do besides economics and thought maybe you'd put in a good word at *Scribe*."

I played with the froth on my coffee some more. "Sure, I'll put in a word." I glanced up at him. The last time we met had been the night we discovered the true identity of The Raven. "Have you had a chance to talk—?"

His jaw flexed and he rested his camera on the table with a light *thunk*. "I tried."

"And?"

"I didn't know what to say, so I rambled on about basketball for longer than anyone wants to hear."

Had he also been heavy with nervousness? Had his limbs felt as if they'd never feel normal again? "Were you nervous?"

He chuckled and veered his gaze away from mine. "Ah, fuck it," he said picking up his drink. "I was shit scared. All I could think was, dude, I've known you my whole life, how could you not tell me about this? And suddenly, I didn't want to hear the answer." He shrugged, and gave a cursory glance toward his legs.

"Maybe it will go better next time."

"Maybe." He took up his camera again and stared at the screen. "You want to tell me what's wrong?"

"Nothing's wrong." I brought my foam-covered finger to my lips, but it seemed too much of an effort to lick it. I used a napkin instead.

"Come on. Spit it out."

I shook my head even as I began spilling every detail about the BCA competition. "I just—I thought for sure . . . What's wrong with them?"

"Them the judges? Because it's obvious, a lot."

"Them, my articles."

Heat sprang at the backs of my eyes, an unfamiliar feeling. I closed them and kept swallowing until it was under control. When I opened them, Hunter was pushing his way around the table. He used his buff arms to yank me toward him and held the back of my head firmly as he pressed his forehead to mine. "You're fucking beautiful, you know that? Right now you make me wanna cry. I'm sorry the BCA thingy turned out to be a dud, but you're gonna be awesome, Liam, and I'm stoked I'll be around to see it."

"Thanks," I murmured as he slowly pulled away. "It's . . . I mean . . . when I get your texts . . . I look forward to seeing you."

He waggled his brows. "I tend to have that effect on people."

THE BUCK BOOZER was exactly what it sounded like: a party selling beer for one dollar per polystyrene cup. Quinn, who rarely drank at parties, gave me a funny frown as he shared the back-door step with me. "Drinking beer now?"

"It tastes horrible," I said and took another bitter sip. "I thought you were hanging with Shannon."

"Yes, well . . ."

We stared into the dark yard, toward a large maple with a couple draped over a tire swing.

"She's that upset with you?"

"Yeah," he said, pulling on his ear. "I wish she'd let me talk. I'm afraid I've really disappointed her."

"Sorry. I'm sure she'll come around." I twisted the beer cup in my hand, and drained the last drip of beer.

"Have any cash I could borrow?"

I felt for my wallet in my jacket pocket and handed it to him. "Take as much as you need."

He opened to the flap where I kept my bills, slipped all twenty-five dollars out, and crammed them into his pocket.

"Great," he said. He handed me back my wallet, as empty now as I was feeling.

Huh. "What do you need it for?"

"Insurance."

"I'm sorry?"

Quinn steered his gaze toward me, half his face shadowed by the night, the other side glowing dimly in the light that seeped through the fogged window of the back door. "Insurance against you getting drunk because you're upset at something."

Oh. Well, in that case, perhaps he had good foresight. Not that I planned to get intoxicated, but I didn't care about how the night turned out. I hadn't even written any notes for my column.

"So, what's going on, Liam?"

"Just a bit off today." I counted the swings of the tire as it swung in our direction, and when it stopped swinging, I tried to map out the branches of the maple—darker blotches against an inky sky.

Quinn inched nearer. Axe and toffee wafted over me. "Blue days suck," he said.

I stopped counting branches and started counting how many times Quinn blinked. His eyelashes lowered as he dropped his gaze to my mouth, as if wanting to kiss me. Or perhaps waiting for me to respond. Maybe both.

My lips parted and my heavy breath slipped out, making a sigh. I followed it up with a shrug, and pulled out my notebook. "They are not fun, no."

Quinn pinched the end of my notebook. "Can I help you come up with an angle?"

I handed him the pen. Tonight, it was just too much effort. "Go for it."

He took my pen and scribbled a quick note in the margin, which I read over his shoulder. *Sorry about the BCA results*, it read.

"Hunter's a bigger mouth than I thought." But I was glad he talked to Quinn. Maybe it meant they'd be fine.

Quinn bumped his shoulder against mine and stared out into the night again, tapping my pen to the notebook. "That's Hunter, he's the epitome of selflessness, even at the cost of being a big mouth."

"I like it."

"Me too." He pushed to his feet, and cocked his head toward the back door vibrating with music. "Now let's get your angle."

CHAPTER SEVENTEEN

Quinn and I sat at opposite ends of the dinner table, both plugged in to our laptops. It was Monday evening, and I was wrapping up my party page column, ready to draft up my feature article. I curled my bare feet around the chair's legs.

"Yes!" Quinn pumped a hand in the air, looking over at me with a wide grin as he sank triumphantly against his chair. "Done."

I fished around for specifics. "Your essay? Or is this a *Dungeons and Dragons* thing?"

He cut a glare. "My essay."

In that case, maybe he shouldn't be cheering quite yet. I saw his last essay. All of those stray and completely absent commas tampered my nod of approval. "Send it my way," I said, closing my document. "I'll proofread."

Quinn shifted, lips poised to comment, and then he shook his head and rapidly started pounding at his keyboard.

A few minutes later, his email and attached essay popped into my inbox.

You're fucking gorgeous sitting there, grinning away as you work. Makes me want to sweep our laptops off the table and have you on it.
Q.
P.S. What about Thanksgiving? Going to come with me?
P.P.S. I damn well know I have a problem with commas. Your constant choice in grammar-oriented T-shirts has not been subtle.

I replied:

Give me an hour on your essay, and then I will carefully remove my laptop from the table. After which, you can ravage me as you please. But don't mistake it for anything more than sex.
Liam
P.S. Too much to do this weekend, I'm going to pass.
P.P.S. It must be working. The grammar in your mail was spot-on.

Quinn bit his lip, which didn't hide his flushed cheeks. He typed something, then lurched up and disappeared to the bathroom.

I refocused my attention on his essay. Certainly the grammar had improved since the last one. But improved didn't mean great.

A few minutes later another mail came into my inbox, and Quinn was back, squirming in his chair.

Re. Ravaging. Only sex. Got it. (For now.)
Then this is how it's going to go and not to worry: it'll be a laptop-friendly

pillaging:
I'm going to start by stealing under the table and taking your big toe into my mouth. I'll suck it hard and good as I slide my hand to your crotch and rub through the taut material of those slacks you're wearing. You'll sag at the sensation, and I'll take my opportunity, sliding you under the table with me, where you will beg me to get you off. A warning, I'm going to make it slow. I'm going to make sure every scrap of clothing is off both of us, and then I'm going to lather our dicks in lube, then lie on top of you, hard and solid. I want to feel you arch and rut against me. I want to hear you pant. I want to watch you come. Afterward, I'm going to kiss you until we're stuck together, right? And then I'm going to ask again if you'll come for Thanksgiving.

"Quinn, I really do have too much to do—" I looked up, and Quinn was gone.

A shuffle came from under the table.

A hand latched around my foot, and a hot wet mouth engulfed my toe . . .

WEDNESDAY MORNING, before Quinn, Hunter, and Shannon left for their Thanksgiving weekend, I stole Hunter away for a quick coffee. We met at our usual spot, Crazy Mocha Coffee.

"You sure you're not coming back with us?" Hunter asked, arms folded, the hummingbirds at his wrists peeking out from under his cuffs.

"Not this time," I said, picking up my bag and searching for my first draft on how the internet and mass media support student involvement in environmental protection. The printed pages were a smooth weight in my hands, and I slid them over to Hunter.

"Would you do something for me?"

"Why not this time?"

I gestured to the pages. "This needs rewriting in parts. After you've read it, give me your honest thoughts."

Hunter raised a brow. I added, "Would you mind?"

Hunter glanced at the title and scanned the first page, and then he rested it on the table again. "I can tell you my honest thoughts on this already."

He'd barely read a quarter of it. I sank lower into my chair. I'd listen to the criticism, let it soak in, and then do whatever was necessary to strengthen it over the long weekend. "Go ahead."

His index finger played at the top corner of the pages, bowing the paper. "It's smart as hell, but I think you should write about something else."

A dry laugh left me hollow. He was kidding. Had to be. This was a feature article—correction, *the* feature article. I couldn't whip up anything with the quality I needed in only a week. Not if I wanted to do the proper research and interviews—no one was around this weekend. It'd leave me only Monday to Thursday, with Friday to write it.

Then again, that was the world of journalism. Tight deadlines and the pressure to make every report perfect. I could do it. Of course I could.

So long as I had an angle worth exploring.

Tentatively, shifting in my seat, I asked, "What, exactly?"

He scratched his upper arm, sleeve shifting to show the wings of the turquoise hummingbird at his wrist. With a tap of his fingers on the arm of his chair, he said, "Write about me."

I leaned in to comment, and he held up his hand.

"Let me finish. Not about me, per se, but about my experience. Experiences in general in the dating world as a differently-abled guy. Loads of guys on my basketball team would be open to talking to you about their relationships, successes and failures. Most are gonna be level with you. They'll tell you all of it. The obvious. The downright scandalous."

I slid my hand into my pocket, gripping the shaft of my pen, my finger touching the top. *Click. Click.*

He continued, "You could make us more approachable, Liam. So many people are afraid of dating us, afraid of saying the wrong thing—afraid of even telling us if they like us because they just don't know enough. Your readership is wide, man, and I think your writing will have just the right amount of punch to make an impact."

Hunter held my attention with his level stare and a shrug. *Click-click-click.*

The paper was stained and dented, scrunched at one side. It looked as old and tired as the idea I was forcing onto it.

He was right. The truth didn't taste pleasant on my tongue, but it was there nevertheless. And hadn't I in some way wondered the same myself? Why else had I such an urge to show this to Hunter?

I'd wanted his no-bullshit analysis.

And I got it. More than that, I got a new idea. A *brilliant* idea, wonderful, and I really wanted to do it. But Quinn intensely disliked it and gave me the cold shoulder when I had tried to use him as an angle before. "I want to do it," I said to Hunter. "But Quinn wouldn't want me using you as a means."

Hunter smiled and shrugged. "You're not using me. And even if you were, I know what this features position means to you. I would look the other way. Quinn would too. The question is, does Quinn know why you *really* need this?"

The café door opened and Quinn entered, Shannon at his heels. Shannon moved stiffly to the counter, and Quinn flipped his keys over his finger as he threaded his way to our table, a dimpled grin lighting his face. "Thought I might find you two in here."

Quinn, between Hunter and I, braced a hand on the back of my chair. His thumb casually stroked my back as he told Hunter he should drive his van around to the apartment so they could follow each other.

"Louisville, Kentucky, here we come," Hunter murmured, glancing toward Shannon balancing two drinks. "So," he said, "maybe we could change things up? When Shannon or you are driving, one of you could sit with me in the van, right?"

"Miss us already, do you? Or did you want to pry for information about the guy who asked her out on a date?"

"The latter for sure."

Quinn let go of my chair and dragged another chair over from the neighboring table. He settled himself on it and leaned conspiratorially toward Hunter. A thumb jerked in my direction. "Did you manage to change his mind?"

Hunter laughed. "Better luck next time, Sullivan."

I picked up the pages from the table and slipped them into my bag, offering my chair to Shannon. She barely looked at me as she nodded and took my place.

I settled my bag strap over my shoulder and said to Hunter, "Well, I'm not sure if I will take that angle, but it wouldn't hurt to do some preliminary research."

Hunter smirked. "Just do it. Quinn will get over it."

"Get over what?" Quinn asked, looking between us.

"I've told him to use me as an angle," Hunter said, puffing out his chest with a large breath.

Shannon hummed, sitting tense in the chair. Hunter glanced at her, as if expecting her to get defensive, but she said nothing.

"Angle?" Quinn's brow furrowed.

"Yes," I said as I squeezed out from between Quinn and Shannon. "It bothers me you're not okay with it, but it really is a good idea, and I am going to do it."

I clasped Quinn's other shoulder and bent down, kissing him quickly on the lips. "I have to get everything I need for the weekend from the office. Drive safely. I'll see you on Sunday."

Quinn, Hunter, and Shannon blinked at me.

"Oh, and happy Thanksgiving." I gave them a wave and left, resettling the bag strap on my shoulder.

CHAPTER EIGHTEEN

Drenched from rain, I let myself into apartment twenty-three, flicked on the light, and shucked off my jacket and shoes. With cold, stiff limbs, I dropped onto the couch, my bag wedged uncomfortably behind my back.

With a groan, I stripped out of my wet clothes and padded to the bathroom to dry my hair. The warm air didn't help me forget the email I'd sent my father.

My *Happy Thanksgiving* message had come back with an auto-reply.

Thank you for your message. I am currently out of the office over the

Thanksgiving weekend. I will be returning on Monday, the first of December. If you need urgent assistance, contact me at . . .

I switched off the blow dryer. Maybe I could try contacting him, though the matter could hardly be qualified as "urgent."

Back in my living room, I pulled out my notebook and moved back to the couch. *Dating the Differently-Abled.* I jotted down some of the observations I made about Hunter and Mitch, and I expanded on the questions and answers I already had.

"Definitely need more interviews," I said, and my voice bounced off the arched windows and back to me.

I stopped note-taking to draw the curtains. Leaning against the window frame, I stared out into the night. Lamplight peppered the length of the street, and car tires *chuuurred* over the wet road. Quinn should have arrived in Louisville by now.

A step back, and the reflection of me alone in the room winked back at me. The apartment seemed bigger, colder without him. My stomach rumbled, empty—*hungry*.

I popped a slice of bread into the new toaster Quinn bought. *I ought to write a report on the blessings of an attentive roommate . . . friend.* Boyfriend?

A small shock shot up my middle, and I prepared the toast with shaky hands.

Sitting at the end of the table, I ate slowly while reading the current *Scribe*. I scanned the opinions page and Jack's report on the reopening of the 32nd floor of the Cathedral of Learning, which ended with a mention of the black-tie event that Mitch had invited Hunter to. Sounded like my type of party. But that Friday wasn't going to work for me, unless I got my feature article to the chief before that. Considering all the interviews I would have to schedule this week, I didn't think the black-tie event would be a possibility.

I shut the magazine and pushed it to the middle of the table. Its *churr* echoed loudly. Staring at the other end of the table at what had become Quinn's chair, I revisited my reasons for staying home.

I came to the painful conclusion that I'd made the wrong choice.

I WOKE up to the smell of the neighbors making *pancakes*, of all things. On Thanksgiving Day, I thought most families would skimp on a large breakfast in favor of the turkey extravaganza later.

I rolled out of bed and took a quick shower. I slipped into a maroon robe, and when I stepped out of the bathroom, the thick scent of pancake goodness tickled my nose.

And then came the distinct sound of shuffling.

I froze for a second before striding to the kitchen—

"Gah!" It wasn't my imagination. He was here, making pancakes. Quinn.

He twisted from the pan, wielding a spatula in his right hand, a sheepish grin twitching his lips. "Morning."

The window was hitched open a crack, and I drew my robe tighter at the draught of winter-spiced air. "What are you doing here?"

He focused on the pancake, taking a moment to flip it. Then he pointed the spatula at me as if it explained everything. He added, "You kissed me in the café. In front of everyone."

I followed the rise and fall of the spatula. "I did."

Quinn fished the pancake out of the pan and set it atop the others. "I liked it."

He looked sincerely at me, like he could see through me, somewhere deep that I only occasionally visited. I hooked my thumbs around the robe belt to tighten it.

He poured the last of the batter into the pan and set his

spatula on the bench. He lessened the distance between us. Closer. Closer. Closer.

"A *lot*, Liam."

He took my hand and drew me into the kitchen until he was pressed against the bench and I stood between his opened legs. His jeans were coarse against my skin, prickling against my hairs.

"I couldn't stop thinking about it the entire drive home."

He brushed a kiss over my bottom lip and pulled back to stare, mesmerized, as if my lip could sparkle. I curled my lip in, tasting the warm spot.

"You crossed my mind a fair bit too," I said. "The place feels so much more comfortable with you in it."

The next kiss came to the top of my head, matting short hairs to my forehead. "It's so hard for me not to ask you again."

I stilled a moment. He meant *us*, our relationship—being more than friends. More than just having sex. A relationship meant the development of an emotional connection. I teetered on answering him immediately, but reined in the urge. I needed to be one hundred percent sure, and that meant thinking through the repercussions should things turn out horribly in the end.

What would it mean for our friendship? Would this beautiful thing vaporize before my eyes, leaving me alone, grappling at thin wisps in the air?

And then there was Hunter. Quinn and he had been friends forever. Hunter's allegiance would, and rightly so, be with Quinn.

I'd be back to Liam Davis, reporter for *Scribe*, with no friends outside of the magazine.

I remembered going to the Nightmare on Shady Avenue party, wanting to prove there were worse nightmares out there than mine. Instead I'd proven a dream had been missing. Now that I knew it, I didn't want to mess it up. *Friendship* was the relationship most lacking in my life.

"Would you still live with me if I decided that I'd prefer us to stay friends?"

His body tensed, his hands clutching tighter around my upper arms. He took his time, swallowing before he answered softly, "I want to have you around." He rubbed my arms. "Is that your answer?"

"I'm not sure yet. I like having sex with you."

A laugh tumbled out of him and he turned me, pressing me tight against the bench, his arousal nudging at my lower stomach. He reached around my side, took the spatula and flipped the last pancake. It was a good example of multi-tasking, even if the pancake was close to burned.

"So, you came back," I murmured, pressing a hand to his chest and playing with the peak of one nipple bumping his T-shirt.

"I said hello to my family and then found myself saying goodbye, hopping in my car, and driving back here."

"They'll be missing you then."

He turned off the stove, slipped the last pancake onto the plate behind me, and kissed my lips. A soft kiss that felt delightfully unfinished.

He ripped up a pancake and fed me bits, pushing the pad of his syrupy thumb into my mouth and scraping over my teeth.

"I hope this leads to a ravaging of sorts," I said after the next bite, rubbing the heel of my hand against my length.

Quinn's pupils dilated. His arms came quickly and firmly around me, fingers digging into my ass as he urged me to wrap my legs around him. He walked me purposefully toward his bedroom. "Is it okay to break the wall if you're the one helping me do it?"

"Yes."

His laugh tickled at my throat.

"I can't think straight when you do that."

Quinn paused in his doorway, arms flexing with the weight of carrying me. I squirmed to my feet, relieving him of the pressure.

"Was that a joke?" he asked as he brushed a thumb over my nose to the edge of my mouth. "Did Liam Davis just crack a joke? The end of the world must be coming."

My robe had come loose and I shrugged out of it, letting the soft material sink to a puddle at my feet. I stroked myself. "Not the coming I want to concentrate on right now."

His voice tensed, and his lust was undeniable. "Another one. Shoot."

"Really?" I said, linking our hands and pulling him toward the bed. I kissed him quickly and flung myself over his semi-made bed. "Because I could, you know."

He pounced on me, pinning my arms above my head. The bottom edge of his T-shirt fell softly against my shaft as he leaned in and bumped our noses together. "Going to tell me exactly what you want, Liam?"

"You naked for a start."

He scrambled off me, and I hooked my fingers behind my head as he shucked out of his jeans and almost fell, stomping on the ends to free himself of their hungry grip. The T-shirt came off in record time, followed by his socks.

He paused at his boxer-briefs, stretching the waistband with a teasing wink.

"You can keep them on if you want," I said, sitting up and shuffling to the bedside, where I pulled Quinn forward. His legs flexed as I dug my hand in the flap of his boxers, gripped his cock and pulled it out. I leaned forward and tasted him. Salty. His velvety foreskin rubbed against my lips.

His moan came long and surprised. "Liam," he gasped. There was something infinitely motivating about that sound, and I fed more of him into my mouth until the head of his cock was nudging the far roof. The angle was somewhat awkward, so I slid off the bed to the floor.

Quinn curled his toes against the sides of my knees as I stroked and sucked him. He let me lick and explore while he gifted me with little noises of appreciation. He pulled out of my mouth, stripped off his briefs and tugged me up onto the bed.

The bedding cushioned my back as Quinn climbed on top of

me and locked me into a deep kiss. I arched against him as our tongues danced and Quinn's fingers slid between our hips and rolled my balls. My grip, splayed over his shoulder blades, tightened as I eagerly drew him closer. *More. More of that.* I angled my hips and Quinn sought deeper until he was rubbing along my entrance. "Yes, that's it. That's what I want."

Quinn rutted against me as he wriggled the tip of his finger and popped it into my ass.

"More, Quinn. Turn me over and put your cock in there."

Quinn groaned and drew back onto his haunches, reaching to his side drawers and pulling out lube and a condom. "Are you sure, Liam? I mean, I really want to, but I don't have to. There are a thousand other ways we can get off."

I stroked my cock. "I don't say things unless I'm sure about them. And I'm sure I want you behind me. In me."

His cock twitched and his gaze grew hooded. He touched warm fingers to my side and I rolled over onto my stomach, stretching my arms out on either side of me, palms open against the sheets.

"All right," he said, uncapping the lube and dribbling the cold liquid in a line down my ass. "You can change your mind any time, and if you don't like something—"

"I'll tell you."

Quinn chuckled. "Yeah, I know you will."

His hand came down at my shoulder and squeezed, and then he massaged his way over my back to the base. A light kiss hit between my shoulder blades as his finger drew over the lube, running over my entrance to the base of my balls.

I arched my ass up toward him and, on his path back up, Quinn dipped his lubed finger right where I wanted it. He was thorough with preparing me, which I appreciated on a logical level, but which teased me almost to the point of yelling at him to hurry up and slide in already.

Perhaps he guessed my thoughts, because he chuckled lightly

and finally lowered his length over me. He nuzzled my neck as he firmly rolled his fingers down my arms and linked our hands. He squeezed them as he rubbed his cock between my cheeks. The condom was on, but the lube was plentiful and he glided back and forth as he breathed heavily in my ear. "You feel so good."

An electric, beaded shiver had me thrusting harder against the sheets and urging my ass back so he would take me.

"Okay, Liam," he said, and shifted, one hand coming off mine as he gently angled my ass and aligned the tip of his cock at my entrance. He pushed in, his head popping inside, stretching me. I drew in a breath and clenched my fingers tighter around his hand.

"Keep going."

He pushed in carefully, filling me with his thick length as he fed me encouraging little strokes with his thumb.

It stung a bit, but I'd had no illusions it wouldn't. He gave me a moment to adjust to the full feeling and then drew back a short way and thrust slowly, gradually increasing the length and speed of his thrusts.

At first, most of the pleasure came from the thought that Quinn was deeply seated in me, that we were so *close*. I derived pleasure from the trust and from hearing how much it undid Quinn; the way he groaned and panted, the light nips on my ear when he held himself still for a moment, trying not to spill too early.

My body accepted and anticipated the rhythm, trying to arch back and thrust into the sheets at the perfect moment. My cock grew hard again and with even more zeal and impatience than before. Quinn shifted our positions slightly so we lay more on our sides. My feet pressed against his for leverage, and he gripped my cock and stroked it in time to his thrusts.

His mouth opened on my shoulder and bit down gently and suddenly I needed Quinn to move faster, harder—

He moved as if he read my thoughts, and then he rolled his

hips, and a burst of sensation had me whimpering against my arm. "That. Again."

He rocked against the spot again.

"Keep doing that," I panted, pushing a hand against the bed to increase the friction as I pitched faster on him.

"Oh, fuck. Liam!"

His hand jerked me faster, and he nipped again at my shoulder all the way up to my neck, where his body tensed and froze around me. His cock pumped with his orgasm, and the combination of mental and physical pleasure of it sent my climax hurtling out in five powerful ropes, splashing over my chest.

Our rapid breaths slowly calmed, and Quinn drew his arm tight around me for a moment until his cock slipped out and he rolled back to take care of the condom.

A kiss met the back of my head, and air stirred as Quinn got up and left the room. He came back a minute later with a warm washcloth.

"How are you doing?" he asked, and wiped my chest clean.

I flexed my ass. "Tender, but I'm thankful for it."

He laughed, and strategically folded the washcloth and placed it on his bedside table. The bed dipped and bowed as Quinn lay down again and folded the blankets around us from the sides. "I'm thankful for you too."

He kissed my cheek and rearranged himself so he stared up. The sunlight blotting through the tree and into the window made shadows play across the cream ceiling.

He said quietly, "I'm sorry for our beginning, though. I should never have made assumptions about you before I knew you. The strange thing is, even when I was saying them, I still felt this thing."

"Thing?"

"The thing that led to the pathetic crush."

"Attraction, you mean?"

He rubbed his eyes. "Yeah. Since reading your first description of me in that damn notebook."

"If I had it here right now, I'd jot down a few other adjectives. You're really quite the sight."

Quinn rolled over suddenly, fanning cool air between us. He turned back with a pen. "Go ahead."

I shifted onto my side and took the pen, pressing the tip on his arm. In cursive, I wrote:

Disheveled. Rakish.

And then, thinking of the sex we'd just had:

Strong. Safe. Tender.

The pen slipped when Quinn spoke: "Hunter gave me more details about the idea for your article."

I continued with *Considerate.*

"I think he's right. You should do it."

"I was going to, anyway," I said, and after a moment added, "but it makes things . . . better that you're okay with it."

He stilled his hand over mine on the pen and drew it away, shifting to hold my gaze. "Remember when I came to this apartment the first time and you told me it belongs to your dad?"

"Yes."

"You said there were no hurt feelings hidden anywhere. That it is what it is. But it's not, is it?"

So Hunter had spilled more than details about the article. "No, it's not."

Quinn glanced to the dancing shadows and back. "I'm sorry, Liam."

I rolled over him to the side of the bed and shrugged. Quinn tried to grab me, but I dodged him. It was time I get up and get on with the day, anyway. "He'll get to know me," I said as I slipped my robe over my shoulders. "I'll score that position." And then—more to myself than to Quinn—I said, "I'm not going to fail."

THE FRIDAY FOLLOWING THANKSGIVING WEEKEND, Hunter rang. "Wish me luck on my date."

I held the phone to my shoulder with my ear as I packed my laptop into my bag. "Don't you make your own luck?"

A short silence, and then, "Make a toast with me: to the most unforgettable night."

I scoured around and picked up a glass of tepid water I'd had at my bedside. "To the most unforgettable night."

I swallowed the water, but it left an acrid taste in my mouth. Closing my bag, I asked, "Have you talked to Shannon yet? Quinn said he tried, but things are still awkward."

I trudged into the living room and grabbed my keys from behind the cookbook stand on the bench. Quinn had marked an eggplant lasagna he wanted to try out on an unwilling me.

"I tried a couple of times," Hunter said, his voice thin down the line. "Both major fails. But I'm sure things will pick up between her and Quinn soon."

As if he heard his name, Quinn, lying on the couch talking on his cellphone, looked my way. He covered the receiver and mouthed, "Off to the office?"

"Tonight's the night." After a week of interviews and research, I'd drafted my article. And it was good. In need of fleshing out, and possibly rearranging in some parts, but I liked where it was going. "*Scribe*, here I come."

Hunter was the first to respond, "Fuck, dude. You'll rock this. If what I saw was anything to go by, you have this in the bag."

Quinn hummed something into his cell and hung up. "And the party of the week? If you like, I can go somewhere and write notes for you?"

I checked my pocket for my notebook and pen. There. There. Good. "I'm pushing that to tomorrow, unless I'm feeling particularly sprightly come midnight."

Hunter snorted in my ear. "Sprightly. Love it. Get cracking on that article, and send me and my buddies a copy when you're done, yeah?"

He disengaged, and I slipped the phone into my bag. Quinn was there the moment it slid into the snug pocket. "No matter what happens with your report, whether or not you get features editor and what your dad does or doesn't say, *I* already think you're amazing."

A soft, brief kiss punctuated his words. "But I know how much this means to you, so . . ." A sudden slap sizzled my ass. "Get cracking, Liam."

THE NIGHT WAS thick and chilled, so of course my bus came late and I climbed on with chattering teeth and my jacket done up to my chin. I could have walked to campus faster, and now that I'd had three self-defense lessons, I was confident enough for it too.

By the time I arrived, the church bells in the distance were chiming eight o'clock. Never mind. At least I'd gone through my outline on my way over and knew exactly how I'd tackle it. It shouldn't take me longer than an hour to finish. And at *Scribe*—the reason I'd packed myself up to go there—I worked best. Something in the atmosphere of the place really kick-started my engine. Besides, this moment I wanted to remember for a long time, so along with the email I'd also lay a copy of the article on the chief's desk.

Outside the ugly concrete block that was my destination, my phone trilled, vibrating in my bag.

Quinn.

I answered, "You miss me already." His chuckle was breezy in my ear. Beeping came down the line. "Are you going out for the night?"

"How'd you know?"

"Street noise."

"Right. Well, I'm heading to that cathedral party."

"Not to interfere with Hunter's date, I hope."

"Nah. Shannon called and told me her date was a bust, he never showed up. So I have to get my ass down there. I'm using any opportunity to get us on the right footing again. I bought her blue roses, her favorites. Any other advice?"

I used my key-card to get inside. "If you dance, let her lead."

"Damn, but I really can't figure out how the steps go in reverse."

"Bye, Quinn."

He grumbled and disconnected.

I climbed to the *Scribe* floor, expecting to have the office to myself this late on a Friday evening, but milky light came through *Scribe*'s fogged glass doors. I let myself inside—

A large grunting sob echoed through the room, tensing my limbs. Stiffly, I searched where the sound emanated from. I was never one to deal well with other people's tears, and when my gaze settled on Jill, head tucked into his elbow at his desk, I was even less prepared.

He hadn't heard me. That much was clear. If he had, he'd have shut up quick—I was the last person he'd want to humiliate himself in front of.

I considered sneaking back out of the office and finding a Starbucks where I could finish my article. It wasn't ideal, but neither was listening to Jill sobbing as I worked.

Of course, the other option was to man-up and go over there. I didn't like the fact it was probably the option Hunter and Quinn would have cheered for most.

That thought had me reluctantly picking my way over to Jill and his heaving back. I kept my stance assertive and packed with as much confidence as I could muster.

But just in case Jill wasn't the victim Hunter thought him to be, I fished for my cellphone and readied it.

"Jill?" I had to make a quick decision—go to his side, or sit at Jack's desk opposite him.

I chose Jack's desk. Space was good.

Jill's body went rigid, and he slowly peeled himself from his arm. He twisted his chair toward the wall where I might not see his face, but from this vantage, I already caught his teary-eyed, blotchy profile.

"What do you want, Davis?" he asked, his voice devoid of its usual sharpness. "Or are you here to rub it in?"

I shifted, my chair squeaking as I leaned forward and placed my elbows on the desk. "I'm the last person you want to speak to, I get that. I'm not thrilled about this either. But . . . something is up with you and has been for the past few weeks. And—let's just put it out there—I'm pretty sure it's got something to do with you liking Jack."

Jill spun his chair in my direction, scowling, angry. "You don't know *shit*."

"You're in the closet then."

His face twitched from a blotchy red to something close to the color of my robe . . . or those tights I wore to the Halloween party. He stuttered, and I thought he'd yell at me again, but instead a gurgled sob escaped his throat.

"It's more than just that," he said, knuckles whitening around a phone.

"You told him, and he doesn't feel the same way."

Jill shuddered and he focused on the phone. A tear seeped from his eye. When he didn't say anything, I rested my cellphone on the table and took out my outline. "Tell you what," I said, "You take your time. Talk if you want. I'm just going to sit here and do some work. But if and when you're ready, I'll be listening."

I unzipped my laptop and started it up.

It was beyond awkward, working across from him as his breath shuddered and he constantly murmured "fuck." I sat stiffly and within quick reach of my phone.

I'd done less than ten minutes of work when he said, "You think I'm the guy, don't you?"

I reached for my phone and brought it to my lap. "The one threatening The Raven? I did."

"That's why that wheelchair dude kept harassing me about my arm."

"His name is Hunter, and he's the best dude you'll ever have harassing you. How is your arm?"

"Just a sprain."

I held his tough-guy gaze that no longer looked so tough, but rather uncertain and pained.

He passed the phone to his other hand and tapped the end of it against the edge of his desk.

"Who do you want to call?" I asked, saving my document. "Jack?"

Another sob. "No. The police."

I straightened, grabbed a packet of tissues from my bag and handed one to Jill. "Are you finally going to tell them about The Night Warrior?"

He snatched it and rubbed his nose. Through a billow of tissue paper came, "He hurt me. He's going to hurt again." He glanced at his arm. "But—but I just can't bring myself to give him up, because . . . because . . ."

"You're afraid?" I said.

He shook his head, choking on a sob.

"You think it makes you look weak?"

"Fuck off."

"Because you're in the closet?"

He threw the tissue between us and banged the phone against the desk. "Because it's *Jack*. Because I'm in love with him."

Silence.

And then it all came crashing into place. How The Night Warrior had slipped the threat into Hannah's mail, how I thought

Freddy had known my name, why Jack had been so cold toward Jill . . .

I clutched my phone. "You need to file a report immediately. And if you think he's going to hurt someone, call the police. Immediately."

Jill rubbed the top of the phone against his forehead. "Don't you think I know that? He wants to teach The Raven a lesson."

"The Raven," I repeated. A shiver wormed its way down my spine to the tips of my toes.

"I'm in love with him. He keeps a spare key taped to the back of his desk drawer." Jill rummaged in his pocket and procured a key. He tossed it between us. "I stalked. Snuck into his apartment, and he has all this stuff on The Raven. He's hated him with a passion for years. I always thought it was because he didn't believe in using violence to stop violence." He glanced pointedly at his arm. "I don't think that anymore."

I leaped to my feet. "Do you think he's figured out who—?"

"Yes," Jill said, pressing something on the phone. "From the stuff I read, Jack's been working with someone to gather information on—and lure out—The Raven."

"Why does he care so much?"

Jill rested the phone and swiveled his chair. He fumbled through a bag and brought out a folder-full of newspaper clippings and photos. "The Raven knocked Jack's brother down and held him until the police arrived. He disappeared just as they pulled up."

I took the folder. "Is this what you found at Jack's?"

"Everything. Call me pissed, but I took it all. Among a few other things."

I marched to the shredder and fed every scrap of evidence about The Raven into it. Glancing out the windows, I was met with the view of Cathedral of Learning lit with featured lights.

The Raven's gonna lose his wings

We'll smile while he sings and sings
Then we'd love to watch him fly
Through a deep, dark, angry sky

Acid rose up my throat as I remembered Jack saying he would be at the cathedral party to work. I sucked in a sharp breath. He was going to attack *tonight*.

Fingers trembling on my phone, I rushed out of the office, dialing the police—

"Someone I know is about to commit an assault . . ." Jill spoke firmly into the phone.

"Tell them that it might be happening at the cathedral party," I said. I barreled for the door. The police would take anywhere from seven to ten minutes to get to the cathedral?

My friends were across the street. I had to warn them.

I ran.

CHAPTER NINETEEN

I kept running.

I made it into the neo-gothic building, skidding around the corridor to the elevators, and pounded on the UP button.

My heart punched against my ribs. "Come on!"

The elevator dinged open, and two women spilled out laughing, one tugging the other by the hand. I squeezed past them and pressed for the 32nd floor, once, twice, three times.

The doors grated shut, and each second passing made it feel like the elevator was being manually lifted. I shifted my weight, my hands clamped into balls at my side. *I'm coming, I'm coming, I'm coming.* An age later, the doors squealed open and I skidded into the party.

Tens of students and lecturers chattered over a live Bach pianoforte, popping *hors d'oeuvres* into their mouths. Through the thick pack of champagne-drinking tuxedos and gowns, Quinn and Hunter weren't anywhere to be seen. Darting around a waiter in a golden waistcoat balancing a tray of caviar, I spotted Hannah near a large bookshelf, leaning against Roger, who was playing with the ends of her hair.

I pushed my way to her, stumbling over my shoelace. "Have you seen Quinn and Shannon? Or Hunter and Mitch?"

Hannah tilted her head. "Are you okay, Liam?"

"No," I said, scanning the crowd once more. "Have you seen anyone?"

"Is Hunter the one in the wheelchair?" Hannah asked. "I saw him and another guy head into the bathrooms ten minutes ago—"

I zipped to the bathrooms, banging my shoulder against the door in my hurry. It swung in. Cold air whistled through a partially open window, but otherwise it was unoccupied—

No.

An empty wheelchair sat in an open stall, a camera bag hanging on the back—

My head pounded, palms sweated, stomach crunched at the terror that ripped through me. All I could think about was that threat. I saw The Raven thrown from the top of the Cathedral of Learning, tumbling, head over heels, screams lost to the rushing wind . . .

"Hunter?" I whispered, pivoting to a sharp arc as a breeze whistled again.

A splotch of blue wedged at the corner of the windowsill caught my eye, furthering the trepidation. Blue rose petals.

Quinn.

With trembling fingers, I called the police again and told them there was an assault in progress. "Hurry, 32nd floor of the Cathedral of Learning."

"Police are on their way."

"They're outside the bathrooms."

"Remain where you are . . ."

A grunting cry stung through the window gap. The phone dropped from my grip and clattered against the tile. I pushed on the foiled glass. Meeting resistance, I shoved my shoulder against it, wedging it open. I thought I'd made a fair amount of noise, but the direction of the wind and traffic and beeping horns below worked in my favor.

A dark, stone balcony stared at me, framed by an inky sky and a smattering of city lights.

"What are you going do about it, *Raven*?"

A judgment and a dare all at once.

Thwack!

A gurgled gasp, followed by a cry.

Sneaking out of the window, I tiptoed to the edge of the building. My hands and cheek pressed against cold, pocked concrete, and I peered around the edge of the cornered balcony.

I absorbed the scene like I had Freddy's punch to my gut. It took all my effort not to fold in on myself and sink into a useless puddle.

Jack stood with a gun pointed toward the ground, his body turned away from me toward Hunter, who'd been dragged into the corner of the balcony and slumped there. Mitch crouched at his side, mumbling repeatedly how sorry he was but claiming he didn't have a choice.

Jack's been working with someone to gather information, lure out The Raven.

Everything about Mitch had been a lie? But he seemed genuine. Seemed like he really cared about Hunter—

Wait. He studied improvisational theater. Was he really that good of an actor? Was he gay at all? Had this whole thing been a set up from the moment we met?

Queasiness flared up my throat.

And I set that upon Hunter.

God, had that moment when he banged into me again at the café been part of this plan?

My weight sagged against the building as if I'd been pushed from behind, but it was Mitch's betrayal that weighed me down. It was the blood dripping from the corner of Hunter's mouth.

I thought of the moment in my office when Mitch casually held my stapler. I wanted to slam my fist down on it and puncture him, the same way he was doing to my friend.

Blinking back something hot and wet, I prayed he would be okay. I'd never prayed before, it didn't seem like a practical thing to do, but right now . . . now I was beyond practical. It was as if I were a puppet and my master was tugging invisible strings—strings that made me want to throw up and cry and punch something.

At least Hunter seemed to be taking this calmly. His blue eyes clasped onto me for a second before he darted his gaze to the side.

I followed it to The Raven, standing in those tightly-fitting boots Garret had mentioned, cargo pants, leather gloves, and a navy jacket with a large peaked hood, angled toward the ground.

From here it was easy to see how she could have been mistaken for a guy.

As she lifted her head, I caught a glimpse of her shadowed face. Now I knew who it was, I could see it. Her. *Shannon.*

Quinn stood to the left, rubbing the back of his head like he'd been shoved hard against the side of the building and had knocked it badly. He braced an arm around Shannon, stepping on the blue rose bouquet choked of life at his feet.

Shannon urged forward, but Quinn wrapped his arms around her waist and held her back. He too was calm, but there was the undeniable glow of fear lighting his face a pale green.

"Don't, Shan," Quinn said softly. "It's too dangerous."

"Is this why you kept trying to prevent me from doing this?" The hood shifted, revealing Shannon's cold blue eyes trained intently on Mitch. She shuddered, and her voice came out strained. "People like them and victims like Travis are the reason I wanted to be out there."

"I'm sorry, but—" She stomped on Quinn's foot and pulled at his thumbs, freeing herself, and lunged toward Jack.

He lifted his gun and pointed at the bird tattoo peeking through Hunter's ripped shirt. "Stay back."

"Let my brother go."

"I'll let him go," Jack said. I glanced toward the window praying for the police to hurry up. "After I've ruined your life the way you ruined my brother's."

My breath shook. What could I do to help the situation? With only a pen, a notebook, and a cellphone, the answer was painful. Not much.

I took out the pen and notebook. At least by annotating the situation, I could give the police the best possible eyewitness account. I wrote faster than I ever had before, leaving out any details depicting Shannon as The Raven. Something I didn't think about, but knew instinctively I had to do.

Quinn's Adam's apple bobbed, and then he spoke carefully, "Don't do anything you'll regret for the rest of your life, man."

Jack swung the gun toward Quinn, his hand shaking, voice pitching. "He was there for me when no one else was. I owe it to him to exact justice."

Shannon swore, "You son of a bitch. Why? Why do you attack men just because they love other men?"

Jack cocked the gun at the same time as his head. "My brother cared about that shit. I only care about who got my brother incarcerated. I figured the best way to find you was by following the trend."

Quinn grabbed Shannon before she lunged, and he held her back against his chest once more. He whispered something in her ear. Perhaps something to cool her down. Quinn said firmly,

"That's your idea of justice? It'll just get you thrown in prison, right alongside your brother."

Jack let out a gurgled sound, as if his emotions were getting the better of him. He loved his brother, that was clear. "Maybe, but I'm going to make sure The Raven goes down with me."

The safety unlatched, a distinctive *click* sounded in the still air, and that's when I knew I had something else with me that could tip the scales.

Surprise.

I dropped my notebook, stole two steps and leaped on Jack's back as his finger went trigger-happy. My momentum knocked him forward as the gun fired.

We hit the ground with a heavy *thwump!* I dug my pen into his weapon-arm with all my strength as he bucked underneath me, trying to chuck me off. Thanks to self-defense lessons, I knew how to throw him off his balance—

"You fuck!"

I locked my hands around his wrist as Quinn yelled. I tipped suddenly, shoulders hitting stone.

The gun clattered as it dropped from Jack's hand, sliding toward Shannon's feet.

Suddenly Quinn was there, wrestling with Jack and shouting at Shannon not to do something that would make her the bad guy.

Jack thrust against Quinn's weight, angry eyes snapping to me. "You," he spat.

"Me," I said, still holding my pen tightly in my grip, my knuckles scraped from the stone. "Why did you attack me, *Freddy*?"

"Fuck you. You should have given up the party page." *Powwach!* Jack managed to land a hook over Quinn's ear. "But at least you led me to the cripple. He made catching The Raven easy."

"Fucker," Quinn swore, snatching Jack into a firm hold as Shannon stepped one of her shit-kickers on the gun. Her gaze was livid, as if static streamed from her. She embodied my definition of rage.

She caught my eye, and I shook my head, clumsily trying to pull myself up. "Quinn's right," I said, with a cough. "You need to stop being The Raven before you become victim. None of us want you to lose your wings."

She blinked, her gaze snapping to her brother who sat stranded in the corner.

Hunter grabbed Mitch's shirt, drew him near and spat in his face. "I don't ever want to see you around my friends or my sister again."

He shoved him back, and Mitch crumpled. "I'm so sorry, I didn't want to. I tried to say no."

"But you didn't," Hunter said. "That's all I need to know. Fuck off."

"I just . . . wish I'd been there to save him the first time," Shannon said, closing her eyes. She took a quivering breath and swept the gun far out of Jack's reach. Jack still struggled under Quinn. "Looks like my brother really can handle himself though."

"And the police are on their way," I grunted, letting them all know it was soon over.

Hunter looked across at her, swiping away the blood on his lip. "Come here, sis."

She came to his side, kneeling where Mitch had been. Mitch, who had disappeared.

I glanced at Quinn pressing his forearm against the back of Jack's neck and hissing in his ear to keep his filthy mouth shut.

"You all right?" Quinn asked me, failing to control the panic in his voice.

I held up my pen as Shannon walked past carrying Hunter. "Really is mightier than the sword."

THE TALL OFFICER with the goatee, holding Jack back, gave us a cursory once-over, his gaze landing inquisitively on Shannon who'd passed her hooded jacket to Hunter.

Quinn stiffened next to me. I wanted to nudge the back of his hand in a gesture of comfort, but now was hardly the time or place. The officers were trying to get a grip on the situation. As soon as someone had mentioned the gun, the female officer sporting a clipped-back perm had dialed in for back up.

"That's The Raven!" Jack screamed, trying to jerk away from the officer. "The one you want on countless cases of assault!"

"Raven?" I asked, pulling out my notebook with my descriptive account of the moments leading up to Jack firing his gun. "I have most of the details here." I offered the page with my notes to Goatee Officer. "I'm a journalist; it's my job to note the particulars. I didn't see The Raven." He glanced over it, and I pushed up my glasses. "Though that would have made a fantastic angle for my next party page piece for Scribe."

"Liar. He's a friendless fucking liar!"

The officer turned back to Jack, changing his grip on him. "Doesn't look friendless to me."

Quinn shifted his weight, pressing his arm lightly against mine. "He's no liar. I didn't see The Raven here, either."

Hunter piped in, "I also didn't see The Raven. Why, is there a bounty on him or something? I could've used the cash."

Goatee Officer glanced back at Shannon, who was blinking hard.

She said, "I thought I wanted The Raven to come and save us when he"—she pointed to Jack—"held his gun at me, my brother, my best friend." She tucked blue hair behind her ear, peeking toward Quinn, her other hand tight on Hunter's chair. "But we managed without them, and now I think it's better that the police are handling it."

"Liars. All liars! I can prove it, I have pictures at home."

No, he didn't.

"Some of us have experienced quite the trauma this evening; I think a trip to UPMC is in order . . ."

Perm Officer was back with a grim smile. "No can do. We can send in the EMTs to treat you, but you'll have to wait for the detectives so we can sort this all out."

SORTING it all out took a couple more hours of being separated and questioned by the detectives, but by midnight we were free to go.

Outside, Quinn was still tenderly touching his head. "UPMC," Shannon ordered.

Hunter agreed, insisting he was right as winter rain, so we took his van.

I didn't even glance up at the Scribe offices across the road as I clambered into the van after Quinn.

The vehicle roared to life and Hunter drove us to the University of Pittsburgh Medical Center. "How's your head?" I asked Quinn, the streetlights outside making a silhouette of his profile.

"Dizzy," he admitted. "But I'll be all right."

"I remember the last time we were doing this," I murmured, slipping my hand over the middle to his.

Quinn rested his head against the headrest, his pinkie playing with mine. A small smile cupped his mouth. "Yeah, you called me your angel."

"I'd been going for *angle*, but turns out that was close enough." I leaned forward and poked Hunter's shoulder over the front seat. "I like that we're friends, Hunter, but I want a relationship with Quinn."

Quinn's hand squeezed around mine, and he shifted sharply in his seat. "Liam?" he said under his breath.

"Ahhh," Hunter said, peering through the rearview mirror at

me. "Did I get hit on the head and not know about it? What do I have to do with you dating Quinn?"

Shannon snorted in the passenger seat. "Hunter just doesn't get it sometimes."

"Get what?" Hunter asked, swerving around a bend that had me toppling toward Quinn. "And be sensitive, the guy I was dating turned out to be friends with a homicidal maniac. I already know I lost a clue or two."

Shannon groaned. "Hey, my date *was* the homicidal maniac."

Quinn was undoing his seatbelt and shuffling into the middle, closer to me. Having had far too much experience with Hunter's driving, I grabbed the middle belt and looped it over his waist for him to buckle in.

Shannon stared at her brother, shaking her head, fondness in her gaze. "Liam doesn't want to lose you if things don't work out with Quinn."

"Not a problem," Quinn said to the whole car, slipping an arm around my shoulders. "I'll make sure things work out."

I pushed up my glasses and met his gaze. "Statistically—"

Quinn's mouth covered mine. "No, don't. And look, even if things don't work out—which they *will*—I'd never pressure my friends to ditch you. Besides that, if I tried, Hunter would tell me to go take a walk off a plank."

"Into shark-infested waters," Hunter agreed.

Quinn grinned, his cheek dimpling the way I liked so much. "And rightly so."

Our conversation short-circuited as the van came to an abrupt stop outside UPMC emergency entrance. "Out," Hunter said. "I'll meet you in there soon."

Things moved smoothly inside, just like they had the last time we'd been there, and soon Doctor Carter was finishing up Quinn's assessment. "Up to you," she said, scribbling something onto her clipboard of paper. "You can be admitted overnight for observation, or I can sign the release forms on the condition one of your friends here checks in on you regularly.

"I'll do it," I said to the smiling Doctor Carter, who had made it clear she recognized us from our previous visit. "I want him to come home with me."

In front of a wall of superhero-doctor pictures, Quinn stood out the brightest and the best. He didn't have a cape on, and he had a slight concussion, but nevertheless he looked about ready to swoop me into his arms and fly me home.

"Yeah," he said, quietly, "sign those release forms."

"QUINN? WAKE UP."

He stirred. "Huh?" Blinking, he pushed up onto his elbows and drowsily glanced at me. The glass of water I held reflected the small bedside light, refracting golden shards onto the bedspread, almost like a small star in an otherwise dark room.

"Just checking you're well. Drink some water."

He took the glass and sipped, sending slits of light to the ceiling. "Thanks."

I plucked the empty glass from his grip and set it on the side table next to his frayed leather wallet and keys, angled so the light played through it more.

Face lined with tired shadows, Quinn smiled warmly and patted the bed for me to hop in.

I rounded the side, peeled back the sheets, and slithered in. It was cool against my bare skin and for a moment I considered replacing my comma-cat T-shirt with something warmer. Instead, I scuttled closer to Quinn, who had pushed himself up and was resting against the headboard.

It was warmer with our arms jammed together. In fact, Quinn's whole man-cave was more comfortable than I'd ever have believed.

Maybe it had something to do with the fact that, although his clothes lay in puddles on the floor, I knew he washed regularly. And I'd seen him vacuum. He actually lifted the clothing to clean underneath it.

I rested my head back on the wooden headboard, cocked my head, and studied him.

"Quite the night," he said. "And I don't know if it was the worst or the best."

"Judging by the boil on the side of your head, I'd go with the former." I sucked in my bottom lip as I replayed the evening. "So how did it happen?"

Quinn shook his head. "My darlin' Shannon." A sigh. "She called me and said her date—Jack—was a no show. At some point after that, Mitch comes up to her saying some guy swore at him that he's a 'fag' in the bathrooms. That sent Shannon into Raven mode. She always goes to a party prepared. She silently followed Mitch for his protection. Only, he was bait. He led her right to the male bathrooms, where Jack had dragged Hunter out of his chair and onto the balcony."

"At what point did you show up?"

"As she was ducking into the male bathrooms. I've been following her for years, backing her up and calling the police when she needs it. I was angry this time. I banged the door in and told her to stop. I told her like I've been trying to for a long time, that this was going to get her in trouble. She was on the edge of backing down until we turned and saw Hunter's chair sitting there, empty. Mocking us." He sighed. "And you know the rest."

"I wonder why Mitch did it?"

"Blackmail would be my guess. He kept apologizing—it sounded like Jack had something on him. Though he kept repeating that he was sorry. That it hadn't started out this way. Something about Jack threatening him at Halloween."

I took it all in, slowly going over the information, a fraction relieved that Mitch might not have been malicious from the start.

I was about to speak when Quinn shifted and said, "The night we first met. The one with Freddy . . ."

I shuddered. "You were there with her?"

"She left the party without me. I only found her once Freddy was crawling away. You asked about it after the hospital. I'm sorry I lied."

"To protect your friend." Honor, something I understood. I moved my leg so it met with his and I wiggled my toes on the arch of his foot. He was there. He was all right. My voice croaked as I spoke, "I was scared tonight. It seized me so tightly. I thought I wouldn't be able to do anything. But when Jack had that gun . . ." I scratched at an invisible itch on my arm. "I'm relieved you're okay."

He held my gaze squarely, but there was a hiccup to his breath. "Liam?"

"Yes?"

"There's something else I want to say. I . . . I . . ." He shut his eyes and expelled his breath slowly before reopening his eyes and feeling for my hand under the sheets. "I like how you allow yourself time to think things through. How you waited until you were sure that you wanted to make this work. Between us."

Fingers curled around mine. "Everything you set your mind to do, you do with a perfectionist's heart. And I know you want to do perfect by your friends too."

I said, "'Aim for the moon; even if you miss, you'll land among the stars.' W. Clement Stone."

He laughed. "That's why I love you, Liam."

I jerked at that and Quinn squeezed my hand gently. Tightness thickened my middle and my throat wouldn't let any words pass. I blinked in his smile and felt the gentle tremors pass from him to me.

He said softly, "It touches me, the way you show your love."

I shifted, lifting my knees and curling my free arm around them. The blanket slipped, but I wasn't feeling the cold anymore.

I'd always been told in the past that I wasn't very good at showing my affection. How could Quinn see it, then? And how could it touch him?

As if he read my mind, he nudged his shoulder against mine, and when I glanced at him, he stole my lips into a soft kiss. "You stole my computer, cracked my password, and finished my essay when I was sick. You go over my work when you're busy with your own." His nose brushed against mine. "You chose to help me instead of finishing *Dating for the Differently-Abled.*"

"It's a good piece," I said, untangling our fingers. "It can still be featured in the next *Scribe*."

Another lingering kiss. His whispered words, falling over my bottom lip and the tip of my chin. "I know what it really meant to you."

I pulled back a bit so I could keep eye contact. "Yes, and in an ideal world, I would have landed the features editor position and got my father to notice me. But—" I brought a hand to the back of his neck and played with his bleached hair, "—tonight it came down to you *or* my father."

"Thank you for choosing me," Quinn said again, rolling his neck at my touch.

My fingers skated to his shoulder. "You were the one there at Thanksgiving. You are the one that makes the apartment feel like home." I looked at him levelly. "This was not a choice, Quinn. I did not need to *hum* and *ahh* over my options. The answer was in bold and circled with a giant checkmark at the side."

I leaned in and kissed his wobbling lip. "It was always going to be you."

EPILOGUE

The chief curled a finger at me from his doorway. Hunter, peeling the stickers off my stapler, sent me a wink. The kind of wink that said *Go get 'em, tiger*, the kind that had every bit of confidence in me.

Confidence I'd lost somewhere in the twenty-eighth ranking of the BCA competition.

Chewing enthusiastically on a mint she'd pinched from my drawer, Hannah grabbed her issue of the *Post-Gazette* and dumped it in front of me with a smile. "You'll do fine, Liam. This article makes you look really good. Chief won't be able to argue with that."

I clapped my eyes on the folded page. Strange how two

columns should sum up the events of the night before, when those few moments felt like a lifetime.

It was woefully inadequate.

I pushed my chair back—

Ompf!

Twisting, I came face-to-face with Jill, who sidestepped around my chair. He stood as if his ass was itching and he couldn't reach the spot. His arms folded and refolded; his gaze met mine defiantly and, with the twitch of his jaw, softened from burning charcoal to mere charcoal.

Across the room, the chief had ducked back into his office. "Make it quick," I said to him, "I've got a meeting with Chief Benedict."

Jill jerked his head to the side, his bangs sweeping out of his eyes. His gaze slipped to Hunter, and a light blush spread over his cheeks. He looked away again. "I just . . ." He pulled out a rolled-up *Scribe* from his back pocket and it landed on top of the *Post-Gazette*. He cleared his throat. "The last few party page columns . . ." He shrugged, again glancing toward Hunter. "They could've been worse, is all."

Hunter placed my newly-naked stapler on my desk and I straightened it next to my inbox trays. "Pain in the ass you are, Jill," I said, "but chief was right to put you in editing. You don't do a half-bad job."

The barest edges of a grin touched his lips, but quickly disappeared behind a grunted, "Thanks."

"Also . . ." Jill said, backing away from my desk only to knock into Hunter's chair, "Shit." He grabbed the arm of the chair and Hunter reached out to steady him with a curious-blue gaze. Jill froze for a moment before coming to his senses and yanking his hand back.

"Also?" I asked, peeking up to the chief's open door as I stood.

Jill shrugged. "I mean, you left your laptop and notes on Jack's desk."

"I've since retrieved them."

"That wasn't what I . . . never mind." He twisted, carefully rounding Hunter's chair. "See you around."

He stormed back to his corner of the office, and Hunter and I shared a stumped look. Then he jerked a thumb over his shoulder. "Get to the chief—and if it comes up, slip in a good word for me, yeah?"

Hannah's phone rang and she hurriedly answered as I clipped my way to Chief Benedict.

He sat in his office chair, reading off some crinkled sheets of letter paper. "Sit."

I sat.

"I don't think it's going to give you everything you're searching for, Liam."

I gripped the metal frame of the seat, palms pushing on the vinyl upholstery. "Excuse me, sir?"

He whisked the paper he'd been reading toward me. "You've got the features editor position. This was brilliant."

Frowning, I picked up the sheets and glanced over them. This was my article. My draft had been shaped up and edited. I blinked down at my words, tweaked in places for flow and impact.

I glanced over my shoulder and through the chief's open door, but I couldn't see Jill's desk. I read over the opening paragraph again, and then the *Dating the Differently-Abled* title, and my name underneath.

My fingers smoothed the paper and I set it down. "Thank you, chief."

"Thank you, Liam, for embracing my challenge to you for the semester. You've grown in leaps and bounds." He stroked his beard thoughtfully, his mouth a worried line. "You wanted this really badly—dare I say, desperately—and I'm concerned you're setting yourself up for disappointment."

He shifted in his seat so I was looking at his profile and the cathedral behind him. He got up and came around to my side, stretching out a hand for me to shake. I took it. His squeeze was warm, comforting. "Whatever you decide to do once you're done here, you'll do splendidly."

"But?"

"But I'm not a fool, Liam. I know who your father is. Everyone knows who he is. I also know that for the last four years you've spent every Thanksgiving in the office."

Except for this year, I wanted to add. Except that wasn't his point and I knew it.

I let go of his hand with an acknowledging nod and slipped my glasses higher. "I'm not going to be disappointed," I said. "I'm still aiming for the moon, but even if I don't get it . . ." I thought of Hannah, Shannon, Hunter, and especially Quinn.

I didn't finish the sentence; I didn't need to.

I stood from the chair, nodded once more to the chief, and headed back out to my friends.

THE END

ACKNOWLEDGMENTS

As always, thank you first to my wonderful husband. Your support is what enables me to write. I love you for it.

Big thanks to Natasha Snow for the great cover! I love how it captures the mood of the story.

Teresa Crawford: cheers for helping me to structure this story, especially during those first developmental stages, when I wasn't quite sure where the characters were heading. Your input was gold.

To my editor Lynda Lamb, for going through and tweaking all those spelling errors and missing words. And for all the emailing back and forth with encouraging words. I value your approachability.

Thanks to HJS Editing for copyediting. It's been a great experience working with you. Your edits helped not only with the grammar and tightening of sentences, but made my American characters actually sound American. Thanks for being so thorough and for all your professionalism. I also appreciated all the laughs we had regarding our British/American language differences . . .

Another cheers to Vicki for reading and offering valuable

feedback, and smiles to Sunne for being one of the first to read, and for catching those plot holes. Thanks also for your enthusiasm. I love that you care for Liam so much—I do too. Finally, thanks to all my friends—you know who and how awesome you are!

ANYTA SUNDAY

Heart-stopping slow burn

A bit about me: I'm a big, BIG fan of slow-burn romances. I love to read and write stories with characters who slowly fall in love.

Some of my favorite tropes to read and write are: Enemies to Lovers, Friends to Lovers, Clueless Guys, Bisexual, Pansexual, Demisexual, Oblivious MCs, Everyone (Else) Can See It, Slow Burn, Love Has No Boundaries.

I write a variety of stories, Contemporary MM Romances with a good dollop of angst, Contemporary lighthearted MM Romances, and even a splash of fantasy.
My books have been translated into German, Italian, French, Spanish, and Thai.

Contact: http://www.anytasunday.com/about-anyta/
Sign up for Anyta's newsletter and receive a free e-book: http://www.anytasunday.com/newsletter-free-e-book/

CPSIA information can be obtained
at www.ICGtesting.com
Printed in the USA
LVHW030313160121
676575LV00006B/1039